The Lambert Series–Book One

THIEF OF HEARTS

Victoria Taylor Murray

AmErica House
Baltimore

Copyright 2000 by Victoria Taylor Murray

All rights reserved. No part of this book may be reproduced in any form without written permission from the publishers, except by a reviewer who may quote brief passages in a review to be printed in a newspaper or magazine.

First printing

ISBN 1-58851-559-1
PUBLISHED BY AMERICA HOUSE BOOK PUBLISHERS
www.publishamerica.com
Baltimore

Printed in the United States of America

DEDICATION AND ACKNOWLEDGMENT

I would like to dedicate my LAMBERT SERIES of books to my one true MASTERPIECE in life- my son, Michael Patrick Murray. Without his never ending love, support, and encouragement, my four book series; starting with "THIEF OF HEARTS," would still be a life-long dream of mine instead of the reality it has now become. Thank you, darling. (ILYTWATC).

I would also like to acknowledge a very special little girl in my life- my grandniece, Michelle Renea, who helped me create a few really neat names for some of the characters in my book. Thank you sweetheart.(ILYTWATC2).

I'd like to give a special thanks to the following people; who each helped in writing this series in some small way- whether they are aware of it or not:
Milford & Mary Taylor- Elizabeth Masengale Taylor- Brenda & Bill Reilly- Anita, Frank & Patrick Thernes- Bradford Taylor- John Taylor- Mary Taylor- Joe Taylor- Tony Taylor- Dan, Lisa & T.C. Taylor- Millie, Joey & Josh Taylor Tonya (cool breeze) Taylor - Tim & Kay Taylor
and Lacey Alexandria Bonner for letting me borrow her really great name! And of course, the always hungry, Herb Murray.

A VERY SPECIAL THANK YOU to my new friend's at AmErica House Publishing for giving my LAMBERT SERIES a shot at the gold.

And last, but far from least, I'd like to say thank you for being a friend, JOHNNIE BENCH! He once told a Movie Producer the only way he would let him do his life story was if the man would let me sing in it. Johnnie used to sing a little country, while I, on the other hand, used to sing a little Rock n' Roll. You're one cool dude Johnnie Bench and not a bad ball player either!

Table of Contents

Chapter 1 5

Chapter 2 13

Chapter 3 41

Chapter 4 51

Chapter 5 57

Chapter 6 63

Chapter 7 71

Chapter 8 79

Chapter 9 89

Chapter 10 93

Chapter 11 107

Chapter 12 113

Chapter 13 123

Chapter 14 125

Chapter 15 127

Chapter 16 131

Chapter 17 141

Chapter 18 147

Chapter 19 155

Chapter 20 157

Chapter 21 165

Chapter 22 167

Chapter 23 169

Chapter 24 171

Chapter 25 173

Colorful Cast
of Characters 184

Chapter 1

Her secret passion for romance is what drove Nouri Sommers to excessively write in her journals night after night: Page after page of passion, page after page of longing, page after page of seductive romance. Her late afternoon rendezvous with her sizzling journals were becoming more like daily rituals complete with tailor-maid preparations and all.

First she would draw herself a hot, silky bubble bath, then pour herself a chilled glass of Asti Spumanti, her beverage of choice for journal writing. The bubbling effervescence tickles her nose, and the taste of little green apples, tart, yet fruity and sweet, help assist in creating just the right tone for an hour of imaginary bliss.

"Maybe tonight I'll create a God!" She mused to herself, as she unlocked the silver-jeweled box that house her most intimate thoughts of passion. "Yeah...a Greek God," she lustfully whispered, while retrieving her latest journal from its guarded location.

After settling into the hot, silky water, her imagination quickly shifted from the bored Mrs. Ethan Sommers to Nouri Sommers: A.K.A... DAMSEL IN DISTRESS!

Out of nowhere he came. Just simply- BANG. He was there...standing directly in front of me.

She continued to write...

His shirt slung over his left shoulder. The scorching sun beating down on his perfectly contoured body. He raised his muscular arm in an attempt to blot the perspiration that was beginning to trickle down his beautiful, yet manly face.

She reached for her glass of wine, took a sip, and then continued to write...

His mocha-brown eyes gazed into mine. So mysterious. So seductive. So mesmerizing. I felt passionately drawn to him. He smiled faintly. His smile lit a flame inside me. My heart was under siege...

Suddenly the telephone rang causing Nouri to jolt back into reality. "Oh, that damn phone!" She complained, placing her journal and champagne glass down on the raised-oriental tile panel above the bathtub. She reached for the receiver.

"Hello," she snapped to the intrusive caller. A hesitant, "uh... hel...hello," came back at her. Followed by the stuttered word "is," whispered by a nervous female voice. Suddenly, the mystery caller snapped the words, "never mind," and sharply slammed the receiver down so hard on her end that it left an annoying buzz inside Nouri's right ear.

"Well, that was rude!" Nouri groaned, rising to her feet and stepping out of the bathtub.

THIEF OF HEARTS

Still rather annoyed over the intrusion, she glanced at the caller ID machine, while reaching for her terrycloth bathrobe that was dangling on a hook on the back of her bathroom door. Recognizing the familiar telephone number to Lambert, she decided not to give the intrusive mystery caller another thought. It was probably just someone wanting to confirm our reservations for this weekend, she thought, as she walked back to the bedroom to put her guarded journals back under lock and key.

Still in her royal blue, terrycloth bathrobe and sipping on her now warm glass of Asti Spumanti, she walked over to the large bay window to watch the storm outside. Nouri loved to watch the rain. It seemed to have a calming effect on her. She pulled back the thin, satin, rose-colored, sheer curtain and gently pressed her warm forehead to the cool-feeling, French-plate glass. Staring out into the storm, her mind soon began to drift back in time. A time she would forever keep secretly hidden in her heart, for all of eternity. She smiled and then released a sigh without realizing it. I miss you darling, she silently thought, unconsciously clutching the neckline of her bathrobe.

She continued to be mesmerized by the storm's beauty. The rain had begun to fall fast and furious. The gusting winds were now swaying violently through the tall, full trees. And the sky had turned an ominous, blackish-magenta color. "A beautiful, but dangerous combination," she whispered, before attempting to bring her attention back to the present.

Just as she turned from the window to glance at the marble clock on the night stand, Mai Li knocked softly on the huge bedroom door.

Mai Li was like an elegant flower, refined in her appearance, in her movement, and in her demeanor. She was mature, but noticeably attractive. Her almond-colored eyes were as mysterious as the well kept secrets she managed to hide inside herself so well. Once Ethan Sommers was informed that Mai Li wanted to come to this country to live, he spared no expense in bringing her into his employ. She was hired to run the Sommers' estate.

Prior to her employment with the Sommers, she worked for the "The House Of Chin," China Royalty, in Beijing, where Ethan's father had met her many years ago. Largely due to his mysterious relationship with Mai Li, Ethan Sommers didn't want her living in the same living quarters as the rest of the staff. So as a surprise, when she first arrived in Boston, he gave her, her own three bedroom house on the estate grounds to call home. He had it especially built for her, three miles east of the estate's tennis court.

No matter how mysterious, or unusual the relationship between Ethan Sommers and Mai Li, it doesn't seem to bother his beautiful wife, Nouri. She's quite aware of her husband's extreme generosity and accepts it as just part of his impulsive nature, especially when it comes to people he cares about. With Ethan Sommers, money is never an issue.

THIEF OF HEARTS

Not jealous by nature, Nouri is, however, envious of her husband's time. But that, too, is something she'll just have to learn to deal with in his super-rich world.

Nouri turned to face the door.

"Yes, Mai Li, come in." Mai Li entered the room, smiling fondly.

"Excuse please, miss," she said softly. Nouri's eyes held Mai Li's warm gaze, as she spoke to her from across the room.

"What is it Mai Li?"

"What time to serve dinner tonight, please," Mai Li nodded politely. Nouri released a sigh of frustration and unconsciously cringed.

"Oh, Mai Li, I'm sorry. I should have said something earlier. Mr. Sommers and I are having dinner at the club tonight." An apologetic look suddenly crossed Nouri's face.

"You need nothing else tonight, miss?" She smiled understandingly.

"No thank you, you can have the rest of the evening off...oh, and Mai Li, tell Fredrick that he doesn't have to worry about driving us to the club. Mr. Sommers can drive us."

Mai Li studied Nouri's lost-in-thought expression, before asking, "Anything else, miss?"

"No, Mai Li, I don't think so." Mai Li nodded and turned to leave. Suddenly, Nouri called out to her, just as she was about to open the bedroom door. "Oh, there is one more thing."

Mai Li turned to face her. "Yes, miss."

"You may as well give the rest of the staff the remainder of the evening off as well... including Mr. Bradford. There's no need for him to wait around just to let Mr. Sommers in. I can buzz him in myself, Okay." Nouri smiled fondly.

"Yes, miss," Mai Li responded, as she opened the door to leave. "*Zai-jian xiaojie*," (goodbye miss), Mai Li added, closing the door behind her.

After Mai Li left the bedroom, Nouri walked over to view the hand-painted, full-length, antique mirror that her husband had given to her on their second wedding anniversary, a month earlier. She studied the elegant mirror's style and beauty. The gift was made of pier glass and marble console, framed with pilasters and cornice with shell finial. A magnificent find, to say the least. Her husband had purchased the rare find while on business in China, several months earlier. He had originally planned to donate the one-of-a-kind treasure to The Metropolitan Museum Of Art, but quickly changed his mind when he was suddenly reminded of he and his wife's special day. After studying the unique craftsmanship of the rare treasure, she decided to take a look at her own beauty. Nouri was hoping to find a possible answer to her husband's lack of interest in their bedroom lately.

His recent behavioral changes weren't just in the bedroom. He was also becoming more absent and more mysterious than his usual norm. Was Ethan bored with making love to her after only just two short years of marriage? Or perhaps he was just too busy with his many business affairs, like his recent bid to take over The Medallion Corporation, Nouri thought to herself, as she continued to silently ask herself more puzzling questions that she had no answers for. Business affairs or not! It was starting to concern her. Nouri wasn't ready to give up on her marriage to her elusive husband just yet, not by a long shot. She released an unconscious sigh, as she raised her hands to her head to pull her long, curly hair up and away from her face. She continued to be lost in thought, as she tied a silk ribbon in her curly, soft hair.

Nouri loved her husband and desperately wanted to try to make her marriage to her mysterious husband work. Even if it meant that she would have to turn to writing in her journals more often. As long as there wasn't another woman in his life, she knew that she would eventually learn to deal with his many business affairs. As she continued to study her reflection in the mirror, she slowly untied her terrycloth bathrobe. It fell into a circle around her feet. She stepped over the robe and closer to the mirror to better examine her now naked body. Her eyes slowly traveled the length of her entire frame. From the head of her curly, brownish-auburn hair, down to the tip of her freshly pedicured, copper colored toenails. She smiled approvingly.

She was the type of woman that truly enjoyed being a woman. She loved being pampered. And she loved pampering herself. She loved the silky, scented bubble baths, the expensive clothing, and the expensive imported perfumes. Yes, Nouri loved being a woman in every possible way. The chase of romance, the flames of desire, and especially the surrender of passion.

Still focused on her reflection in the mirror, she gently brushed the length of her satin-soft arm with one long stroke. Nouri released another sigh, suddenly finding herself wanting to make love to her elusive husband. She closed her eyes tightly in an effort to calm herself, quickly turning away from the mirror when she felt a tear slowly trickle from her eye. "I need you Ethan," she whispered longingly. She closed her eyes tightly again and swallowed hard, quickly reaching down to retrieve her bathrobe. She put it on.

After getting her emotions back under control, she decided to shift her thoughts back to the present. "Now what to wear for dinner tonight," she sighed, entering the large walk-in closet. Nouri was always concerned about her appearance. Image was everything to her husband's super-rich world, second only to money and power. Nouri Sommers seemed to have it all: A life that most people only dream of. That is except for only one thing. That one thing was her driving force: PASSION. She craved it like a child craving chocolate.

THIEF OF HEARTS

She knew for her marriage to work that void inside herself would have to be filled. She missed the fire that her husband used to ignite inside her with only his touch. Now his love making was more like a heated rush. A major disappointment for her to say the least!

Ethan Sommers' many business affairs left little time for romancing his hot-natured wife. So she turned to journal writing to vent her frustration, hoping things between them would return to normal very soon. Writing in her journals seemed to be working, at least for the time being, a temporary, but do-able solution.

Unable to decide what to wear for dinner, she optioned to refill her now empty glass of Asti Spumanti. Before leaving her bedroom, she walked back to the large bay window to check on the storm outside. She was hoping the storm had let up a little, but it hadn't, and that worried her. "I hope Ethan will be all right driving home," she whispered, as she walked away from the window, wishing Fredrick would have driven her husband to the city that morning.

On her way to the downstairs bar, she continued to be lost in thought. Nouri was worried. Before she could set her champagne glass down, the main entrance intercom buzzed loudly, demanding immediate attention. "Who could it be this time of night?" she groaned, glancing at the clock on the mantle above the fire place, and sitting her glass down on top of the bar. She knew it wasn't time for her husband to arrive home yet. Suddenly the thought of something happening to her husband driving home in the storm sent a surge of panic throughout her body. She quickly made her way to the viewing monitor that guarded the front entrance to the estate.

After recognizing the shiny red Mercedes belonging to Clint Chamberlain, she hesitantly released the lock on the gate, allowing him to enter the estate grounds. Knowing it would take Clint at least ten minutes to drive the ten mile stretch of driveway leading up to the mansion, she quickly made her way to the bar. Nouri needed that drink more than ever now. Suddenly, she began to feel light headed. Her heart began to pound rapidly, and her hands were now trembling. Her legs felt as though they were going to buckle right out from under her.

She excitedly reached for the chilled bottle of Asti, not bothering to pour the cold, sweet wine into a champagne glass. She quickly put the bottle to her mouth and drank a half of a bottle before coming up for air. "Oh my God," she squealed nervously, pouring the remainder of the wine down her throat. "Oh my God!" she squealed again, after suddenly realizing she was about to let Clint Chamberlain into her home, and she was naked! Well, almost naked. She still had her bathrobe on. Nouri set the wine bottle back down on the marble bar and jumped to her feet. "I have to force myself to move", she thought, as she struggled to the staircase. "I've got to throw something on before he presses the door bell," was her last thought on the matter, when she finally managed to put her foot on the first step.

Before she could reach the fourth step, the front door bell sounded loudly. "Oh damn!" she muttered nervously, quickly changing directions. She glanced into the large, antique mirror in the wide hallway on her way to the front door. Nouri released a deep sigh and the ribbon from her hair. Shaking her head firmly, she used her fingers as a substitute comb, as she continued to make her way down the hallway to let Clint Chamberlain in out of the storm. She checked the terrycoth belt around her waist to make sure it was snugly fastened around her body. She put her hand on the sculpted door knob, inhaled deeply, silently muttered one Hail-Mary, and slowly opened the door.

Clint Chamberlain was Ethan Sommers' high-powered attorney, and best friend. They had become friends while attending Yale, nineteen years earlier. Through the years, the two bosom buddies have shared numerous things, making the bond of friendship between them unbreakable. That is until the impulsive, and unpredictable, Ethan Sommers married the heart-stoppingly beautiful, Nouri St. Charles from Boston.

Clint Chamberlain was tall, extremely well built, incredibly good looking, and quite charming when he wanted to be. He was also hot tempered and hard to control at times. Nouri knew only too well. She knew Clint better than he knew himself. Nouri was engaged to him before she married Ethan.

Well, technically engaged, that is! Apparently, Clint was a man who was capable of expressing his heart felt passion in the bedroom, but a man of few words on the subject of romance outside the *boudoir*. He just assumed they would marry someday but was in no hurry to set a date. Nouri grew tired of waiting, and Clint soon became a treasured memory in her fantasy journals. That was two years ago.

Her marriage to the dashing billionaire tycoon was a whirlwind romance that ended in marriage only two short weeks after their first date, shocking many people, especially her ex-fieance--Clint Chamberlain. Prior to her marriage to Ethan, Nouri wasn't aware of any involvement between her husband and her EX, past or present. It wasn't until her first wedding anniversary with Ethan that she discovered the shocking news. Fearing the worse, she felt it best not to tell her husband about her past involvement with his best friend. She silently vowed to take her history of Clint Chamberlain to her grave. She made Clint promise to do the same. He reluctantly gave in to her demands of him.

Her past romance with Clint would always be a part of her, and she knew it. A romance so magical, so passionate, once felt by a woman, could never be forgotten. Hidden in the shadows of her heart, maybe. But never forgotten. The bond they shared as lovers was truly a powerful one! So when she decided to leave him, it was very painful for her. Still very much in love with him, she felt leaving him was the right thing to do, at the time. Even today, however, she continues to long for his passionate embrace, secretly in her heart. Why just the thought of him making love to her sends shivers throughout her entire body. Nouri loses all self control, and it becomes very difficult for her to fight the heated passion she so desperately craves. When memories like those arise, she quickly turns to writing in her journals. Nouri writes for temporary solace of past memories she once shared with her former love, the man who still secretly holds the key to her heart. Nouri was still harboring her passion for Clint, and was very vulnerable when she met her exciting husband-to-be.

Ethan zoomed in from out of nowhere and swept her off her feet. And in a flash, their lives instantly became one. Clint Chamberlain suddenly became her past, and Ethan Sommers impulsively became her future. Ethan's polished G.Q. good looks, style and charm, coupled with his air of mystery, power, and strength, but mostly because of his impulsive nature to go anywhere, and do almost anything without prior warning are what immediately attracted her to Ethan Sommers. His spontaneous personality made it quite easy for her to decide to marry him so impulsively. He kept her much too busy to brood over her EX. As far as that goes, he kept her much too busy to think about anyone, except for himself. "What woman in her right mind wouldn't want to be swept off her feet by a dashingly handsome, billionaire tycoon, like Ethan Sommers." Is what she silently whispered to herself, as she impulsively exchanged "I DO's" on her husband's private jet, heading for China. She spent her wedding night at her husband's favorite restaurant, The Emerald Dragon.

Without hesitation, Clint Chamberlain headed his red Mercedes into the direction of the long, winding, macadam driveway that leads to the large Victorian Mansion.

The late spring thunderstorm had come from out of nowhere with no warning at all. Though beautiful to look at, it was dangerous to drive in, especially with the heavy, downpour of rain combined with the extremely strong winds.

Being anxious to get out of the brutal weather, Clint pushed his foot harder on the gas pedal than he actually intended, causing him to almost lose control of his car several times. His mind seemed to be focused more on his business at hand with Ethan, instead of the ten mile stretch of driveway leading to the Sommers' Mansion.

Clint was upset that he hadn't been able to track Ethan down all day. And it was of the utmost importance for him to do so. There had been a major set back in their efforts to takeover The Medallion Corporation, plus there had been a recent rumor that had surfaced. He needed to put an end to it A.S.A.P!

His friend was becoming more and more difficult to track down lately, and that scared him.

"Ah, man, I hope Ethan isn't being influenced by Steven again," Clint mumbled to himself, as he zoomed past the servant's living quarters. "I'll kill him this time, if he is," he sighed, shaking his head in disbelief, as he sped past the tennis court. I thought when Ethan married Nouri he was determined to put everything from the past behind him, was his final thought on the subject, when his car almost slid out of control, as he flew by Mai Li's house. "Pull yourself together, Clint 'ol boy!" He scolded himself, glancing into the rearview mirror. He shook his head in relief and quickly brought his car back under control.

The last time Ethan Sommers teamed up with Steven Li almost ruined Ethan and Clint's friendship. The memory was far too painful to think about. Clint knew that something was bothering Ethan, but he just couldn't corner him long enough to find out what it was. It was his friend's recent behavior changes that triggered his concern.

Clint had just parked his car in front of the Sommers' main house, when suddenly, the image of Nouri Sommers' beautiful face flashed into his brain, causing him to smile. Just the thought of seeing her made everything else seem less important. He released a sigh of anticipation, then quickly opened the door to his car, and jumped out into the brutal rain, running as fast as his long legs would carry him. After trying desperately to avoid the heavy down pour, Clint finally reached the front door. He quickly pressed the doorbell with one hand while firmly clutching his suit jacket around the collar with the other, in an attempt to protect himself from the rain as best as he could.

Nouri finally answered the door on the third buzz. Her hands were shaking. She smiled faintly. Their eyes nervously met.

Chapter 2

The moment Nouri Sommers opened the wide double doors, and their eyes met for the first time in over a year, feelings of remembered love quickly overcame Clint. It took a moment for his rational mind to regain control. Finally he managed a warm "hello." Clint's eyes gleamed a familiar smile. His heart pounded rapidly, and goose bumps quickly ran up his spine. Nouri and Clint quickly sized each other up and hoped that their stolen glances weren't quite as obvious.

She stared at him speechlessly for a moment, feeling as though she were in a dream. During that moment, she remembered his lips, his touch, and his passionate embrace. She wanted to run into his arms and passionately kiss him, but somehow, instead, she managed to respond with a polite, "hi." He noticed the way her heart raced wildly. He could tell by the way her bathrobe would rise and suddenly fall. He noticed the way her eyes held steadfast to his lips, and he found himself wondering if she had noticed his eyes doing the same. He wanted to pull her into his arms, but instead, he lowered his hand to his side with a great deal of will power.

"Come in before we both catch cold," she quickly added, hoping her added remark would make it appear that she was in control of her emotions. She motioned him into the house, as she backed up against the door, allowing him to enter. When he slowly walked past her, she met his searching gaze. For a quick moment, she silently surrendered to a quick fantasy about him, but it was short lived when he suddenly turned to face her. Her expression was one of longing, as though she were remembering. He pretended not to notice. Nouri quickly turned away from him to shut the door. As he stood silently waiting for her to turn around, she nervously cleared her throat as she shut the door. Just the thought of him standing behind her, watching her every move, sent the blood surging through her veins. She finally turned herself to face him. Nouri pretended that she was more in control than she actually was.

Nouri's mind was racing in two directions at one time. Clint could tell by the expression on her face. He knew her very well, even after all this time away from her. He walked over to her without saying a word and put his hand to her face and affectionately brushed her cheek with his index finger. She froze and swallowed hard, too afraid of what he might do next, but secretly hoping it would be to pull her into his arms. He had always been able to seduce her with his passionate kisses and caresses. He was secretly wondering if he still could. She was secretly wondering too. Nouri's heart continued to pound rapidly. Her first thought was to pray. Oh, dear Lord! Please make him leave. The next thought, she was begging him to stay. She suddenly took a step back, only after noticing the hurt, and sadness in his eyes. It was so clear, she could almost feel his pain.

The bond between them was a passionate and powerful one. It both pleased and frightened both of them. Nouri suddenly felt the need to sit down. The decision was based entirely on the inability of her legs to no longer give her adequate support.

"I was going to pour myself a glass of wine. Would you care to join me," she suddenly asked, attempting to break the trance she seemed to currently be under. Not waiting for his reply, she swiftly began to walk across the room. She had her eyes focused on the nearest bar stool, and thinking to herself, "Legs please don't fail me now."

"Sure if it is no bother," he responded nervously. As Nouri continued to walk into the direction of the bar, Clint quickly seized the opportunity to let his eyes slowly roam over her perfect frame. Nouri circled the corner of the bar, quickly reaching for another bottle of Asti Spumanti. And with an urgent need of her own, she popped the cork on the bubbling bottle of wine. She was tempted to impulsively drink from the bottle, which, she thought, would calm her trembling hands. Instead, she poured the wine into their properly chilled champagne glasses.

"No. Of course it's no bother, don't be silly Clint," she said, handing him his glass of cold, sweet, wine.

"Still drinking this sissy stuff, huh?" he remarked teasingly. He intercepted his glass of wine from her unsteady hand and sat down on the bar stool beside her. He smiled as their eyes met for a brief moment. Nouri downed her wine in one fast swallow, quickly reaching for the bottle a second time. She poured herself another glass of sparkling wine. The bottle slightly wavered in her unsteady hand. Clint pretended not to notice her trembling. She downed her second glass before answering his question.

"Girlie stuff, huh." Her tone hoarse and nervous. She forced a small grin.

"Yeah, girlie stuff," he teased, as he noticed her squirm uncomfortably on her barstool.

"Would you rather have something else?" she offered, gesturing in the direction of the liquor bottles. She faked a cough to clear her nervous throat.

"No, Nouri, this is fine. It was a failed attempt at humor." He smiled, reaching for the bottle of wine. He poured himself another, then refilled hers.

"So tell me, Clint, what brings you out on a stormy night like this?" she asked, as she glanced at his handsome face, and then quickly downed her glass of wine.

"I was hoping to catch Ethan at home," he replied, then quickly downed his glass of wine. He reached for the bottle again, accidentally brushing the side of her hand with his pinkie finger. Nouri gasped, hoping he hadn't noticed.

"Why didn't you phone him at his office?" Her glance held a curious gaze.

THIEF OF HEARTS

"I did of course. Actually, I've been trying to reach him all day." He sighed, and shook his head with annoyance.

"I see. Anything I can help with?"

"Yeah," he smiled lustfully, paused, and then added, "but that wouldn't solve my urgent need to speak to your husband. He gazed into her eyes for a brief moment, causing her to quickly glance away and reach for the wine bottle again.

"Whoops!" I guess we need to pop another cork," she laughed nervously, playfully shaking the empty bottle of wine. She then reached for a new bottle of the bubbling wine.

"Here. Let me open it," Clint offered, quickly jumping to his feet. He walked behind the bar, popped the cork, and poured the sparkling wine.

"Your drink my lady," he teased.

She turned a cute shade of pink, and responded, "Thank you kind sir." She smiled briefly, as he circled the bar and sat back down beside her.

"What time are you expecting Ethan," he asked, as he glanced at his Rolex.

"That's almost funny, Clint." Her tone was teasing, but uncertain.

"Yeah, I'd almost forgotten. He doesn't know what day of the week it is most of the time, much less what time of day," he laughed, shaking his head in playful dismay.

"I keep forgetting you know Ethan better than I do." She smiled, and quickly downed another glass of wine.

Suddenly feeling the urgent need to put a safer distance between them, Nouri stood to her feet and gestured toward the large, comfortable sofa and matching chair. "Why don't we sit in the living room. The couch and chair are more comfortable." She forced a smile, and then suddenly realized that she was still in her bathrobe. "Oh, my goodness, I had completely forgotten that I was still in my bathrobe." Nouri blushed, quickly adding, "I had just gotten out of the...

Clint cut her off in mid-sentence. "Nouri, it doesn't matter what you have on, or don't have on. You look incredible," he said approvingly. His eyes gave her incredible body a quick once over. He smiled lustfully.

"You are absolutely shameless! Clint Chamberlain," she playfully responded. "I should run upstairs and throw something on," she said, as she continued to blush and unconsciously clutch the neckline of her robe.

Clint's steady gaze met hers head on. He smiled seductively and then quickly added, "Not on my account. Ready for another drink." He smiled again, taking the glass from her hand. "Please, sit down, Nouri. I'll get our drinks." He quickly refilled their glasses and rejoined her in a flash.

"There you are, sweetness." He handed her the glass of wine. His eyes locked on to hers. She squirmed uncomfortably, and took a sip of her wine. Nouri was somewhat surprised that he had used his old pet name for her.

THIEF OF HEARTS

In an effort to calm the nervous strain she was currently experiencing brought on by the awkward situation presently at hand, she decided to shift the conversation to his wife, Becka.

"Gee, it's been a long time. Sorry you couldn't make our anniversary party last month." Nouri smiled nervously.

"Becka said that you were out of town, I believe. Where did you go?"

Clint took a sip of his drink, and sighed deeply. Finally, he responded in an agitated tone. "She said that, did she?" He stared blankly at his glass of wine.

"Yes. Why? Didn't you go out of town?" she asked, as she slowly circled the edge of her champagne glass with her index finger. She was too afraid to look into his eyes at that particular moment.

"No. Actually, I just didn't feel like going," Clint responded sadly. His eyes stayed focused on his drink.

"Too bad. You missed a good time." She lied. His response was cool.

"Yeah, I bet." He downed his drink, and sat his glass down sharply on the ornamented coffee table, causing her to glance his way. Nouri stayed silent for a few moments, and then leveled her eyes to his.

"What's the matter, Clint? Did I say something wrong?"

Ignoring her question completely, he asked her a question of his own. "So where are you two love birds going for dinner tonight?" he said jealously.

She studied his hurt expression for a moment, before answering, "We're supposed to go to the club tonight. Why don't you join us?" She bit her lower lip, nervously waiting for his reply. He slumped back into the overstuffed chair that he was sitting in, and released a frustrated sigh, as if something were bothering him. He nervously circled the outline of his lips with his index finger, as he carefully selected his next words.

After a few moments of silence, he responded, "No thanks, I'm afraid that I wouldn't be very good company tonight. But I'd like to stay a while and wait for Ethan, if it's okay?" He forced a small grin.

"Don't be silly, Clint. You're welcome to stay as long as you like." She smiled caringly and stood to her feet to go refill their drinks. She continued to speak from across the room. "Clint, if you don't mind me saying, you're a little on edge tonight." Nouri circled the bar and reached for the bottle of wine. She continued to speak, "Are you sure everything is all right?" She glanced at him from across the room.

"Is it your business with Ethan that has you so upset?" She picked up the drinks, circled the bar, and walked back to the living room. "Maybe I can help?" she offered, while setting the drinks down on top of the coffee table.

To deliberately avoid her curious gaze, he glanced at his watch.

"I wish you could help, Nouri, but you can't. It's personal; it's between Ethan and myself. Nothing for you to worry about." He picked up his drink and took a sip.

Without thinking of what she was going to say next, she quickly blurted out, "Personal? You mean business, don't you, Clint?" An uneasy expression crossed her face.

He sighed, quickly belting down his drink, and sharply sat his glass down on top of the coffee table.

"I don't know, sweetness, maybe a little of both." He glanced in her direction. "I don't understand Clint." She squirmed in her seat. "Nothing for you to worry about Nouri." Their eyes held steadfast.

"It's your turn to refill our drinks," she said, as she handed him her empty glass, "Don't want to talk about it, huh?" She smiled nervously.

His answer short, and to the point, "No."

"All right then, tell me Clint, how's things going with you, and your bride of only...What is it now...Ah! yes, I remember, nine months, isn't it!" she asked with a noticeable tone of jealously.

He circled the bar, heading back to the living room with their drinks, wanting desperately to ignore her question about his wife, but decided he should at least give her some sort of remark about her. He stood directly in front of Nouri, as he handed her the glass of wine, accidently brushing the side of her hand with his finger, causing her to suddenly inhale sharply, as goose bumps ran up her spine. She silently prayed that he hadn't noticed the effect he was having on her. She smiled nervously, quickly lowered her eyes, and sat her drink down on top of the coffee table.

In silence, Clint walked back to the chair he had been sitting in. He sat down, took a drink of his wine, and released a deep sigh before responding.

"I'd really rather not talk of Becka right now. If you don't mind." A distant expression suddenly masked his face.

"Trouble in paradise, Clint," she remarked smugly.

"Nouri, I said I'd rather not talk about Becka right now, okay," he said insistently.

She suddenly felt the tension between them rise. So in an effort to calm him, she apologetically remarked, "I'm sorry, Clint. I didn't mean to pry." She smiled, then added, "We're going to Lambert this weekend, so are Genna and Guy, and maybe Stacy and Stuart. It would be nice if you and Becka could make it too." Nouri studied his thoughtful expression and waited for him to respond.

After a few moments of preoccupied thought, he finally managed to answer. "I don't know, sweetness. I'm so busy right now." He forced a smile and glanced at his watch.

"Clint, what's the matter? There's something wrong, isn't there?"

"Forget it, Nouri." He shook his head.

"Have you forgotten who you are talking to, Clint Chamberlain. It's me, Nouri. Remember! I know when you're trying to hide something from me, bucko." She smiled affectionately and continued to watch his expression, unaware that she used one of his pet names, as well.

"Yes, Nouri, I do remember. Only too damn well. As a matter of fact, it still hurts like hell when I visit memory lane. So let's just don't go there, okay." He gazed into her eyes, as his handsome face turned an amazing shade of red.

"Fine!" she snapped heatedly. "Have it your way. Want another drink?" She jumped to her feet, tilted her head upward, and lifted her chin sharply into the air.

"Yeah. Sure. Why not," he responded, lightening up on his tone to her. He smiled amusingly to himself at her childish display of anger.

Clint knew that he was making himself miserable by being so close to her. He knew that he should leave, but he just couldn't go. He didn't want to go. All he could think about was his need to touch her, to pull her into his arms. There were so many things that he wanted to say to her. There were so many things that he NEEDED to say to her. There were so many things that were left unresolved between them. But did he dare!? Would she even care! He thought to himself, as he patiently waited for her to return with their drinks. He still hungered desperately for her. He continued to sit in silence watching her. Aching for what was his, but could never be again.

He suddenly adverted his attention back to the present when he heard her speaking to him in the background of his mind. He squirmed uneasily in his chair, as she handed him the drink. For a quick moment, he didn't know if he should ask her to repeat what she just said to him or not. Just being near her once again was driving him to complete and total distraction. He hadn't heard a single word that she had said.

He wanted to confess what was really on his mind. He wanted to shout his never-ending love for her, a love from the depths of his soul. But instead, he somehow managed to respond, "What took so long, sweetness. Did you have to crush the grapes with your own two feet?"

With her hand on her hip she responded, "If you don't want to talk about it, Clint Chamberlain, all you have to do is say so." There was puzzlement in her tone.

"What are you mumbling about, sweetness?" he asked, suddenly realizing that he must have missed more of her conversation to him than he realized.

"Oh just forget it!" she snapped.

"Forget what sweetness?"

"I'm worried about you, that's all." She smiled affectionately. "Please Clint, tell me what's bothering you."

THIEF OF HEARTS

"I don't think you really want to know, Nouri." He sighed, lowering his eyes to his drink.

"Clint Chamberlain! For Chrissakes! What is wrong with you tonight? Are you all right?" she shouted, as her famous temper suddenly came to life.

With his emotions clearly out of control he shouted, "Hell no! I'm not all right, as you can plainly see, woman!"

"Clint, please talk to me. I care. I honestly do. Maybe I can help," she said, as she walked closer to him. She patted his shoulder lovingly.

"Please don't, Nouri. Maybe coming here tonight was a mistake. I should probably leave." He impulsively downed his glass of wine and stood to his feet.

"Please don't go, Clint. It's still pouring outside; stay and talk to me. I'd honestly like to know what's troubling you," she said caringly.

"All right, Nouri, but only if you pour me a shot of scotch, I need something a little stronger than that girlie stuff you've been feeding me." He smiled faintly.

"Sure Clint, do you want ice in your Scotch?"

"No. Just straight will be fine, thanks."

"Okay, but I'd still like to know what's bothering you. Is it Ethan? Business? Becka catch you in someone else's bedroom?" she asked in a concerned, but playful manner. She quickly walked to the bar and brought him back a double shot of imported scotch. "One double scotch without the rocks," Nouri toyed.

"Please sit down, Clint, and tell me what's on your mind. Okay." She sat down, waiting patiently for his reply.

Clint reached for his drink, and slowly put the glass to his lips. He leveled his eyes to hers and finally responded, "You honestly care, huh?" His tone was disbelieving.

"Don't be ridiculous. Of course I do. I always have, and you know it, Clint! As a matter of fact, as I remember it, that was part of our problem. I apparently cared too much!" she said sharply, squirming uncomfortably in her seat, and nervously reached for her drink.

"Too damn much, huh sweetness? So that's why you jumped into a marriage with mister impulsive. That's rich, Nouri. Really." He shook his head in hurtful disbelief. His words left her speechless for a few moments. He knew she was about to explode. He watched her breathing increase and the sudden rise and fall of her perfectly shaped breasts through her now slightly ajar bathrobe. Finally, he noticed her expression rapidly change from a stunned look to an angry one. He quickly prepared himself for her wordy retaliation.

After what seemed like an eternity to her, she somehow managed to pull herself back under control. I refuse to argue with him, she thought to herself, as she lowered her eyes to meet his.

THIEF OF HEARTS

"Clint, what are you talking about," she said in utter dismay.

"All of your new found concern for me is really quite overwhelming, sweetness. Too bad you didn't feel that way about me before you jumped into marriage with my best friend." His hurt eyes stayed focused to hers.

"Give me a break! That's not exactly how it happened, and you know it, bucko!" she snapped, quickly downed her glass of wine, and jumped to her feet to go for a refill. Without asking him if he would care for one, she rudely grabbed his empty glass from his hand. He glanced at her with a startled expression.

"Just forget it, Nouri," he snapped back, shaking his head in disgust, when she dashed away from him in a huff.

"I don't think so, bucko. You're the one that feels the need to open old wounds. Maybe you're right in wanting to do so. We should discuss it. Maybe that way we'll finally be able to put it behind us, once and for all," she barked back from across the room. Clint heatedly jumped to his feet and walked to the large bay window to check on the storm outside. He pulled back the thick, plush drapes and then the thinner, sheer lining. He stood silently staring out into the storm.

Nouri quietly walked up behind him. "The storm is really beautiful to watch, isn't it," she said, as she glanced out the window from over his shoulder.

"Umm, but dangerous," Clint softly replied. He glanced down at her and smiled. Nouri sighed sadly.

"A beautiful, but dangerous combination." She looked up at him then added, "Sounds like us, don't you think?" She smiled faintly and slowly turned away from the window. Nouri walked over to the fireplace and tossed on another log. Clint turned away from the window to watch her, as she walked to her cozy spot on the large, comfortable sofa.

He answered her from across the room. "This is no time to discuss how great we were together in the bedroom, sweetness."

"Another failed attempt at humor, mister funny man?" She toyed back, as she turned to look at his handsome face.

"You have to admit, sweetness, our love making was pretty explosive," he said, as his eyes found hers. He smiled lustfully.

"Don't go there, Clint. I feel awkward enough as it is." Nouri swallowed hard and squirmed uncomfortably.

"Nouri, can I ask you something," he said, as he walked back to the chair that he had been sitting in.

"I don't know, I suppose so." She smiled nervously and reached for her glass of wine.

He swallowed hard, sank down deeply in his chair, and nervously glanced at her before replying, "Are you really happy being married to Ethan?" She was stunned by his question, and took longer than she should to respond to his question. Nouri was still lost in thought when he interrupted.

THIEF OF HEARTS

"Well, are you, Nouri," Clint said insistently.

She blinked herself out of her stunned state of mind, finally responding, "Ah...um...what the hell kind of question is that, Clint Chamberlain!" She downed her glass of wine and set her empty glass firmly on top of the coffee table.

"What's the matter, sweetness. Your marriage to his highness isn't everything you thought it might be?" he asked hurtfully. Her expression was one of complete disbelief.

She responded, "What the hell kind of question is that to be asking me?"

"You've already said that sweetness," Clint said, as he glared into her eyes.

"Oh, Clint Chamberlain. Honestly!" She lowered her eyes and shook her head. She stared at her empty glass.

"What's the matter, Nouri?" "Nothing is the matter."

"Why won't you answer my question about your marriage to Ethan?"

"Because Clint, it's a stupid question, that's why."

"Stupid!"

"Yes, Clint, it was a stupid question, and you know it."

"If it's such a stupid question, sweetness, then why are you writing in your journals again?" He lowered his eyes to her again and waited for her to respond.

"I have absolutely no idea what you're talking about. Do you want another drink, mister question man?" She faked a smile, while reaching for his glass.

"Ah, yes you do, Nouri. And yes, I'll have another drink, thanks." She continued to talk to him, as she made her way to the bar, and back again.

"For your information, you pompous jack-ass, I don't have to resort to writing in my journals anymore. With Ethan, I don't have to. My love life, not that it's any of your business, is just fine. Thank you very much!" She lied unconvincingly.

Clint accepted the drink from her trembling hand. His only response: "Liar." He knew she was lying. He knew her very well. The only time she drank Asti Spumanti was before, and usually after, she had been writing in her fantasy journals. A habit she had picked up while she was in college. In the past, he remembered the few times she had been bored, or had felt neglected by him. He smiled at the sudden remembered thought of her and her fantasy journals, sitting in a hot bubble bath. He shook his head fondly and smiled again.

After a few moments of silence between them, he responded, "So, you're saying what, Nouri? That I drove you to write in those damn journals of yours? Or perhaps you're trying to imply that you enjoy sex more with Ethan than you did with me. I...I wasn't man enough to satisfy you sexually, is that it Nouri?" His tone was hurtful and sharp.

"Clint Chamberlain, your silly question and answer session is starting to get on my left nerve. I implied no such thing and you damn well know it, bucko." She squirmed in her seat, as she reached for her glass of wine.

"I'm still waiting for you to answer my damn question, Nouri?"

"Clint Chamberlain, so far your silly questions don't seem to warrant an answer." She faked a yawn and stretched, trying to give the impression of boredom.

"Sweetness, I've missed that." He chuckled.

"What have you missed Clint, getting on my last nerve." She returned the smile.

"No sweetness. Watching that famous temper of yours come to life." He smiled that incredibly sexy smile of his that she could not resist in the past.

"My temper, huh? We sure had our fair share of disagreements, didn't we?" She laughed and shook her head playfully.

"Remember how great our make up sessions were after one of our silly screaming matches, baby?" He lustfully sighed and gazed into her incredible hazel colored eyes.

"Clint, don't go there. Let's have another drink, okay?" She squirmed uncomfortably again, fighting the urge to run into his arms. She handed him her glass for a refill. When she glanced up, their eyes met. Her heart began to race. Her breathing increased, and her hand trembled. Clint noticed and smiled, happy to know that he still had that type of effect on her.

"What's the matter, sweetness? Did your earth just move," he said knowingly. He intentionally brushed the side of her hand with his finger and smiled. She blushed. Her response was guilty as charged.

"Damn you, Clint." She bit her lower lip and suddenly clutched the neckline of her robe, again.

"What's the matter, Nouri? Truth hurt." He continued to stare into her eyes.

"Let's don't do this, okay," she said softly, but reluctantly, inhaling deeply and releasing the air slowly, in an effort to calm herself.

"Do what, Nouri? Talk about the obvious feelings we still have for one another. The same feelings we should've dealt with before you jumped into marriage with mister impulse? Those feelings?" he said coolly.

"Stop it, Clint," she said excitedly. Her heart began to pound rapidly, again.

"I don't want to stop it, Nouri!" he said stubbornly, as his desire for her continued to escalate.

"What if Ethan would..." He cut her off in mid sentence, "FUC..."

"Stop it, Clint, please don't," she interrupted.

THIEF OF HEARTS

    Nouri watched his wide, provocative mouth close shut and the wide angle of his jaw tighten. And she knew from her past history with him, that he was on the verge of verbally exploding. Much to her surprise, instead of exploding, he calmly turned away from her and walked over to the bar with out saying a word. "Can I freshen your drink sweetness?" he said politely, but puzzling, as he walked behind the bar.
    "Sure," she responded in return. Stunned by his apparent change of mood.
    "Earth shattering isn't it sweetness?" Clint said calmly and seductively.
    "What?" she asked in a confusing tone.
    "Us." He smiled, shaking his head in dismay.
    "More like thunder and lightening." She teased and then smiled.
    "What do you mean, Nouri?" he said smiling, handing her the glass of wine.
    "In a word...Explosive!" She returned the smile.
    "I'm not talking about us in the bedroom, sweetness." His look was seductive.
    "Ha, ha...very funny, Clint Chamberlain."
    "I was only teasing. What I actually meant was our tempers," he said, glancing at his watch.
    "So did I, mister smart man."
    "No, you didn't, sweetness."
    "I most certainly did too."
    "I don't believe you." He arched his eyebrows questioningly.
    "Sorry about your luck, mister." She returned his smile.
    "No, sorry about yours." He met her gaze. They both squirmed uncomfortably and reached for their drinks at the same time.
    Suddenly the phone rang, breaking the playful, but tense mood between them. "I'd better get that," she said, jumping to her feet and turning towards the hallway.
    "If that's Ethan, I'll tell him that you're here," she said, glancing back over her shoulder.
    Suddenly, Clint jumped to his feet and called out to her from across the room: "No! Don't tell him that I'm here!"
    Nouri stopped walking, and turned to face him. "What's that all about?"
    "Just answer the damn phone, Nouri. I'll explain when you get back." He sounded anxious and upset.
    As Nouri made her way to answer the phone, Clint made his way back to the bar and poured himself another double shot of imported scotch. He swallowed it in one drink and quickly refilled his now empty glass. He glanced at his watch.

THIEF OF HEARTS

The caller was Ethan Sommers' private secretary, Anna McCall. She was phoning to inform Nouri that her husband had to cancel their dinner date. He was unavoidably detained and wouldn't be home until late, if at all.

Clint couldn't help but to over hear Nouri shout out disappointedly, "Oh, no Ms. McCall, not again." Her tone was one of disappointment. Clint shook his head in disgust.

"Damn you Ethan," he whispered.

Nouri stood inside the hallway beside the telephone stand for several moments, pulling herself together. It was the third time that week he had canceled a date with his lovely wife, and she was extremely upset over it. "Damn you, Ethan," she mumbled just as Clint popped his head around the hallway entrance to check on her.

"Is everything all right?" he asked, as he watched her wipe a tear from her eye. He walked closer to her waiting for her to respond.

"Oh Clint," she said hopelessly, running into his arms.

"What is it Nouri?" he asked again, as he held her tightly in his arms. He gently stroked her hair. He continued to embrace her for several long moments. Finally, he spoke.

"Nouri, let's go back to the living room. I'll fix us a drink, and you can tell me all about it, okay?" He suddenly felt the need to put a safer distance between them, not wanting to take advantage of her vulnerable state.

"I'm sorry, Clint. There isn't anything to talk about. Really. I'm just disappointed. It's Ethan. He's canceled another date with me, that's all. I'm afraid I overreacted." She took a deep breath and headed back to the living room.

Clint continued to talk to her as they made their way through the long, wide hallway. "So your tears are just tears of disappointment?" he asked.

"Yes, Clint, that's all." She lied.

"Ethan can be such a jerk sometimes." He shook his head in disgust.

"I wouldn't go that far, Clint," she said defensively.

"Well, maybe fool would be more appropriate," he said, leveling his eyes to hers.

"Clint, please." She lowered her eyes to her empty glass.

"Please what, Nouri. It's the truth isn't it?" His tone was sharp.

"Enough about my boo-hoo's, Clint. Let's have another drink. What do ya say?" She handed him her glass and smiled. Disappointment still covered her face.

He nodded in agreement and accepted the glass from her hand. She sat back down in her cozy spot on the sofa, and he went to pop the cork on another bottle of Asti Spumanti. He rounded the bar with the fresh drinks in his steady hands and smiled at her when he handed her the fresh glass of sweet wine.

"Feeling better sweetness," he offered as polite conversation.

THIEF OF HEARTS

"After a few more bottles of Asti I will be," she replied with hurt still apparent in her voice.

Clint watched Nouri squirm, fidget, and down another full glass of wine. Finally, he asked in a concerned manner, "Is everything okay between you and Ethan?"

"I'm not sure. I think so. But to tell you the truth, Clint, I really don't feel much like talking about my husband right now, okay," Nouri said, forcing a smile.

"Not a problem, sweetness. But if you want to talk, I'm here all right." He smiled and gently reached over and patted her shoulder caringly.

Nouri suddenly felt flushed and light headed. She quickly realized that she had consumed entirely too much wine and should have something to eat. If she intended to keep up her pretense with Clint about things being better than they appeared to be between her and her husband, she would have to pull herself together, and quick.

"Clint, I have a splendid idea. Why don't I have Mai Li whip up one of her wonderful Chinese pastas for us. I feel like nibbling on a little something." She smiled. Clint couldn't resist the temptation to tease her.

"You want to nibble on a little something, huh?" He smiled lustfully. "Yeah. How about you, Clint?" Their eyes met; she smiled innocently.

He lustfully responded, "I've got something you can nibble on sweetness, but it isn't Chinese."

Nouri instantly blushed, as the naughty image that he had just suggested entered her brain. She quickly dismissed it, responding, "Ha, ha. Mister funny man. Shall I ask Mai Li to fix us a pasta?" She smiled.

"Sure. Why not? It's still pouring outside, and I'd hate to drive in it. But I'll have to use the phone first." He returned her smile.

"Have to check in with miss thing first. Huh?" Her tone jealous, but teasing. She arched her eyebrow and smiled wickedly.

"You have no idea," he laughed nervously. "Becka left word with my answering service earlier that she had run into a friend in Lambert and decided to stay a few extra hours. She wanted to have lunch, or something, I don't know. Anyway, I was supposed to meet her at the airport, but I had forgotten all about her until just a few minutes ago. She's probably home by now." He cringed.

"Whoops." Nouri teased.

"You've got that right!" He cringed again and shook his head unbelievingly.

"Well, Clint, you shouldn't keep miss thing waiting any longer. Help yourself to the phone, and I'll run upstairs and throw something else on. Maybe something a little less comfortable," she laughed, as she glanced down at her bathrobe. She stood to her feet and started to walk in the direction of the hallway. Clint's eyes were glued to her every stride.

"What's wrong with what you have on, sweetness? I rather like it," he said, stopping her in mid-step.

She turned to face him. "I bet you do." She smiled, knowing what was on his mind. That being she was naked under her robe. Nouri turned to leave the room when he stopped her again.

"Your robe is more reveling than you think, Nouri," he said seductively.

She turned to face him once again. "Oh please, mister fashion man," she said, putting her hand on her hip and laughing.

"It is, sweetness." She could feel his eyes burning into her flesh. She swallowed hard before answering.

"What do you mean?" She knew exactly what his statement had meant.

"Well, I know that you don't have anything on under your robe," he teased.

"You figured that out all by yourself, Einstein?" she playfully replied.

"Not exactly," his tone arrogant and knowing.

"What do you mean?"

"Ah. When you stood up to go answer the telephone earlier..." He paused, his look wanting.

"Yeah?" She blushed. Their eyes locked. She bit her lower lip nervously.

"Well. I sort of..." he grinned sheepishly.

"Don't even go there, mister," she said, cutting him off before he could finish.

"I still get to you, don't I, sweetness?" he said, after recognizing the familiar look of longing in her eyes.

"You wish." She blushed.

"Okay, enough said, feed me woman." He teased, as he tried to lead his mind into a direction other than her magnificent body, and his hunger to have it.

She turned to the intercom to ask Mai Li if she would be kind enough to fix herself and Mr. Chamberlain one of her wonderful pasta dishes, when she suddenly remembered she had given everyone the evening off. "Oh, damn!" she exclaimed, turning to face Clint again.

"Now what's wrong?" he said, shaking his head.

"I forgot!" She cringed.

"Forgot what, Nouri?" he asked, as he studied her expression.

"I forgot that I gave everyone the night off." She sighed helplessly.

"And Mai Li?"

"Yes, her too." She smiled and shrugged her shoulders.

"You mean you're in this huge house all by yourself?" His look showed concern.

"Well, you're with me."

THIEF OF HEARTS

"What about when I leave? I just don't think you should be in a house this size all by yourself, that's all." He shook his head and put his hands on his hips.

"For goodness sake, Clint, you're beginning to sound like my father." She laughed and then added, "Anyway, it would only take ten minutes or so for Mai Li or one of the other staff members to get here, if I really need something. Plus we have the best security system money can buy. Clint, please stop worrying about me. I'll be fine." She smiled and walked back to her cozy spot on the sofa.

"Does Ethan leave you alone, like this, very often?" he asked with concern still in his tone.

"Oh, Clint, please." She nervously walked back to the bar.

"I'm serious, Nouri. Does he?" he asked insistently. "

It's not his fault. He's a very busy man." She explained, defensively.

"That idiot!" he snapped, as he watched Nouri set their drinks down on the coffee table.

"Please, Clint. I've got other things to worry about tonight." She smiled teasingly.

"Oh yeah? Like what?" He returned the smile, but concern still on his face.

"Like our Chinese pasta. I'm starving!" She smiled and patted her stomach.

"For Chrissakes, sweetness. How hard can it be to boil water?" He teasingly shook his head and added, "Never mind. I suddenly remember your cooking ability." He laughed loudly.

"Hey bucko! I resent that," she teasingly snapped.

"You mean resemble that, don't you sweetness?"

"Okay, mister smart ass, just for that remark, you can be the one to cook our dinner tonight." She laughed with her back-at-you atyitude.

"No problem. If you remember correctly, I can make a mean spaghetti and meatball dinner." He smiled, as he teasingly reached his arm over his shoulder to give himself a pat on the back.

"Yes I do remember, and you don't have to convince me any further. The job is already yours. Mister chef man." She shook her head playfully.

"Sweetness, you go change if you like, and I'll go make the pasta." He teasingly laughed, as his eyes trailed the length of her body lustfully.

"Clint Chamberlain, you are absolutely shameless. You do know that, don't you?" Her eyes met his penetrating gaze; she smiled nervously.

"When you're finished changing sweetness, join me in the kitchen, and we'll see what we can cook up!" he said, as he continued to tease and embarrass her.

He enjoyed toying with her, watching her get excited, watching her face flush a cute shade of healthy pink, and the way her eyes would childishly sparkle, and the way her breasts would erotically rise and suddenly fall every time her breathing would increase. He smiled lovingly, as he waited for her to respond to his last teasing remark.

"The only thing we will be cooking up and serving tonight will be pasta, mister chef man. Got that?" She toyed back, as her heart suddenly began to race out of control. The remembered image of the last time Clint Chamberlain fixed a spaghetti dinner for them suddenly flashed inside her brain. She was still living with him.

He was in the kitchen cooking spaghetti and meatballs, with salad and garlic bread. He was wearing an apron that read: *kiss the cook.* She was only wearing her birthday suit and was sitting at their dinning room table that he had decorated with a red and white checkered table cloth with two long-stem red candles...She had been the appetizer before the gourmet meal. She smiled lovingly at the envisioned memory, before blinking herself back to reality.

Clint quickly recognized the familiar look of remembered longing in her eyes and smiled.

"Hey, sweetness. How about another drink with me before I start dinner and you go upstairs to change." He smiled that ever so sexy smile of his that she could not resist in the past.

"Are you trying to get me drunk, Clint Chamberlain?" she teasingly remarked. Their eyes met for a quick moment.

"Why, Nouri St. Charles Sommers, I've never been so insulted in my entire life!" he teased and then added, "And anyway, sweetness, I hate to be the one to break it to you, but I do believe you're already a tad, on the, shall we say, just to be kind of course, a little on the tipsy side." He laughed amusingly.

"I most certainly am not! I'll have you know, bucko," she playful snapped.

"If you say so sweetness. But..." He stopped talking, almost as though his mind drifted away.

"But what, Clint?" she asked with a puzzled look on her face.

"Nothing, Nouri." His tone sounded depressed again.

"What is it Clint. What were you going to say?" She smiled.

"Nouri, can I ask you a personal question?"

"I don't know, mister question man. We tried that earlier, and it didn't work out very well." She smiled nervously.

"I'm serious Nouri. We keep skirting around issues that we both agree we should finally try to deal with, but we keep getting side-tracked, and that isn't solving anything between us." His tone shifted to serious.

THIEF OF HEARTS

"Do we have to do this tonight Clint? I'm afraid that our conversation will just lead to one of our famous screaming matches."

"Nouri, please. I want to talk now. Do you understand?" He forced a smile.

"Only if you promise that our conversation won't turn into a fight between us. I don't think I could bear that. Not tonight anyway." She squirmed uncomfortably.

"Before I make that promise, maybe we should make a few definitions perfectly clear." He smiled.

"Like what, mister attorney man?" She glanced up at him.

"For instance, you, of course, realize that talking passionately about something and arguing about something are quite similar, agreed?" He smiled that famous legal eagle smile of his.

"Your point is noted, sir. Please continue."

"Nouri, all jokes aside. I just want a few honest answers from you. That would be nice." He sighed.

"Clint, first you asked if you could ask me a personal question, and now you say a few honest answers would be nice. Which is it? A personal question, or a few personal question?" she remarked smugly.

"All right, miss smart ass, several. How about that? Can you deal with several?" he said sharply.

"Well I don't know, mister question man. Ask me and we'll see," she playfully responded.

"I'll ask you again, Nouri. Are you going to be completely honest with me?" He leveled his eyes to hers.

"Clint, what the hell is wrong with you tonight? Are you and miss thing fighting again, and you came here tonight to take it out on me, is that it?" Her tone was hurt and confused.

"Forget it, Nouri. Forget the whole damn thing!" he hurtfully snapped.

"See, this is exactly what I mean. You're mad again, and I haven't done a damn thing!"

"Well, you started it, damn it!" he shouted.

"Started what, Clint?" she asked, shaking her head in disbelief.

"Why the hell didn't you come back to me that night, damn it!" His emotions clearly out of control.

"You know damn good and well why I left, Clint Chamberlain!" She leveled her hurt eyes to his.

"Yes, but you always came back. Until that night. Why?"

"Because I got tired of waiting for a real commitment from you, that's why, Clint." She felt the tears begin to form in her eyes. She quickly tried to stop them.

"What the hell are you talking about, Nouri? I gave you a ring. That's what you wanted, wasn't it?" He looked at her. His eyes...sad.

"Yes, but I also wanted to actually get married. That's what marriage is you know." Her tone laced with hurt.

"Well, I thought that was understood between us." He squirmed uncomfortably.

"Well, you thought wrong, mister! You thought I'd wait around until hell froze over. Admit it damn it!"

"No I didn't, Nouri. I just couldn't figure out why the rush. Surely you knew how much I loved you." He lightened his tone of voice to her.

"How? You sure never said the words." She glanced down at her empty glass of wine.

"I was so stupid. I'm so sorry. I just assumed that you knew. The way I melted every time I saw you. Melted every time we made love. God! Nouri, you were my world. I just thought you knew." He hung his head.

"Clint, what the hell do you want from me?" A tear rolled down her cheek. She secretly fought with her emotions, desperately wanting to run into his arms.

"Nouri, I love you," Clint remarked softly.

"It's a little too late for the 'I LOVE YOU' words now, don't you think?" Another tear rolled down her face.

"God baby. I hope not!" He fought back his own tears, desperately longing to hold her in his arms.

"Clint, please don't talk like that. I can't handle it."

"How the hell do you think I feel, Nouri?"

"Clint if only you would have told me when I needed to hear those words." She hung her head sadly.

"So what are you saying, Nouri? If I would have verbally expressed my love for you, then you wouldn't have left me?" He looked for the answer in her eyes.

"Maybe. Maybe not. I don't know anymore."

"So you're implying that by me not confessing my love for you, drove you to impulsively marry my best friend?"

"Clint, I'm sorry if I hurt you. I didn't mean to. Everything with Ethan and I happened so fast." She shook her head in dismay.

"Too damn fast!" he snapped, shaking his head in amazement.

"Well maybe, Clint. I don't know. But you know damn good and well that I had no idea that you and Ethan even knew each other. How could I have known something like that for chrissakes. But you, mister-can't-keep-it-in-your-pants, are a different story!" she said sharply, placing her hand on her hips and leveling her hurt eyes to his.

"What the hell are you talking about, for chrissakes?"

"You have nerve coming here raising hell with me over my marriage to Ethan. You couldn't wait to jump into marriage with miss thing now, could you?" Anger in her tone.

"Nouri, I married Becka Adams to hurt you." He confessed with dread.

"Give me a break Clint Chamberlain!" She shook her head unbelieving.

"It's true. I swear it!" He stared into her hurt and angry eyes.

"Yeah, right. You went and jumped into your own whirlwind marriage with a drop dead, gorgeous blond, just to punish me. Oh, poor baby. Did I forget to mention her to die for body?" she remarked sarcastically.

"Believe what you want. But it's the truth. I knew how much you hated her, and rightfully so, I might add."

"I tried to warn you about her, but you wouldn't listen." Nouri shook her head smugly.

"Yes, and now I'm paying the ultimate price, believe me." Clint shook his head in disbelief.

"We are about pitiful, aren't we?" She smiled faintly.

"I'd say that's the understatement of the year, sweetness."

"So you're not happy with Becka?" she asked, giving him her full attention.

"Nouri, I didn't come here tonight to talk about my problems with Becka. I came here first of all to see Ethan. I have to admit that I honestly didn't expect him to be here. But in all fairness, I was hoping that he might be. We have some major problems with this corporation that he is trying to take over. But that aside, I truly wanted to see you. Let me rephrase that. I truly needed to see you. I'm lost without you. When you left me, I almost died. The only way I survived was to keep telling myself that you would come back."

"Please, Clint, don't."

"Nouri, please let me finish."

"NO, Clint I... I can't deal with this right now, I'm sorry."

She jumped to her feet and walked to the bar. He walked up behind her, slowly slipping his arms around her waist, and gently laying his head on her shoulder. His emotions needed no words. His pulse began to beat rapidly, as one of his arms loosened just enough to gently turn her around to face him. He gently kissed her temples. Her ear. And her eyelids. "Please don't, Clint," she whispered hopelessly.

He ignored her quiet protest, as he tightened his embrace and lowered his head to kiss her. He brushed his lips ever so gently across hers. "I love you, Nouri," he whispered the words seductively across her mouth with his warm breath, and then he raised his head. Reluctantly releasing her from his tight embrace, he walked over to the large bay window to look at the storm.

After a long silence, he spoke. "Sweetness, do you really love Ethan?" He paused for a moment and then continued, "I have to know." He glanced over his shoulder to look at her.

"Clint, I seem to be at a complete loss for words, or thought, right at the moment. Please let's don't do this. Not right now." Her expression was filled with mixed emotions.

"Nouri, I need to know." His tone was insistent.

"Clint, the reason I can't answer that now is because I don't have an answer for you. To be completely honest with you, I...I'm not sure anymore. I'm confused. I want to love Ethan, and I want to make our marriage work, on one hand, but on the other hand, it's getting more difficult for me. He's never at home anymore. He constantly breaks our dates. It's almost like I've married a person who doesn't really exist. He's definitely not the person that I thought I was marrying. I don't know what I'm going to do." She sighed and then reached for her drink.

Clint walked over to the large sofa and sat down beside her. Silently, he pulled her over into a protective embrace. She pulled her legs up under her, and laid her head on his well-built shoulder. He was surprisingly understanding of her need to just be held. The image of her sadness affected him deeply.

She allowed herself to feel the strength of his embrace. It calmed her inside. For a few silent moments, she was able to feel safe and protected, shielded from all the hurt, loneliness, and disappointments in her life with Ethan. She released a sigh.

Finally, Clint spoke. "Nouri, I'm sorry you're going through all of this uncertainty with Ethan." He gently stroked her hair. His tone was soft and understanding.

"I'm so glad you stopped by tonight, Clint," she whispered hoarsely, as she wiped another tear from her cheek.

"Me too, sweetness." He pulled her even closer into his embrace. He gently kissed the side of her head.

"Oh Clint, I'm so confused," she cried.

"I know, sweetness. Do you want me to talk to Ethan for you?"

"No, Clint. It's something that I will have to figure out for myself." She sighed sadly.

"Nouri there is a lot about Ethan that you don't know." She lifted her head to look at his face. He had her complete attention at that point.

"Like what, Clint?" Her eyes bore attentively into his.

"Nouri, Ethan is a very complex man. To tell you the truth, I've known him for almost nineteen years, and I still don't know the complete man." He sighed.

"I don't understand," she replied confusingly.

"Sweetness, my bond of friendship with Ethan won't allow me to talk about certain aspects of him, or his life, especially his business affairs. But I will tell you this, he's not the man for you. I wish you had never married him. You have no idea what you've gotten yourself into." He sighed and shook his head sadly.

"What do you mean, Clint? Please tell me." Her expression suddenly looked tense.

"Nouri, there was a reason I never introduced Ethan Sommers to you when we lived together. Quite simply, I didn't want you to know someone like him. He's...well, he's..." Clint suddenly stopped talking as if his current thought had changed directions.

"What is it, Clint?" she asked with a stunned expression plastered across her face.

"You know sweetness, you honestly don't know what Ethan is capable of. It wouldn't surprise me one bit if he deliberately..."

"Deliberately what, Clint?" she asked with concern, after releasing herself from his embrace. She stood to her feet to freshen their drinks.

"Baby, I better feed you. We both have had a lot to drink. Maybe you should run up stairs and throw on some jeans or something. I'll phone Becka, then I'll fix us dinner, okay?" He smiled, deliberately changing the subject.

"Clint, I absolutely hate it when you change the subject like that on me. I'm not finished talking to you. I have a lot of questions. And I need answers to them, do you understand?" she said insistently .

"In the first place, I can't answer most of your questions about Ethan. Sweetness, and in the second place..."

She cut him off before he finished making his point to her. "You mean you won't answer them. Isn't that what you meant to say, Clint?" Her tone was one of disappointment.

"Maybe. All I want to tell you, Nouri, is that we both have a lot to think about in the next few days. I love you. I always have and I always will. You're my woman damn it! You should have never married Ethan Sommers. You belong to me. I know it, and, damn it, you know it too! Now go up stairs, woman, and put some clothes on before I lose all self control and make love to you right here, right now! Do I make myself perfectly clear, Nouri?" His passionate outburst surprised not only Nouri, but also himself.

After the initial shock of his passionate outburst wore off several moments later, and Nouri regained control of her ability to finally speak, she remarked, "That's about the fourth time you've left me speechless tonight, Clint Chamberlain." She smiled longingly.

"Nouri, I meant every word that I just said." He returned the smile. His emotions, again, began to rage out of control. He thought, "Please Nouri, run while you can. I can't fight my desire to have you one moment longer."

"Clint. I...I..."

He quickly interrupted her, "You've got ten seconds to leave, or I promise you Nouri....I...I will get up off this sofa, and I will make love to you!...nine seconds." He glanced down at his watch.

Nouri quickly clutched the neckline of her robe, and gave Clint a seductive look, as she fled past him, on her way to quickly throw on her jeans.

She still loves me. I know it! He thought to himself, after she left the room. He walked over to the fireplace and tossed on another log. He went to the bar for another shot of imported scotch. With his drink in hand, he walked over to the large bay window to look outside.

Even with the loud crackling sounds of thunder, and the blinding flashes of lightening, Clint's mind swiftly drifted away. The colorful images still clearly embedded in his mind. It was his and Nouri's last evening together. The last time he had held her in his arms and made love to her. God! I was so stupid, he thought, as he continued to remember. Earlier that evening they had argued, one of their famous screaming matches. He had just given her an engagement ring. She was beside herself with excitement. He was not. It was something that she had wanted from him for a long time. She had driven him nuts dropping hints for one. He continued to remember and smiled.

She was anxious to set a date for their marriage. He was not. He loved her deeply. Passionately. But he was afraid of commitment, at least the permanent kind. He was afraid of losing her, and God knows, he didn't want to do that. So to make her happy, and to show her how much he loved her, without saying a word, he surprised her with the ring that she had wanted for so long. Unable to set a date, she flew into a fit of anger. What should have been a happy occasion, turned out to be the beginning of the end for them. One word led to another. One action led to a chain reaction of events. Many of which he later regretted.

He heatedly slammed the door behind him, as he stormed away from their apartment. He later ran into one of his many old flames, Anita Maree. She was really quite lovely, and turned out to be just the right medicine he needed to help cure him of his reoccurring ailment: Pre-wedding jitters, A.K.A. a life time commitment with the same woman for all of eternity.

After taking his sexual frustration with Nouri out on the lovely Ms. Anita Maree, he headed back home to the woman that he really loved, heavily burdened with guilt. He quietly tiptoed into the apartment and headed directly to the bathroom for a quick shower. He was anxious to make sure that the promiscuous Ms. Maree hadn't left any noticeable love marks on his body. She was quite famous for branding her unsuspecting victims. God knows that she had given him his fair share of love bites in their short lived, heated past together.

"Thank God!" He sighed in relief, after finding no little love bruises anywhere on his body. He quickly showered and quietly entered their bedroom. He had originally planned to sneak into the bedroom, grab a pillow and sheet, and sleep on the couch that night. He wasn't prepared to be so overtaken with desire for Nouri, as he walked into their bedroom.

He stood in the doorway of the bedroom, watching the beautiful woman that had captured his heart sleep. She looked like an angel lying there. He sighed longingly. She was lying on her stomach and snuggled up with his pillow on his side of the bed. Her beautiful, curly hair had fallen around the sides of her face, adding a child-like innocence to her expression. He moved closer to her. A wave of emotion quickly came over him, as he continued to walk closer. God! She's beautiful, he thought to himself, as he sat on the bed beside her. Unable to speak, he lovingly leaned down and gently pressed his lips to hers. She slightly stirred and stretched seductively. The next moment, his desire for her raced out of control.

"I want you, sweetness," he whispered, as he brushed the outline of her ear with his warm tongue.

"Mmm," she responded, moving her hand behind her back in an effort to find the man behind the words and pull him closer to her. Even in her sleep, she wanted to respond to him. To his touch. To his kisses.

"I'm sorry, sweetness," he whispered in her ear with his warm breath.

"I know you are, darling," was her sleepy response.

He craved her for reasons he couldn't explain. Every time he would touch her, he would get caught up in a renewed desire, over and over again. Her touch held a sort of magic over him. He never fully understood why his need to have her was as important to him as the air that he breathed. He couldn't get enough of her. Her love. The true passion he felt when he touched her, and the way he felt inside when his body would enter hers. No other woman had ever been able to have that effect on him. He honestly loved her, even though he had never actually told her with words.

"I should have told her," he whispered to himself, as he continued to remember about the last time he had made love to Nouri. He wanted to recall every intimate detail. Just like he had so many times since.

"Oh darling," she whispered softly, as he began to lovingly caress her sensuous body. He gently caressed her perfect shaped breasts. She moaned longingly. He gently lowered his hands to travel over her soft, perfect frame. She moaned again.

"You're so beautiful, sweetness." He remembered saying to her before she opened her eyes and pulled him into her arms. They deeply and passionately kissed for an eternal moment. His urgent need to have her cut his foreplay plan short. "Oh, God! Nouri, I have to have you right this second, or I'll surely die," were the last words he had said to her for over a year. After they made love that night, and Clint had fallen asleep, Nouri quietly got out of bed, packed her bags, and disappeared into the night. Leaving her diamond and gold engagement ring on her pillow, in place of a good-bye note.

Clint sighed deeply as he put his treasured memory back inside his heart. "I was so stupid to let her go," he whispered, as he went to the bar to fix himself another shot of scotch. He glanced at his watch and began to wonder what was taking Nouri so long.

Suddenly, the image of his wife, Becka, entered his brain. "Damn," he muttered, quickly making his way down the hallway to where the phone was stationed. The image of her angrily pacing back and forth in front of the fireplace sent an immediate surge of dread through his body as he reached for the receiver. The God awful rage his wife was capable of was beginning to scare him. He never knew what she might do from one moment to the next...Her spurts of anger were becoming more and more violent. Raging completely out of control most of the time, surpassing any form of anger he had ever seen before. He cringed at just the thought of her rage. He changed his mind about phoning her and quickly slammed the receiver down. "I'll deal with her later," he said as he went to the kitchen to prepare the pasta dinner.

Clint Chamberlain married Becka Adams out of spite. It was his way of getting even with Nouri Sommers for impulsively jumping into marriage with his best friend. After all, she did marry his best friend first.

Becka and Nouri used to be best friends at one time. Clint hadn't actually known Becka then. He had only heard about her and her wild escapades some years later. Clint took it upon himself to find a way to be introduced to her, after he found out the shocking news of Nouri secretly getting married to his best friend, a year after they had been married.

Clint was devastated when he learned that Ethan's mystery bride of one year was none other than his ex-lover, Nouri. He was invited to their first wedding anniversary party last summer at the Sommer's Estate. The mystery bride was to be officially *unveiled* on this festive occasion. And Ethan wanted to make sure that his best friend sat right next to him at the unveiling. He and Nouri were both speechless when their eyes met for the first time in over a year.

Somehow, they both managed to fake their way through a most uncomfortable evening. Clint was introduced to Becka Adams, courtesy of Ethan Sommers, of course. Ethan had heard through the grape vine earlier that evening that Clint was dying to meet her. Once Clint said hello to Becka, Nouri silently began to fume!

Nouri and Becka were once partners in an Interior Design Business. When their friendship turned sour, they sold the business, and both women went

THIEF OF HEARTS

their separate ways, only seeing each other socially. On those rare occasions, Nouri forced herself to appear civil, but it wasn't easy.

Becka was insanely jealous of Nouri. She used to copy Nouri in almost every way. She would buy the same style and types of expensive clothing, bubble bath, and perfume. She would drive the same type of automobile. She even went to Nouri's personal hair dresser, Michelle. She seemed to want everything that Nouri had, even a few of her former dates. Becka's continued obsession with Nouri's life, ended their friendship.

Clint had remembered Nouri telling him about her former obsessive friend, but after meeting her, and seeing how beautiful she was, Clint thought that Nouri's version of what transpired between them must have been largely exaggerated. He quickly got the idea to give Nouri a taste of her own medicine. He married Becka immediately, actually faster than Nouri married Ethan. Clint had only dated Becka for less than one week when he proposed. She immediately said yes. They were married two days later.

In only nine months of marriage, Clint had realized what a horrible mistake he had made by marrying Becka. He had found out the hard way. She was not the beautiful woman he had hoped she would be. Nouri had been right about her all along. He should've listened to his wiser head.

Aside from her sexy body and being incredibly good-looking, she made Clint's life a living nightmare. She was a real wacko! Her, anything but normal, behavior was completely out of control, and getting worse by the day, it seemed.

At first, Clint didn't mind a good shouting match with her from time to time. At times, making up had been worth it. But as the days slowly turned into months, her anger worsened, slowly turning into ungodly displays of rage. Her behavior was not only unacceptable but down right scary.

Her obsessive nature had gotten worse, as well. He didn't know how much more of her insanity he could, or would endure. Especially after she rejected his suggestion to see a therapist. He had suggested it after their last fight a week ago, when she threatened to cut his heart out with a knife if she ever caught him cheating on her. The same thing he has suspected her of doing all along. He just wasn't able to prove it yet. He had recently heard a rumor that his wife was having an affair with none other than his so-called best friend.

It was a rumor that's been buzzing around Lambert for quite sometime, but had just recently come to his attention. Other than the fact the rumor, if found to be true, might hurt Nouri, he could have cared less. He was actually hoping the rumor had, in fact, been true. It would be the perfect excuse to rid himself of her once and for all. Something he had dreamed of doing for the past six months. That thought alone had given him reason to smile.

What the hell is taking that woman so damn long, Clint said to himself, as he glanced at his watch. He shook his head. "Women!" He sighed, while rolling his eyes.

He then went into the living room, the smaller one. It was set up to accommodate a smaller, more intimate group of people, around twenty or so. Where the larger dining room was used for more social functions holding up to several hundred people at one sitting.

Clint shook his head amusingly, as he entered the small, but vast dining area. "Well, I suppose we'll just have to make do." He jokingly sighed before he lit the long stem candles that were already stationed in the center of the enormous, but quite magnificent mahogany table. After Clint set the table, and opened a French bottle of red wine, he then made his way to the footing of the long spiral staircase.

"Sweetness, chow time, come and get it." He playfully shouted. There was no response. "Sweetness, dinner is ready," he shouted once again. Still no response. "For chrissakes, your dinner is getting cold." He shouted one final time before he decided to run up the dreadfully long flight of stairs.

After reaching the top of the staircase, he shouted her name one more time. There was still no response. "Damn it woman!" he moaned, as he walked over to the master bedroom. He dreaded having to go inside. Being that close to her and a bed, at the same time, was almost too much temptation for any man to have to endure. "God please give me the will power to behave myself," he mumbled, as he put his hand in the custom-crafted, gold door knob.

Once inside her bedroom, Nouri realized just how tipsy she had become. She decided to lie down for a few moments before changing into her jeans. She knew it would take Clint awhile to prepare dinner, and she needed a few moments to collect her thoughts, as well as her emotions, anyway. With so many different images and conflicting emotions swimming around inside her brain, she instantly fell into a sound sleep without meaning to.

Clint knocked on the door the same time as he opened it. "Sweetness," he said softly before noticing her asleep on the giant sized bed. "Poor baby," he whispered, walking closer to her. She looked like an angel snuggled up with her pillow cradled in her arms. He sat down beside her on the giant bed. Instantly filled with desire for her, he sighed hopelessly.

Clint was hypnotized by her beauty. He sat on the bed for a long time, fighting with his need to touch her. To kiss her. To pull her into her arms, and, oh, how he longed to do just that. Memories of their past romance quickly flooded his mind with crystal clear images of them together making love. "God how I miss you baby," he whispered, as he continued to reminisce. He smiled longingly when she slightly stirred. Her robe had come loose when she rolled onto her back and stretched. His eyes quickly seized the opportunity to admire her incredible body.

His eyes stopped to examine her perfectly shaped legs. He smiled lustfully when he suddenly remembered how wonderful her shapely legs had felt wrapped around his manly hips, when she used them as a tool to pull him deep inside her. He released a sigh of remembered bliss.

Clint was jarred back to the present when Nouri suddenly rolled onto her side. I'd better go while I still have enough strength left to leave, he thought rising to his feet. He leaned down and softly pressed his lips to hers, thinking to himself, "It's far from over between us, sweetness." He caringly pulled a sheet over her body before leaving her bedroom.

"My friendship with Ethan Sommers be dammed," Clint mumbled, while running down the long spiral staircase. He quickly made his way to the bar. He needed a drink more than ever. As he sat on the bar stool, his mind seemed to be racing in two different directions at one time. Lost in thought and out of habit, he bit his lower lip, suddenly remembering how sweet Nouri's lips had tasted when he tasted the fruity wine from her kiss. He smiled lovingly.

Clint quickly downed several double shots of scotch before going to the fireplace. Still heavy with thought, he tossed on another log and glanced at his watch. He walked back to the bar and set down his empty glass, and picking up the bottle of scotch in its place. With bottle in hand, he went over to the over stuffed chair that he had been sitting in earlier and sank deep into it. He began to stare into the golden embers of fire dancing around in the fireplace.

His mind was still racing in several directions at once. Torn between a love that was his to begin with and the bonds of friendship with a man he never fully understood. "What to do? What to do?" he mumbled to himself before downing several large drinks of reddish-brown liquor. He continued to stare into the beautiful flames, unsuccessfully trying to organize his scattered thoughts and mixed emotions. He continued to stare at the golden embers of fire burning in the fireplace. The heat from the beautiful flames only added to his desire for Nouri. He downed another long drink of scotch. The more he drank, the more he wanted to go upstairs and make love to her. He felt the need to reclaim what was rightfully his. "Damn you, Ethan!" he cried, as he wiped a tear from his eye. "God, I have to get out of here!" he drunkenly spattered, before adding, "God, help me, I've lost all self control." He jumped to his feet and without any further hesitation, he knew it was time for him to leave.

He quickly grabbed the bottle of scotch and staggered out the front door, forgetting that his car keys were still inside the mansion on top of the bar. He swiftly shut the door behind him. The door would automatically lock itself every time the door closed.

"Damn it!" he suddenly moaned, after realizing his mistake. He began to slowly stagger his way down the ten mile stretch of driveway, heading for the nearest motel to spend the night.

Chapter 3

Nouri Sommers was startled from her tipsy state of sleep by the bothersome ringing of the telephone. The sudden jolt of her arms swinging caused her to knock the telephone onto the floor. "Damn," she complained, as she glanced first at the time then at the caller ID, with one eye open. "Who the hell could be calling so late," she moaned after recognizing the phone number from Lambert. She squirmed half way off the bed, attempting to retrieve the phone. Her effort was in vain. She fell off the bed and onto the full shagged carpet, hitting her right ankle on the side of the night stand. "Damn it!" she squealed, attempting to untangle her curled body. She eagerly reached for the tender spot, anxious to rub the small purple bruise.

After another curse word or two, she, at last, managed to hoarsely respond to the late night caller with a cranky, "Hello!" A few seconds of silence followed her cranky greeting.

Finally, the voice on the other end, also in a not so pleasant mood, responded, "Hello, Nouri." It was Ethan. He continued, "Sorry to wake you."

Still half dazed, she yawned and stretched.

"Ethan, it's late. Where are you?" she asked, forgetting about the caller ID machine.

"I'm in the city," he lied, paused, then continued. "I decided to stay at the condo tonight. I have several early meetings tomorrow," he said convincingly.

"I can't believe you're not coming home again Ethan," she sighed in disbelief.

"Nouri, I need to get at least a few hours sleep tonight. If I drive home, I won't get any!" Ethan's impatience grew.

Nouri coolly replied, "I see."

"No, you don't see! I can hear it in your tone of voice," he remarked sharply. There was silence on the other end.

"You're angry, aren't you?"

"No, Ethan. I'm not angry. A little disappointed, maybe." She rose to her feet and walked to the window to check on the storm.

"Nouri, I'm getting a little tired of you moodiness," he scolded.

"Oh please, Ethan. Give me a break." She rolled her eyes, as she continued to glance out the window.

"You knew that I was a busy man when you married me!"

"Yes, Ethan, but now..."

He interrupted her. "That's just the way it is, Nouri. You should be used to it by now."

"Well, I'm not!" Nouri snapped.

THIEF OF HEARTS

"Well, that's a problem you're just going to have to deal with," he responded arrogantly.

"You're right Ethan. I'm sorry," she said, turning from the window. She excitedly continued, "Ethan, I have a wonderful idea!"

He shook his head annoyingly. "What's that, Nouri?"

"Why don't I have Fredrick drive me to the city? I could be there in an hour or so!" She smiled eagerly.

"Damn it, Nouri! That's ridiculous! If you came here tonight, I wouldn't get any sleep at all. You understand, don't you? Anyway, we're going to Lambert this weekend. We'll have plenty of time to be together then." Nouri sighed. "Nouri, I didn't call you tonight to upset you, damn it! I just wanted to say good night and let you know that I wouldn't be home."

"Ethan, I think we need to talk," her voice was filled with sadness.

"I tell you what Nouri, Have Fredrick drive you to the city tomorrow, and we'll have lunch. I'll have Ms. McCall make the reservations and phone you with the time and location."

"I'm not one of your damn employees, Ethan!" she barked hurtfully.

"What the hell does that mean?" His irritation grew.

"Time and location, really, Ethan," she said sarcastically, rolling her eyes and releasing a frustrated sigh.

"Nouri, I'm getting a little tired of your attitude," he scolded.

"I'm sorry, Ethan."

"Good. Now be a good girl and go back to bed. And if you're a real good girl, I just might have a little something special waiting for you when we meet for lunch, all right?" he said in an effort to humor her.

After Ethan's offer of a bribe for her obedience, Nouri suddenly felt as though the wind had just been knocked out of her. She wasn't sure if she wanted to laugh or cry at that point. She just quietly mumbled the words, "Good night, Ethan," and quickly put the receiver down without waiting for a response.

The nerve of that man! She angrily thought, shaking her head in dismay, while quickly making her way to the bathroom. She wanted to take something for the explosion currently going off inside her brain. She also needed to rid her mouth of the stale taste of wine from a few hours before.

After she brushed her teeth and digested several aspirins, the image of Clint Chamberlain downstairs cooking pasta suddenly popped inside her pounding head.

"Oh my God! I forgot all about him!" she blurted, quickly running out of the bathroom. She anxiously went to the dresser and swiftly retrieved a pair of jeans and a loose fitting sweater. However, just before reaching the staircase, she suddenly realized that she had forgotten to throw her sweater on. "Oh damn!" she moaned, quickly making her way back to the bedroom.

"I'm sorry," she said as she entered the vacant kitchen. She walked into the dining room. No Clint. The living room. The library. The pool room, but still no Clint Chamberlain to be found.

"Where the hell is that man," she whispered, making her way to the bar. He's got to be somewhere, she thought, as she picked up his keys, and playfully tossed them into the air and caught them.

Still lost in thought, wondering where he could be, it suddenly dawned on her to see if his car was still parked outside. What a crazy night this has been, she thought, after noticing Clint's car, but no Clint. "Surely, that man has to be somewhere, but where," she mumbled wonderingly.

The rain had stopped, but the air was damp and quite cool. She stood outside for a few moments, calling out his name. Her efforts were in vain. After no immediate response, she decided it would probably be best for her to acquire the assistance of Fredrick to look around the estate grounds. Knowing Clint as well as she did, Nouri suddenly worried that he may have decided to walk to the nearest motel, which was almost twenty-five miles away. Yes. That's exactly what he tried to do, I just know it, was her last thought, before picking up the telephone.

"Hello, Fredrick. I'm sorry to disturb you so late."

"Yes, madam. Is everything all right?" her chauffer said with concern.

"Yes, Fredrick. I just need a favor."

"A favor madam?" He blinked his blurred eyes several times, trying to read what time the clock read on the nightstand on his bed.

"Yes Fredrick. I need you to look around the estate grounds for Mr. Chamberlain. He's here somewhere."

"Mr. Chamberlain, madam?"

"Yes, Fredrick, that's right. Mr. Chamberlain."

"Are you sure that everything is all right, madam?"

"Everything is fine, Fredrick. I just need you to try and find him for me. He's had too much to drink this evening, and he may need a ride home. Do you understand, Fredrick?"

"Yes, madam. Anything else?"

"Be sure to let me know when you find him. I need to know that he's okay."

"Yes, madam."

"Oh, and Fredrick, I'll need you to drive me to the city tomorrow. I'm meeting my husband for lunch."

"Yes madam, goodbye."

"Now where did I see Mai Li put the ice pack?" Nouri mumbled to herself, holding her head, trying to calm her migraine. "Ahh yes. Now I remember." She continued to mumble, as she suddenly realized that she had seen it next to the box of black rum tea inside the kitchen cabinet. Mmm. Black rum tea, that sounds good, she thought to herself as she entered the kitchen. Just as she opened the cabinet door, the phone rang. Nouri stopped what she was doing and turned to face the phone. She glanced at the caller ID machine. Recognizing the home number of Clint and Becka Chamberlain, she quickly reached for the phone. Nouri was hoping that Clint was calling to let her know that he had made it home okay.

"Hello. Clint, I'm so glad..."

Becka Chamberlain quickly interrupted. "No, Nouri, it's me Becka, not Clint."

"Becka? What is it? Is something wrong? Is Clint all right?" Nouri said, beginning to panic.

"Slow down, Nouri. What the hell are you talking about?"

"I'm talking about Clint. Is he all right?"

"Why the hell wouldn't he be?"

"Becka, I just thought... never mind what I thought. Why are you phoning?" Nouri responded sarcastically, as she massaged her aching temples.

"I was trying to track my husband down, and from the sound of your excited tone of voice, its a good thing I decided to call, huh, Nouri," Becka jealously remarked.

"I don't know what you mean."

"Sure you do, Nouri," she responded accusingly.

"I'm afraid I was never any good at reading minds, Becka."

"Really? As I recall it Nouri, you thought you were good at almost everything," she snapped coolly.

"What the hell does that mean?" Nouri remarked heatedly, shaking her head in disbelief.

"Nouri, stop playing games and put Clint on the phone!"

"Becka, he's not here."

"Don't hand me that. I said put my husband on the goddamn phone!" she shouted into the reciever loudly.

"What part of he's not here don't you understand Becka?"

"Listen to me, you bitch, I said put my husband on the phone now, do you understand?" her rage began to escalate.

"Becka, Clint is not here. He was earlier, but he's not now." Nouri's tone flashed a hint of her short fuse.

"What do you mean he was earlier?"

"You are unbelievable! Too much. Really, Becka." Nouri shook her head in dismay.

"I asked you a question, Nouri," Becka stated sharply, as she stormed over to the bar and poured herself a double shot of brandy. She quickly downed it, and then slammed the glass down on the bar, cracking the side of the brandy snifter.

"And I answered your question, Clint had business earlier this evening with Ethan, and now he's gone. It's that simple Becka." Nouri rolled her eyes in disgust and released a frustrated sigh.

"Listen bitch, I'm not as dumb as you seem to think I am."

Nouri laughed amusingly. "Oh really, Becka! I find that hard to believe." She walked to the cabinet and pulled out the box of black rum tea. She then walked over to the stove and turned the tea kettle on.

"I resent that remark," she snapped, as she poured herself another double shot of brandy.

"Okay, Becka, enough of this nonsense!" She put her tea bag in a cup.

"I know that Clint didn't go to your house to see Ethan."

"Yes, he did, Becka." She poured the hot water into her cup and set down the kettle.

"No he didn't! He came to your house to see you, admit it, damn it!" Becka poured herself another double shot of brandy and quickly downed it.

"Becka, calm down for chrissakes, he was here to see my husband, honest."

"You liar!" Becka said, as rage surfaced in her voice.

"Becka, for the last time, he was here to see Ethan."

"That's impossible, you lying bitch," she accused.

"What do you mean?" Nouri asked, shaking her head with impatience.

"Clint couldn't have seen Ethan today because Ethan was with me in Lambert!"

"What the hell are you babbling about Becka?" she said, giving Becka her full attention.

"You heard me, miss wonderful. I was with your husband today. We had lunch. A few bloody marys. Shall I go on?" Her tone was hurtful, arrogant, and sure.

"You're lying, Becka."

"Are you really that sure, Nouri? I even caught a later flight because your husband asked me to."

"I don't believe you," Nouri said, as a knot began to form inside her stomach, after suddenly remembering the phone number of Lambert flashing on the caller ID machine, when Ethan had phoned earlier. She continued to remember that Clint had told her earlier that evening that his wife was taking a later flight out of Lambert.

"Where the hell do you think Ethan is right this very minute, miss smart ass?" Becka laughed coldly.

"He's... he's spending the night in the city. At the condo." She sighed deeply and then bit her lower lip nervously.

"Really? Trouble in paradise, Mrs. Sommers?"

THIEF OF HEARTS

"That's very funny, Becka. It sounds to me like there's trouble in your own damn paradise." She took a sip of her tea nervously.

"Nouri, you're so gullible. Honestly, you slay me." Becka wickedly laughed.

"What the hell are you implying? That you're having an affair with my husband? In your dreams, Becka," she snapped.

"Ethan is lying to you. He's in Lambert, you moron!"

"Stop it, Becka."

"Don't want to hear the truth, huh?"

"I said stop it! I don't want to hear anymore of your nonsense." Nouri's hands began to tremble.

"Nonsense? Then answer me this miss perfect; why did Ethan lie to you about his spending the night in the city, when in fact, he's in Lambert?" Her laugh was cold and knowing.

"He... He didn't lie. I just assumed," she lied, not wanting to give in to Becka's flight of fantasy. At least she hoped it was fantasy.

"I have an idea Mrs. soon-to-be-ex Sommers. Why don't you phone him in Lambert and see for yourself?"

"Unlike you Becka, I trust my husband. I... What the hell am I doing trying to justify myself or my husband to you for?" She suddenly stopped talking, took a deep breath, and took a sip of her tea, and continued to speak. "You know, Becka, you really are a piece of work." She shook her head in disbelief.

Becka began to fume. She quickly poured herself another double shot of brandy and downed it before replying, "You know Nouri, I really would make a better Mrs. Ethan Sommers. We have so much more in common. Don't you think?" Becka's laugh was ugly and cruel. Nouri stood to her feet and walked over to the kitchen cabinet and retrieved the bottle of aspirins and an ice pack.

She finally responded, "No, Becka, I'll tell you what I think. I think you should do yourself a favor and see a shrink."

"We'll see just who needs to see a shrink miss smart ass, by the time I'm finished with you!" She sharply slammed her glass down onto the bar.

"Ya know, Becka, I have a friend that could probably get you a nice discount on a large script of prozac. How does that sound?"

"Don't fuck with me, Nouri, or you will regret it!"

"Is that a threat, Becka?"

"No, that my former friend and associate, is a promise!"

"Listen, you insane whacko, I've had enough of you for one night. So why don't you just..."

Becka interrupted, "Nouri, if I catch Clint with you I'll... I'll..." Her voice began to shake with rage. "Just stay the hell away from him!" ahe screamed, and then sharply slammed the receiver down in Nouri's ear.

THIEF OF HEARTS

Nouri stood frozen with the receiver still held to her ear with a stunned expression plastered across her face. "What a lunatic!" she finally muttered, as she placed the receiver back on its hook. "Poor Clint. I had no idea. Becka's craziness has definitely gotten worse," she continued to mumble to herself, while filling the icepack. She digested two more aspirins and went into the living room, wondering to herself if Fredrick had tracked Clint down yet.

After pacing back and forth in front of the large bay window, driving herself nuts with worry over Clint's odd disappearance, she finally decided to lie down on the sofa in an attempt to calm the explosion still going off in her brain. She instantly fell asleep.

"Ahh!" Becka Chamberlain screamed violently, after slamming the telephone down so hard that she broke a freshly manicured fingernail. "Damn you Nouri Sommers, you bitch!" She continued to scream out of control, heatedly throwing her cracked brandy snifter into the fireplace. "I'll get rid of that arrogant bitch if it's the last thing I ever do!" she viscously snapped, storming back to the bar and pouring herself another double shot of firewater. Rapidly swallowing the strong tasting liquor, she violently slammed the snifter glass down on the bar. This time it broke in her hand, cutting the inside of her pinkie finger. You and that love sick husband of mine will surely pay for this!, she irrationally thought, while sucking on her cut finger. "Shrink! I'll show you which one of us needs a shrink. You...you overly pampered slut! And Clint, you two timing bastard! You have no idea what I intend to do to you. I'll show you exactly what the phrase 'until death do us part' really means," she idly chattered, making her way to the bedroom.

After entering her bedroom, she quickly turned down the violet silk sheets on her bed. She angrily tossed her husband's pillows onto the floor, as she remained in her own sick world of thought. She stared blankly for a few moments at the shinny pillowcases now lying on the carpet. Finally, she walked over to the terrace balcony and opened the French glass sliding door. Still in her trance-like state of mind, she walked out into the cool, damp breeze.

If I can get rid of Clint and Nouri, then I can have Ethan Sommers all to myself. After all, he loves me, not her. I know it. He's been making love to me for the past nine months now. Hell, he'd rather make love to me. He says I bring out the animal in him. She smiled unconsciously, as she gently rubbed a few of the new bruises he had put on her body earlier that day while making love. She continued to be lost in thought.

What man in his right mind would prefer to eat jello, if they could eat hot-fudge cake with all the trimmings, she insanely mused, as she walked back inside her bedroom. And who did he make love to, with his very own wife right in the next room, on their first anniversary, ME, that's who. So you see, Becka, he does love you and not miss perfect, was her last thought, as she headed off to the bathroom for a hot shower.

THIEF OF HEARTS

After stepping out of the shower, she walked over to the wide, marble mirror stationed above the sink. She began to stare into the looking glass, but instead of own reflection gazing back at her, her imagination flashed the images of her former friend and her husband tightly embracing. She blinked her eyes several times in an attempt to stop them from touching so passionately. Once again, her blood rapidly began to boil, soon engulfing her with ungodly rage. She impulsively reached for her husband's expensive bottle of cologne and violently threw it at the beautiful marble-trimmed mirror. The extreme damage scarcely allowed her enough time to dodge the flying pieces of glass.

"You useless bastard!" she screamed at her absent husband. Suddenly finding herself wanting to have angry sex with him. She heatedly raged back into the bedroom and slammed her body down on her husband's side of the bed, crying hysterically. She cried herself to sleep, while planning her sick method of revenge against both her husband and Nouri Sommers.

The heavy downpour of rain had stopped around midnight. The gusting winds were now a light breeze. And the fresh scent of wild roses and mint filled the cool, damp, evening air.

It's really quite refreshing for a post midnight walk, Clint Chamberlain thought to himself, as he continued to stagger his way down the ten-mile stretch of driveway. His mind was still heavily burdened, wondering what his next course of action should be concerning Ethan Sommers and the woman of his dreams. Suddenly, he noticed the headlights of a car almost upon him. He stopped in his tracks and turned to face the on coming car. He excitedly began to wave his bottle of scotch above his head like a flag, silently praying that it was Nouri coming to get him. Finally, the beautiful white Rolls Royce pulled up beside him. Fredrick quickly jumped out of the car.

"Hello, Mr. Chamberlain. Need a lift sir!" He nodded respectfully.

"Thanks, Fredrick, if it's not a bother," he sheepishly smiled.

"None sir, my pleasure. Shall I drive you home, sir?"

"No, Fredrick. The motel in Covington will be fine. Thank you so much." He jumped into the back seat.

Fredrick closed the door behind him, as he continued to speak. "Yes sir, but..."

"But what, Fredrick?" Clint said, as Fredrick entered the car. Their eyes met in the rear view mirror.

"Mrs. Sommers, sir."

"Yes Fredrick, what about Nouri. I mean Mrs. Sommers." Fredrick studied his expression from the rearview mirror.

"She's worried about you, sir." He smiled.

"Don't worry about it, Fredrick. She's probably asleep by now. I'll phone her tomorrow, okay."

THIEF OF HEARTS

"If you think that's best, sir." They drove in silence for several miles.
Suddenly, Clint leveled his eyes to Fredrick's in the rearview mirror and asked, "Fredrick," his tone rather shy, but curious.

"Yes, sir."

"Uh...uh, do you think..." he paused.

"Think what, sir?" He looked at Clint with a puzzled expression.

"Do you think, Nouri, I mean Mrs. Sommers is...uh...is in...uh..." He paused again.

"In what, sir?"

Clint nervously loosened his necktie, sighed, and responded, "Never mind, Fredrick. Just forget it, okay." He squirmed uneasily in his seat.

Fredrick realized that Clint was skirting around trying to ask him something personal about Mrs. Sommers. He smiled knowingly, and responded, "Forget what, sir?"

"Nothing, Fredrick. Maybe I should just close my eyes for awhile." He began to slowly slur his words.

"Yes, sir, maybe you should." He smiled.

"Let me know when you get to Covington, Fredrick." His eyes slowly closed.

"Yes, sir. It will be about thirty minutes."

"Thanks, Fredrick."

"You're welcome, sir."

Chapter 4

"Honey-suckle, wild roses, lilacs, and salty sea air. What a wonderful combination of fragrant scents filling the air on this beautiful evening, Rob."

"Yes, Kate, and have you had a chance to check out the spectacular sunset?"

"I enjoyed a quick walk along the beach before I came to work tonight. It was magnificent! Almost to breathtaking for words," responded news anchor woman Kate Anderson of W.B.E.R.T. Channel 21 News Station in Lambert.

Seventeen-year old, Kirsten Kamel suddenly jumped to her feet and impatiently turned the TV off. She shouted from across the room to her lover who was in the bathroom taking a shower.

"Baby, damn it! You gonna be in there all night long, or what?" She rolled her eyes and walked back to the bed, quickly jumping onto it.

Reaching for his white, monogrammed terrycloth bathrobe that was lying on the sink next to a wrapped birthday present, Ethan Sommers shouted, "Just a minute, Kirsten. I can't hear you. I'll be right out." He slipped the oblong gift into his robe pocket and reached for another towel.

"I'm growing older by the minute," she subtly dropped a hint, hoping he hadn't forgotten her birthday. She quickly added, "By the time you get out here, I'll be as old as your 'ol lady, for chrissakes," she said, then went back to biting her finger nails.

Ethan amusingly chuckled, shook his head, and called out, "What did you say?"

"I know you heard me, baby." She rolled her eyes and continued to bite her fingernails. He knew that she was extremely jealous of his beautiful wife and enjoyed getting a rise out of her every now and again.

Shaking his head amusingly, he shouted, "For your information, smart ass, my wife is only twenty-six."

"Yeah. Well, she's still old to me," she snapped jealously.

"Enough about my wife, Kirsten. I'll be out in a minute." His mood suddenly changed. He quickly popped a couple of pills.

"Spoiled bitch," Kirsten mumbled under her breath, not noticing Ethan entering the room.

Still drying his hair, he responded, "What were you mumbling about." His look was serious.

After noticing his sudden mood change, she squirmed uneasily before answering his question, "Nothing baby come to bed. I've been waiting for this all day." She smiled nervously.

"Yeah, I bet you have, Kirsten."

"Baby, I've got something very special for you tonight." She laughed wickedly and patted the spot on the bed next to her.

"Like I said, Kirsten, I just bet you have.' His look angry and his tone of voice jealous. He added, "Get up and fix us a drink. Make mine a double shot of Russian Vodka. Just an ice cube or two." He gestured to the bar with a wave of his hand. She glanced at him hurtfully before walking to the bar. He quickly hid her birthday present under the pillow. Kirsten rounded the bar swiftly and returned carrying their drinks.

She smiled and handed him the vodka. Giving her another serious look, he remarked, "Now tell me Kirsten, who was that muscle bound jerk hanging all over you in the lounge this afternoon!"

"What are you talking about, baby?" She squirmed uncomfortably and took a sip of her drink.

"I saw you today." Ethan glared into her eyes.

"Saw me what, baby?"

"Damn it! You know exactly what I saw. Now, I ask you again, what's the jerk's name?"

"Baby, what's got you so hot under the collar all of a sudden?"

"Kirt. Kirt Jarett. That's his goddamn name. Isn't it, Kirsten?"

"For chrissakes, Ethan, I'm a barmaid. It's my job to flirt, and you damn well know it!" she snapped nervously.

"I told you two weeks ago, Kirsten, that I didn't want you to see anyone else anymore. Didn't I?" he scolded.

"Yes baby, but..."

Ethan sharply interrupted, "There are no buts, Kirsten. Tomorrow morning, I'm informing Otto and Olivia Lambert that from now on, you're exclusive. My property! Got it!" His expression needed no other words.

"Calm down, baby. I didn't want anyone else except you. You know that. Don't you baby?" She lied convincingly.

"Good. Make sure you remember that." His voice suddenly lost its edge. She smiled and patted the side of the bed again.

"Now come to bed baby and make love to me," she said seductively.

"Not yet, Kirsten. I'm not finished talking to you." His eyes held to hers.

She squirmed again and picked up her drink. "What is it now, baby?" She forced a smile.

"Kirsten, I've got a lot of money already invested in you, believe me. You don't want to fuck with me. Do you understand?"

Deliberately wanting to make him jealous, she remarked: "Baby. Not that I ever would or anything like that, but what...what if I..."

He immediately interrupted her. His tone was frightening, and his eyes glared at her, scaring her half to death. She trembled with fear. "Let's just hope you never have to find out what I would do to you." He continued to glare at her with his icy stare.

She swallowed hard before responding. "Baby, I was only kidding. I love you baby. You know that, huh?" She smiled.

"Kirsten, you have no idea what I'm capable of. If it wasn't for me, Lambert would have you working in one of his other businesses, and you know what that means. Do I make myself clear?"

"I know, baby. I wouldn't have anything if it wasn't for you. Mr. Lambert wouldn't even let me tend bar until you got me a phony ID. But he told me..."

He cut in sharply. "I know all about Otto Lambert. You let me take care of him. You just behave yourself when you're working." He paused, then continued, "And if you are a real good girl, and do what you're told, I just might buy you your own bar someday, okay." He forced a grin.

"Oh baby!" she squealed with delight.

"Now Kirsten, tell me have you been sleeping with Kirt Jarret?" He glared through her.

"Well, uh...uh, no baby, just..."

"Just what goddamn it!" he shouted.

"Calm down, baby. I... I haven't been sleeping with anybody," she lied, swallowed hard, and nervously downed the rest of her drink.

"What is it Kirsten? Is Lambert fucking with you again?" he asked sharply.

"Uh..." She paused. Fear overcame her. "No, baby, of course not." She lied again.

"You're sure." He studied her scared expression. "If I ever catch you lying to me, Kirsten..." He stopped talking and quickly downed his drink.

"I...I wouldn't lie to you, baby, honest." She smiled nervously and began to bite her fingernails.

"Okay, Kirsten, I'll take your word for it." He stared at her a few more seconds before walking closer to the bed. He threw aside the towel that he used to dry his hair and reached for the belt to his bathrobe. "Now, if I remember correctly, you said you had something special for me tonight." He smiled wickedly.

"Oh, I do baby. Something very special." She patted the spot on the bed beside her again.

"Well, I have something special for you too." He smiled, paused, then added, "Look under your pillow, Kirsten. I know it's a few more hours before your eighteenth birthday, but what the hell."

Kirsten's eyes widened and an excited grin crossed her face, as she eagerly tossed the pillows off onto the thick carpet. She excitedly reached for the gift.

"What is it, baby?" she squealed excitedly.

"Open it and find out, for chrissakes." He shook his head teasingly.

Like a child on Christmas morning, she excitedly ripped the elegant wrapping off of the box. "Oh my God! Ethan, it's...it's...beautiful, and so...so expensive." She gleamed with utter delight. She quickly jumped to her feet, throwing the royal-blue, satin sheets onto the floor, and ran to the full length mirror across the room. She began to jump up and down with excitement. "Oh baby, come here," she exclaimed, as she turned to face him with her stretched out arms. But Ethan didn't budge. He continued to stand in the same spot beside the huge bed, enjoying his view of her young, bouncing body. He smiled lustfully, shaking his head approvingly.

"So you love the diamond necklace, huh?" He folded his arms over his muscular chest.

"Oh, I more than love it baby." She continued to jump with joy.

"How much do you love it, Kristen?" He smiled wickedly. She quickly fastened the diamond necklace around her neck, glancing into the mirror at it one final time. Suddenly, she dropped to her knees, seductively saying, "Why don't you come over here, and I'll show you." She smiled wantingly and sensually licked her lips.

Ethan let his robe fall to the floor. He quickly stepped over it, eager to accept her appreciative offer. By the time he crossed the room, his body was immediately hard. He heatedly reached down and helped himself to a handful of Kirsten's champagne-blond hair in an attempt to help her guide her young, inexperienced, thirsty mouth to his rapid body movements. She soon began to drive him lustfully out of his mind. Her kisses were deep and passionate, his movements commanding and wild, her mouth hot and wet. He began to moan with sheer delight. "God, Kirsten, don't stop he begged!" She continued to excite him. "Please, God! Don't stop!" He lustfully squealed, again and again.

Suddenly, Ethan cried out in pain when his young, inexperienced lover got too carried away.

"Damn it, Kirsten! Watch the goddamn teeth!" he complained. She quickly loosened her suckling hold.

"Ahh, that's better. Now watch it. You know I have to make love to my wife this weekend, and I can't do it with a sore dic..."

She suddenly stopped pleasuring him to respond, "Okay, I get the picture," she jealously replied. After a few more minutes of oral bliss, Ethan finally screamed with moans of contented completion. He quickly pulled her up into his arms. They passionately kissed. He finally carried her to the bed with her legs snugly wrapped around his waist.

He kissed her again before she jumped out of his arms and onto the bed. She giggled. "How was that, baby?" Her tone was childishly eager.

"Not bad, for a little foreplay." He smiled arrogantly.

"Foreplay, huh?" She looked hurt.

"All right, don't pout. It was okay. You're getting better at it, but damn it, Kirsten, you've got to watch the damn teeth, okay." His remark was selfish, and his look was stone cold.

"Okay, baby." She smiled and nodded.

"Now, Kirsten, what else do you have for me tonight?"

"Anything you want, baby." She unconsciously began to bite her nails.

"Are you sure? It might hurt again," he said as he walked across the room toward the bar.

"That's okay, baby, I'm getting used to the pain. But you have to get me really hot first, okay." She smiled nervously.

Here, drink this. I'll get the acid and the coke. I'll get you so high, you won't care what I do to that young, bouncy body of yours," he said, then quickly went to retrieve a suit case from the closet. "I'll be right back. Fix us another drink," he ordered.

After several moments, Ethan returned with a suitcase full of every type of drug known to man. First, he gave Kirsten two hits of acid, his personal favorite. Then he gave her two lines of coke. He joined her. "Here baby, now down this. That's a good girl. In a few minutes, you won't care what I do to you. You'll probably be pissed off when I finally stop." He laughed wickedly.

Kirsten excitedly jumped back into bed, anxious to let Ethan have his way with her. "Baby, I hope you didn't forget to bring the Chinese oil that you told me about last time?"

"No, Kirsten, I didn't forget, I have it right here. When I enter that tight little rear of yours, you won't feel a thing." Their eyes met.

"Yeah right, baby, that's what you said last time." She glared nervously at him.

"Well last time was your first. It gets easier and better each time. Before long, you'll be begging me to enter that tight little bottom of yours." He laughed amusingly.

"What ever makes you happy, baby."

"That's my girl. Now bring that young body over here!"

After several hours of violent, rough sex, Ethan and his young lover passed out into each other's hot, sweaty arms.

Chapter 5

The loud buzzing of the alarm jolted Becka Chamberlain from a deep, angry sleep. She had set the alarm a few hours before, hoping she would rise early enough to catch Nouri Sommers and her husband together at the Sommers Estate. She yawned, stretched, and massaged her temples, trying to ease the pain inside her head. "Ugh," she groaned, as she rubbed the sleep from her eyes, suddenly remembering why she had wanted to set the alarm so early to begin with. "Oh, yes. I remember now," she mumbled, jumping to her feet, and darting to the bathroom. She quickly showered and dressed. Not even taking the time to have a cup of coffee, she immediately flew out the door. She slammed the front door so hard behind her, that it shattered an entire section of the expensive, antique pane of glass. As she continued to walk to the car, she glanced over her shoulder to see how much damage she had done. She smiled wickedly, knowing that her husband would be furious. His old Victorian House was his prized possession.

She quickly entered her car and raced to the freeway, anxious to catch Nouri Sommers in a bare face lie.

The soft voice of Mai Li interrupted the fantasy dream that Nouri was having. She slowly stirred.

"Miss." She thought she heard someone say. She stirred again. "Miss." Someone said once again. Nouri yawned and stretched. Mai Li gently patted her shoulder. "Good morning, miss. Everything okay?" Nouri slowly opened her eyes.

"Oh, good morning, Mai Li," she responded hoarsely.

"Are you all right, miss?" Mai Li said with a puzzled look on her face, surprised to see Nouri sleeping on the sofa.

"Yes. Thank you," she replied, wiping the sleep from her eyes.

"Coffee miss."

"Yes, thank you, Mai Li." She made her first effort to sit up. "What time is it?" She stretched again and then suddenly grabbed her pounding head.

"Eight o' clock, miss."

Nouri took a sip of her coffee, then instantaneously spit it half out. "Oh damn!" she squealed, as she quickly jumped to her feet. A startled expression quickly covered Mai Li's face.

"What is it miss?" she asked in a concerned tone of voice.

Nouri rushed to the staircase, talking to Mai Li from across the room. She glanced over her shoulder. "I'm sorry Mai Li. I'm in a hurry. I had almost forgotten to meet Mr. Sommers in the city today. We're having lunch." She smiled.

"But it's only eight o' clock, miss." She shook her head.

"Yes, I know. I want to surprise my husband. I want to try and get to the condo before he leaves this morning." She massaged her temples.

Nouri was hoping that her husband's lie, about where he was phoning her last night, was only a small white lie, that he could easily explain, and that he would indeed be at the condo when she arrived later that morning. She crossed her fingers, hoping he would have a reasonable explanation for fibbing, especially about something so ridiculous. And as far as what Becka said about her husband, she chose not to put any credibility what so ever into it. She quickly dismissed the hurtful words as fantasy.

"You don't want any breakfast this morning miss?" Mai Li asked.

"No, Mai Li, thanks. I'll just have some coffee in my bedroom, please." She smiled and turned away from Mai Li, quickly running upstairs. Nouri was anxious to take her shower, get dressed, and leave.

Clint Chamberlain was jogged into an awakened state of consciousness by a loud banging on the door of his room by large motel maid. He quickly grabbed his pounding skull, desperately trying to quiet the marching band parading in his head. He tried to open his eyes, but only managed a squint. He glanced at the clock on the night stand. He groaned with pain.

"Eight o' clock!" he complained, just as the maid entered the room. "What the hell!" he shouted, as he noticed the stunned maid frozen in mid-step, staring lustfully at his nude body, which happened to be sprawled across the bed. She gulped and blushed an amazing shade of crimson red.

"Do you mind, miss!" he barked sharply, quickly reaching for the cotton white sheet. She swiftly blinked herself back from her momentary fantasy of him.

She responded, stuttering, "Sorry! Sir, I...I didn't know anyone was in here." Her expression masked a look of guilty desire.

"Yeah, fine," he barked sarcastically. She swiftly turned her back and started to leave. Just then, Clint called out to her. "Just a minute miss." His voice was filled with pain.

With her back still facing him, she hesitantly responded, "Yes, sir." She nervously jingled her set of keys in her right hand. He finally managed to sit up in bed.

"How about you have someone bring me some strong black coffee." He paused, then added the word, "Please." He began to massage his throbbing temples.

"Yes, sir." She quickly left the room, shutting the door behind her. Clint forced himself out of bed and headed towards the bathroom, tightly clutching his throbbing head. He was anxious to jump into a cold shower. He had accidentally turned on the heat to his room the night before, thinking that it was the air conditioner. He was wringing wet with perspiration and could hardly breath.

THIEF OF HEARTS

"Damn it, Clint! You can be so stupid sometimes." He scolded himself, as he slowly began to recall his actions from the evening before. He began to try and put together a mental list of things he urgently needed to do that morning. His hangover was so severe that he quit trying to think after only several seconds. "To hell with it," he muttered, quickly shutting the water valve off. As he stepped out of the shower, he could hear the nervous motel maid calling out to him from outside his room.

"Sir, sir...I have your coffee." He wrapped a towel around his waist and popped his head around the bathroom door.

"Why don't you bring it inside the room for me, please," he responded, as he continued to towel dry his hair.

"Yes, sir." She called back. He heard her key go inside the door to his room.

"Just put it down anywhere," he said, then added, "Hey, listen miss, I'm sorry I barked at you earlier. I'm sort of nursing a hang over. You know what that's like, huh?" He called out from the bathroom. His tone was much calmer. He wanted to make an effort to soothe her hurt feelings, if indeed he had caused any.

"Yes sir," she answered softly.

He suddenly poked his head out from the bathroom and said, "Hey, listen miss, would you please try and track me down a couple of aspirins for me. And maybe some tomato juice and hot sauce." He smiled. "I'll also need a cab or a limo...someone to drive me somewhere, okay."

"Yes sir," she politely responded.

The maid turned to leave when he called out to her, "Wait a minute, miss." He walked out of the bathroom, still wearing the white, terry cloth towel snugly wrapped around his sexy, masculine frame. She blushed and swallowed hard. Her eyes traveled the entire length of his perfect body. He noticed and smiled amusingly.

"I want to give you a little something for your help." He smiled that incredible sexy smile of his. The motel maid blushed again.

As he walked closer to her, she responded with a shocked expression on her face, "That...uh...won't be necessary, sir." Suddenly realizing what she must have thought, he blushed himself and chuckled, quickly walking past her. He reached for his pair of slacks and pulled out his wallet.

"A tip, miss. I...wanted to give you a tip." He smiled again.

Still red in the face, she responded, "That won't be..."

Clint interrupted her by handing her a one hundred-dollar bill, saying, "Please, I insist." Their eyes met briefly.

"Thank you, sir," the motel maid responded, as she gratefully accepted the large tip of appreciation. She turned and walked towards the door.

THIEF OF HEARTS

"I'll be right back with your aspirins and tomato juice. It will probably take thirty minutes to get a cab, though," she said, and then closed the door behind her, as she left his room.

Humm. Thirty minutes, huh? Clint thought to himself, glancing down at his watch. "I better try to reach Ethan before he leaves the estate," he mumbled to himself, reaching for the telephone.

Nouri Sommers quickly ran down the long flight of stairs with the silver coffee pot in her hands, calling out to Mai Li. Mai Li came running to answer her summons.

"Yes, miss," Mai Li nervously responded.

"I'm sorry, Mai Li. I didn't mean to frighten you." She smiled, then handed her the coffee pot.

"Here Mai Li, put this in some kind of container to go. I'll take it with me."

"Yes, miss," she answered, accepting the pot from her hands.

"Mai Li, have you talked to Fredrick this morning?"

"Yes, miss," she nodded.

"Did he mention anything about Clint...I mean Mr. Chamberlain?" Nouri said with concern.

"Yes, miss. He was washing car."

"Who, Mr. Chamberlain?" A puzzled look crossed her face.

"No, miss. Fredrick wash car. He say Mr. Chamberlain stay in motel in Covington last night. He drive him, miss."

Thank you, Mai Li." Nouri smiled with a relieved look on her face. Mai Li turned to leave when Nouri called out to her once again. Mai Li turned to face her.

"Oh, Mai Li."

"Yes, miss."

"You know that wonderful hangover remedy of yours." She smiled needingly.

"Yes miss."

"I'd love one of those to go too, okay."

"Yes, miss. I have Fredrick bring out to you in limo with coffee. Have nice day, miss." She nodded and headed off to the kitchen.

After Mai Li entered the kitchen, she quickly began to toss her secret ingredients into the blender. She carefully blended secret amounts of various vegetable juices, lemon juice, Chinese spices, American seasonings, along with Tabasco sauce, Worcester and horseradish sauce, celery seed, poppy seed, and a squirt of lime. Finally...one raw egg. She blended it thoroughly for thirty seconds, then added ice and put it into a chilled container to go.

THIEF OF HEARTS

Fredrick waited patiently for Mai Li to hand him her famous cure-all. He rushed the magic medicine out to the anxiously awaiting Nouri, already seated in the limo. She quickly downed every drop in one long swallow.

"Hopefully, that will do the trick," she said, handing Fredrick the empty container. God, I hope her cure-all works soon, Nouri thought to herself, as she sat in the back seat of the limousine, massaging her throbbing temples. The explosion going off in her brain was unbelievable.

Every few minutes or so, Fredrick would glance back at Nouri. Finally, Nouri responded, "Fredrick, is something on your mind?" She smiled.

He returned her smile. "Yes, madam."

"What is it, Fredrick?"

"I...I dropped Mr. Chamberlain off at a motel in Covington last night, madam." Their eyes met for a brief moment.

"Yes Fredrick, I know, thank you. I appreciate it." She smiled warmly.

"You're welcome madam." He then added, "Which office of Mr. Sommers would you like for me to take you to, madam?"

"I want you to go to the condo first. Would you phone ahead and inform Heidi and James...Oh, and Fredrick, would you ask James to meet me downstairs. There's no reason to keep you in town all day. I'm sure after my disturbing you so late last night that you must be exhausted."

"Yes, madam." He nodded and reached for the cell phone. Nouri laid her head back and closed her eyes. She quickly dozed off.

Chapter 6

On her long drive to the Sommers Estate, Becka could only keep her mind on one thing. And that one thing was her husband being in the arms of his lover. Her arch enemy, Nouri Sommers. Her blood soon began to boil, as the crystal clear images repeatedly kept flashing over and over inside her sick mind.

"That's okay, miss perfect. We'll see just who has the last laugh!" She angrily muttered to herself, glancing into the rearview mirror. She continued to talk to herself insanely, making no sense at all.

"I can hardly wait to see your face when I tell Ethan about your affair with my husband. His best friend. Better yet, I can't wait to take Ethan away from you. I'll dump Clint, and Ethan will dump you. And I'll have mister mega-bucks all to myself," she said, once again staring into the rearview mirror. Becka suddenly began to laugh hysterically. "I told you bitch, but you just wouldn't listen. Now see what you made me do. We'll finally see who needs that shrink now, won't we, miss wonderful," she angrily thought, as she continued to rehearse the lines that she desperately wanted to say to Nouri. She concentrated more on the rearview mirror, looking at herself, than the dangerous freeway that she was driving on.

Suddenly, a police officer forced her to pull her Mercedes over to the side of the road. After a rather heated debate with the uniformed policeman, Becka was lucky to be released with only a verbal lecture and a warning citation.

"Front desk. How may I be of service to you this morning?" The motel clerk asked Clint Chamberlain.

"Good morning. I'm trying to get an outside line, but all I seem to get is a busy signal." He shook his throbbing head.

"Is it a local call, sir?"

"Yes, it is."

"Just dial nine, the area code and then the phone number, sir." The motel operator smiled over the telephone. He was obviously a young man that seemed to enjoy his job.

"Great, thanks."

"You're welcome, sir." Clint quickly hung up the phone and began to dial again.

"Good morning, Mai Li," Clint responded after she said hello.

"Good morning, Mr. Chamberlain, sir." Her tone was soft and kind.

"Is Mr. Sommers in?"

"No, he not here."

"Where did he say he was going, Mai Li?"

"He didn't. He not come home last night, sir."

"I see." He paused, then continued, "I realize that it's early, Mai Li, but I'd like to speak with Mrs. Sommers, if she's awake." He glanced down at his watch.

"She not here too. Went to city this morning."

"Do you know where she was going?"

"She going to have lunch with Mr. Sommers today."

"Did they say where they were having lunch, Mai Li?"

"No, didn't say, sir."

"Okay, Mai Li, thanks."

"You welcome, Mr. Chamberlain, sir."

"Oh, Mai Li, by the way, I'll be over in an hour or so to pick up my car, okay."

"Okay, sir."

"I almost forgot. Tell Fredrick I said thanks for the lift last night when you see him, okay."

"Yes. Will do sir, zai-jian." (good-bye)

"Zai-jian, Mai Li."

After Clint told Mai Li good-bye, he phoned Ethan's answering service. He was hoping to find out where he would be dining for lunch that day, but instead, he was informed that Mr. Sommers was still in Lambert and wasn't expected back in his office until late in the afternoon.

"Damn you, Ethan," he muttered after hanging up the receiver. "Poor sweetness," he whispered and sadly shook his head. I bet the selfish prick will stand her up again, he thought to himself, as he downed his tomato juice with hot sauce.

He continued to think. Why the hell did she marry that unstable bastard. You, Clint Chamberlain. You idiot. You drove her to it, that's why. "God I was so stupid!" he muttered, as he brought his attention back to the present, when he heard the taxi driver blow his horn. I'll make it up to you sweetness, I swear, was his last thought on the matter, as he stood to his feet and walked to the motel door.

He glanced around the room to make sure he wasn't forgetting anything, when he suddenly remembered the lustful expression on the maids face when she saw him sprawled out naked across the bed. He smiled amusingly, shook his head, and quickly made his exit.

A magnificent late spring morning followed the brutal thunder storm from the night before. The air was crisp and fresh, heavily scented with mint and pine. Clint inhaled deeply. A warm breeze rustled through the century old trees. There was no sound, just the calming whisper of the light wind blowing its warm breath on newly reborn leaves.

"Wow! This place is sure something, sir. Do you live here?" The taxi driver asked Clint, as he brought his cab to a complete stop in front of the main entrance gate to the Sommers' Estate.

"No, a friend of mine does. I'm just here to pick up my car," he said, as he rolled his window down a little farther.

"I'll talk to the intercom."

"This is Mai Li. How can I help you please?"

"Hi, Mai Li. This is Mr. Chamberlain. *Ni hao ma*?" (How are you)

"*Hao xiexie*." (All right, thank you)

"I'd like to come in and get my car, *qing*." (please)

"*Hao* (all right) come up please."

"*Xiexie* Mai Li." (thank you)

Mai Li released the lock on the entrance gate to the estate, and the cab driver quickly headed up the ten-mile stretch of driveway.

"Like I said, sir, this place sure is something else." He smiled and shook his head enviously.

"Yes it is, cabby." He smiled and then laid his head back on his seat and closed his eyes, trying to calm the pain still inside his brain. Soon his mind drifted away from his current problems with Ethan, Nouri, and his whacko wife.

In his thoughts, there were only he and Nouri. He smiled unconsciously, as he continued to remember how they first met. They had first met at an art exhibit. It was a private showing for a friend of hers. Nouri stole the show, not meaning to, of course. Instead of her friend's art being the center of attention, she was. She was magnificent. So beautiful. So sexy. So seductive. The moment she entered the room, Clint knew he had to have her.

The very instant their eyes met for the first time, it was inevitable. Something that was meant to be. He smiled again, as he continued to be lost in thought. Her gown was spectacular. It molded to her body to show off every curve. The color of her gown matched her incredible hazel-colored eyes. Too much temptation for any man to be forced to deny himself. He quickly went up to her and introduced himself, only to be crushed when he found out that she was dating the artist. But artist or not, Clint was determined to have her.

He found out all he could about this breathtaking beauty through a mutual friend, who was also at the showing for the young artist with a great deal of talent. Talent? Yes. Class? No! He continued to remember every little detail of the memory. She didn't belong with that temperamental jerk. She belonged with him, and he was determined that she would. Sooner or later, she would be his. After discovering that she had just went into business for herself, the interior design business, he went out the very next day and purchased an apartment downtown for her to work her magic on. At that point, she was completely unaware of what he had done, or his intentions for doing so. As a matter of fact, the bed in that old apartment embraced many a young woman before the lovely Nouri St. Charles. He smiled again at her original reluctance to accept his *large* job assignment for her.

Nouri had finally agreed to accept his generous job offer, only after most of her money from the sale of her other business with Becka Adams was almost gone. She soon realized that it was expensive supporting a starving artist, as well as herself. Clint Chamberlain turned out to be a complete distraction for her, making it hard for her to stay on time with her agreed completion date.

When she was close to him, she couldn't think clearly. Her mind seemed to be focused more on him, and his incredibly sexy body. His manly scent. His seductive smile, and his penetrating eyes. When he would accidentally brush up next to her, she could barely breathe. And he seemed to somehow know it, which would completely infuriate her.

He smiled again, as he continued to remember. He was quite the ladies' man. And she was determined that she would never become apart of his harem of women. She seemed to have one problem after another with the enormous project he assigned her to. Money was never an issue, which seemed to make matters worse. He just constantly seemed to keep adding more and more things that he wanted done to his huge, five-bedroom apartment. First, he wanted this wall knocked out, then that one. Add this, and take away that. He couldn't make up his mind. He was driving her crazy, and he enjoyed doing so. He left her no time to accept other assignments. Of course, he had planned it that way. He wanted her undivided attention to be solely on him, and no other. Morning after dreaded morning, she would arrive at his apartment, ready for work, only to be met at the door by some different bimbo he had just met the night before. However, his apparent appetite for sex was very impressive to her, to say the least! Unlike her young, inexperienced artist friend, that she had occasional sex with and who barely seemed to know where his zipper was.

Nouri soon began to wonder if Clint would be as good a lover as her first real man, Charles Mason. To date he was the most amazing lover she had ever had.

Clint Chamberlain reminded Nouri a lot of Charles Mason. They were both older, more mature, and very sexy. But an older lover was usually more controlling and demanding, and usually wanted to rush into marriage and that frightened her. That's why she left Charles Mason and that's what frightened her most about getting involved with Clint Chamberlain. That's why she began to date younger guys, more her own age. She could control things, but they couldn't control her. Life was less complex that way.

But still, she was getting to the point that she was growing more and more curious about Clint Chamberlain. Not just as an exciting man, but as a lover as well. She was becoming attracted to him, and he knew it, and that scared her. It also made her mad that he didn't really know her, but yet, he could read her so well. Which was another reason she continued to fight her desire for him.

THIEF OF HEARTS

The fact was that he did indeed know that she was falling for him. But not half as much as he was falling for her. He was determined to wait as long as necessary. The best things in life were worth both the risk, as well as the wait. In the mean time, his body may embrace other women, but he knew, from the first moment their eyes met, that Nouri St. Charles was, without a doubt, the woman of his dreams.

"Here we are sir, shall I wait for a moment," the cabby said, as he pulled his taxi around to the front entrance to the mansion. Shaking his head slightly, to bring his attention back to the present, Clint responded, "No thanks, cabby, that won't be necessary. Here, this should cover it. Keep the change." He smiled as he tossed two, one-hundred dollar bills down on the front seat of the taxi.

"Thank you, sir! Have a great day," the cabby responded, quickly reaching for the money down on the seat beside him.

"You're welcome. You have a nice day too." Clint nodded departing the taxi.

Mai Li was standing inside the doorway of the mansion, sweetly smiling, as Clint walked up to the front door.

"Hello again, Mai Li," he said, leaning down to kiss her on the cheek. He smiled fondly.

"Here's your keys, sir," she said, extending her right arm towards him. She added, "You like something *chifan* (eat). *Kafe* (coffee), or perhaps some *cha* (tea)?" She smiled.

"No *xiexie* (thank you). I don't have time, but I will leave a note for Mrs. Sommers if you don't mind Mai Li." He paused, then added, " *mei guanxi* (never mind)." He turned to walk away. Mai Li reached out to touch his arm. He turned to face her.

She said with a puzzled look on her face, "*duibiqi, wobudong*, sir (sorry, I do not understand, sir)?"

"*Mei guanxi* (never mind), I don't have time. I'll *dianhua* (telephone) her later."

"Okay, sir. *Zia jian*." She smiled politely and nodded.

"*Zai jian* Mai Li." He returned the smile and the polite nod of the head.

Clint was eager to get home before his insane wife had a chance to get out of bed. He knew that on most any day of the week, including weekends, that she never got out of bed much before noon, if in fact then. And with her getting home late the night before, he figured she probably wouldn't get out of bed before late afternoon..

Somewhere between last night and the present, he had made up his mind to leave Becka. He wanted a divorce. And with her many obvious affairs, she must surely want one too, even if she wouldn't admit it for whatever reasons.

67

THIEF OF HEARTS

His plan was to sneak into the house while Becka was still sleeping, pack a suitcase, grab a few other things, and leave a Dear John note with his attorney's phone number on it. Simple. No muss, no fuss! Avoiding an ugly confrontation with his out of control, whacko wife was now paramount. The last thing he was in the mood for was a fight with her.

Being in such a rush, Clint quickly exited to the right of the front gate, leading out of the Sommers Estate. He stepped on the gas pedal harder than he intended, causing the right tire to momentarily spin out of control.

Becka Chamberlain quickly brought her car to an immediate stop, as she saw her husband leaving the Sommers' Estate. She slammed on the brakes so hard, and so quickly, that she would have went through the front windshield had she not had her safety belt on. Luckily, the police officer that pulled her over earlier made her put it on. Normally she wouldn't have. She had a life-long phobia about being restricted. Clint Chamberlain swiftly reacted, bringing his car back under control, but not before peeling rubber for almost a quarter of a mile He was in too much of a hurry to even notice his wife's car not far behind him.

Becka quickly freed herself and jumped out of her car. With a look of complete astonishment and completely at a loss for any normal reaction, she began to uncontrollably shout obscenities at her husband. Who was now out of sight.

"You bastard!" she screamed hysterically. Shaking her fist in the air. "Just divorcing your two-timing ass isn't good enough!" She continued to wail. "No...hell no! I warned you what I would do if you ever cheated on me. Now, I'm going to cut your goddamn heart out!...and...that two-bit slut, you're in love with too! I told you, bitch! I warned you both, goddamn it! Now, believe me, you're going to pay dearly!" Suddenly, she began to shake violently. It lasted several long minutes. Finally, she somehow managed to calm herself down enough to get back inside her car.

After staring at herself for a few moments in the rear view mirror, she decided to confront Nouri Sommers face to face. She pulled her car up to the front entrance of the estate and pressed the buzzer to the intercom.

"Mai Li, how may I...

Becka rudely interrupted her. "Yeah. Yeah. Buzz me in Mai Li. This is Mrs. Chamberlain."

Mai Li hesitantly responded, "Mrs. Sommers not home."

"Oh really. Where is she? I ...I was supposed to meet her and my husband here this morning."

"Mr. Chamberlain not here too. He just leave."

"Really? Did he say where he was going?" Her tone icy.

"Not say miss."

"And Mrs. Sommers. Where did she go?"

"To city. Be home later."

THIEF OF HEARTS

"I see...well Mai Li, buzz me in anyway, I want to leave Mrs. Sommers a note." Mai Li had second thoughts about letting her enter the estate grounds, but she reluctantly released the lock anyway. Becka suddenly got the idea on how she was going to punish her arch-enemy Nouri Sommers and her two-timing husband, both at the same time. I told you both not to fuck with me, didn't I. You should have listened, she thought, as she flew by the staff quarters, tennis courts, and Mai Li's house.

Her thoughts of revenge were growing stronger and stronger, as she continued to make her way to the estates' mansion. She glanced into the rear view mirror and grinned wickedly. I'll kill that two-timing husband of mine and frame his two-bit slut for the murder. She continued to organize her new plan for revenge in her mind, while driving the ten mile stretch of driveway. All I have to do is steal a few personal items of the soon to be Ex-Mrs. Sommers, kill Clint, and place the slut's personal items beside the body, and voila: two birds killed with one small stone. Bye, bye Nouri. Bye, bye Clint. Ethan will be mine, all mine. What ever will you do, miss perfect? She laughed hysterically.

Suddenly, she began to shake uncontrollably again. She quickly slammed on the brakes to her car and shut the ignition off. Mai Li came running out to the car.

"*Xiaojie* (miss). *Xiaojie*. Are you *hao* (all right)?" Mai Li quickly opened Becka's car door and repeated what she had just said to her.

Becka's cruel response, "For chrissakes, Mai Li! If you're going to live in this country, the least you could do is to speak better English." She heatedly jerked her door out of Mai Li's hand. A hurt expression quickly masked Mai Li's face.

"Mai Li, don't just stand there staring at me for godsakes! Do something. Coffee. Get me some coffee. I apparently need it! I'm going to the study to leave Mrs. Sommers a note. Bring it to me there!" she coldly snapped.

Mai Li shook her head in disbelief, as Becka stormed past her and headed towards the front door. She pushed the latch down on the door, but it wouldn't open. She tried again, getting angrier by the moment.

"Damn it, Mai Li! What the hell is wrong with this goddamn door?" she barked

"Key, miss. I have to unlock," Mai Li politely responded, as she quickly reached into her apron pocket to retrieve it.

"Well, that's just great!" she remarked sarcastically, putting her hands on her hips, impatiently waiting for Mai Li to open the door.

"For chrissakes, Mai Li, get the lead out will you. I haven't got all day!" She huffed. Mai Li smiled inwardly, as she slowly made her way to the front door. Becka rudely jerked the key out of Mai Li's hand.

THIEF OF HEARTS

"My Lord, Mai Li. If I wait for you to unlock the damn thing..." She suddenly stopped talking when the door flew open, taking her with it. "Damn it!" she angrily shouted. Mai Li held in her grin.

"I go fix coffee, miss," she said, not bothering to help Mrs. Chamberlain up off the floor. She just quietly walked passed her and went into the kitchen. She was dying to laugh out loud.

While Becka went into the study, Mai Li quietly tried to phone Nouri at the condo. But she hadn't arrived yet. Mai Li left word for her to phone the mansion as soon as she arrived. She wanted to report Mrs. Chamberlain's odd behavior to her.

On her way into the study, Becka glanced beside the telephone stand in the hallway. She spotted Nouri's jeweled lipstick holder and a diamond cocktail ring. Both items had her initials monogrammed on them. Becka quickly swiped them and slid them into her loose fitting pocket. She went into the study mumbling the word, "perfect" to herself.

Once inside the study, she immediately noticed Nouri's antique hair brush that Ethan had given to her as a surprise gift upon his return from China, several months earlier. It too had her name monogrammed on it. Becka smiled wickedly as she quickly slid the hairbrush into her other skirt pocket.

"My work here is done," she triumphantly whispered to herself, while reaching for the telephone. After listening to the endless ringing of the telephone in her ear, Becka finally slammed the receiver down.

"Damn you, Clint," she complained, where in the hell he had gone to when she saw him flying out of the Sommers' Estate. "That's okay, baby. You can run, but you can't hide. I will find you, you unfaithful bastard," was her last thought of him, as Mai Li entered the study carrying a silver tray with coffee on it.

"Your coffee, miss," she said, as she quickly did an inventory of the study.

"Forget it, Mai Li. You took entirely too damn long. Now I don't have time to drink it!"

"Sorry, miss," she responded, thankful that the miserable woman was about ready to leave.

"I hope you realize that I have no other choice but to report your lack of accommodation to Mr. Sommers," she barked, walking past Mai Li.

"Yes, miss, as you wish." She hid a smile and shook her head instead.

"You know, Mai Li, you wouldn't work for me for five minutes, I wouldn't put up with...Oh, just forget it." She turned to leave the study. Mai Li smiled, not bothering to give Becka's rudeness a second thought.

Becka quickly rushed to the front door, hoping Mai Li hadn't noticed the slight bulge in her right pocket caused by the hair brush. She turned to face her. "Mai Li, I decided not to leave Mrs. Sommers a note. I'll phone her later," she said before she walked out the door.

Chapter 7

Even with all the outside noise caused by the heavy traffic on the freeway, Clint Chamberlain's mind swiftly shifted once again back in time, somehow needing to recall special moments that he once shared with the woman of his dreams.

Several months after she was hired to renovate his five-bedroom apartment, Nouri arrived for work at his apartment just like she had for many mornings before. With dread. But this time would prove to be different. Instead of one of his many bimbos answering the door to let her in, he answered the door himself. Her beautiful, hazel-colored eyes sparkled with joy to see him. His expression showed a man with something on his mind. Their eyes never left each other as he gestured her inside. He smiled seductively. She nervously swallowed and gasped for air. He pretended not to notice and smiled to himself. He was pleased he had that effect on her. He finally said, "Good morning, Miss St. Charles." His eyes still held hers captive. Nouri fought the piercing ache inside herself to run into his arms.

With a great deal of effort, she coolly remarked, "And why are you here?" Nouri blinked several times to break the spell she currently seemed to be under. She quickly turned away from him, suddenly needing to put a safer space between them. She walked into the living room, not waiting for his reply.

Ignoring her question to him, he simply stated, "You're just in time for breakfast. You'll join me, of course." His expression was insistent. Without giving her an opportunity to decline, Clint motioned her into the dining room. He had gone to a great deal of trouble to impress her. How could she refuse? He had set the table so elegantly, and the aroma of the omelets cooking made her stomach slightly growl.

"It smells wonderful. What is it?" she asked, deliberately avoiding his penetrating gaze.

"Western-style omelets. I hope you like it. I put everything but the kitchen sink in it," he said, as he walked to the table and pulled her chair out for her.

"I love omelets. It really smells wonderful." Nouri smiled. Clint continued to talk to her from across the room.

"I like my bloody Mary's spicy. I hope you do too. I premade a batch."

"Yes, I like mine spicy too." She squirmed uncomfortably.

"Your drink, my lady." He teased.

"Thank you, kind sir." She toyed back.

"A toast." He insisted, gently clinging his glass to hers.

"If you insist. But I thought you were supposed to cling the glasses after the toast." She smiled. He chuckled, as his eyes locked onto hers once again.

THIEF OF HEARTS

"You're probably right. I don't make that many toasts," he said and then added, "Sometimes you find the most amazing things in the most unexpected places. To you, Nouri." Their glasses touched. She blushed. Too surprised to speak, she felt glad that she was already sitting down. If she hadn't been, her legs would have buckled right out from under her.

Clint noticed her trembling hands and smiled, as he gently brushed his coiled index finger against her cheek. Nouri knew he touched her. She saw him do so, but she couldn't seem to actually feel it. Her body was completely numb. She swallowed uncomfortably, trying to get her voice back. After a few long moments, she finally managed to respond, deliberately changing the tone of things. " Shall we eat, I'm starved." He smiled knowingly and answered her with a decisive shake of his head. He went to the kitchen, returning with a colorful assortment of fruit arranged temptingly inside a crystal bowl.

"Here start on this. I'll be right back with the omelets," he said, leaning over to place the fruit in the middle of the decorative table.

"Mmm. You're very handy in the kitchen it appears," she remarked, reaching across the table to help herself. He smiled appreciatively and returned to the kitchen to retrieve the omelets.

As he placed her omelet in front of her, he said, " Your omelet, my lady, but be careful, the plate is still quite warm." He circled the table and seated himself.

During breakfast the conversation was kept light and pleasurable. One bloody Mary lead to another. Both parties enjoying the company of the other. It was several hours before Nouri noticed that the two of them had been alone all along.

"Oh my goodness!" she exclaimed. "It just dawned on me. Where the hell are all the workers!" A stunned look crossed her beautiful face.

He smiled. "Relax, Nouri. I gave everyone the day off."

"But why? There's still so much that still needs to be done."

"You've been working much too hard. You need a few days off. Forget the damn deadline. You don't want your workers to start calling you a slave driver, do you?" He smiled and handed her another bloody Mary. "Here, drink with me. I like the company." His expression was lustful.

"How dare you..." He cut her off by impulsively pulling her into his muscular arms. He heatedly kissed her, taking her completely off guard. Her first instinct was to push him away, but she didn't want to. His kiss was much too exciting. Thrilling, actually.

One kiss lead to another. Each new kiss more passionate than the one before. His tight embrace had her body molded erotically to his. She softly moaned unknowingly. Clint was pleased.

THIEF OF HEARTS

"God, Nouri, I've wanted to do that from the first moment I saw you at the art exhibit." He finally managed to whisper, when he was forced to stop kissing her to come up for air.

Suddenly Clint's brain sent an alarm signal to him, forcing his mind back to the present, warning him that he was almost home. A quick surge of panic began to creep up his spine as the image of his wife's angry face suddenly popped inside his brain. He cringed just thinking about her and the god awful rage she was capable of.

He pulled his car into the driveway and sat quietly inside. Silently praying that she was still asleep, so he wouldn't have to deal with her face to face.

Becka was unpredictable. He never knew what she would do from one moment to the next. She was more than capable of doing some pretty unthinkable things. He desperately wanted to be in and out of the house before she had gotten out of bed. But in reality, he somehow knew that she was inside, wideawake, just waiting to shoot him. OR worse! After wishfully thinking, he knew he may as well get out of the car and get the dreaded confrontation over with. He released a deep sigh of dread.

Clint knew that Becka would fight the divorce that he so desperately wanted. He also knew that it would be expensive. But no matter what the cost, it would be a price well worth it! Even if it meant losing his only prized possession: his old Victorian house. He loved that old house. He regretfully sighed, as he approached the front door to the old mansion. He stopped walking when he noticed the broken pane of antique glass on the front door and the splattered pieces of broken glass on the ground beneath it. His face instantly turned red with anger. His jaw muscle jerked. His body tensed, and his blood quickly began to boil.

"Damn you. You crazy bitch!" he shouted as he heatedly put his key into the lock. Fumbling his effort to unlock the door, only made him angrier. Finally, the door swung open, allowing him to enter.

"So you want to fight, do you? Well, come on bitch, let's get it on!" He continued to shout, making his way into the living room. His fists were angrily swinging in mid air.

"Where the hell are you? You fucking psycho!" He raved, quickly doing a room to room search for her. After realizing that she was no where to be found downstairs, he swiftly darted upstairs, making their bedroom his first stop.

He slammed the door to the bedroom so hard, that it almost fell off the hinges.

"Becka, damn you. Where in the hell are you?" He shouted one final time before realizing that she apparently wasn't at home. He suddenly collapsed on top of the bed. He began to uncontrollably laugh at himself. Taking several moments to finally calm down.

"Damn you, Becka. You're making me as crazy as you are," he hoarsely whispered, as he forced himself off the bed.

"I've got to get out of here!" Was his last remark to himself. He reached for a pad of paper and a pen. He scribbled his Dear John note to her:

> Becka,
> *I refuse to live like this anymore. I want a divorce. My attorney will be in touch. Don't call me. It won't do any good. Name your price at any cost. It's a price paid. Well worth it! I'm out of here, thank God!*
> Clint

Clint laughed at his note and quickly put his whacko wife out of his mind. He went over to the large walk-in closet and grabbed several suitcases, quickly filling them with some of his personal belongings. He glanced at the clock beside his bed and swiftly reached for the telephone.

"Good morning, Sara. This is Clint Chamberlain. How are you today?"

"Oh, good morning, Mr. Chamberlain. I'm fine thanks, and you?" The young receptionist at Ethan Sommers' head office responded.

"I'm just perfect, thank you. Listen, Sara, I know that Mr. Sommers isn't in his office, but I'd like to speak to Ms. McCall if she's not too busy."

"Just a sec, and I'll connect you. You have a nice day now, Mr. Chamberlain." She smiled.

"You, too, Sara, thanks."

"Clint. Anna, here. What can I do for you?"

"Anna, it's been a while, huh?"

"Yes it has, Clint. Too long. We should do lunch soon."

"I'd love to, and we will soon, I promise," he lied.

"Yeah sure, that's what you said six months ago," she teased.

"I'm sorry, Anna. I'll make it up to you soon. I swear. Okay?" He humored.

"Okay, Clint. What can I help you with? Something I'm not supposed to be telling you, I'm sure!" She laughed.

"No, not really. I just need to know where Ethan plans to have lunch today. I understand he will be having lunch with his wife."

"Yes, I made reservations for them at 1:00 at the new French Restaurant, downtown. 'Le Massionette'."

"I know where it is. I dined there last week. Thanks, Anna."

"You're welcome, Clint. Is that all you needed?"

"Yes, that should do it." He smiled

"Wait a second, Clint."

"Yes, Anna?"

"What are you going to do about the problems with the Medallion Corporation?"

"I don't know. I haven't discussed it with Ethan yet."

"Well, I don't know if Ethan has mentioned it to you yet, but rumor has it that the FBI is secretly investigating certain branches of it for illegal activity."

"No, I didn't know. Thanks, Anna. Maybe we should just back out of our bid to take control all together. The last thing Ethan needs right now is for the FBI to put him and his many business affairs under a microscope." He sighed.

"That's true, Clint. I understand the investigation has something to do with misuse of economic power."

"Fabulous." He sighed, shaking his head.

"Thomas Sphere is checking into it."

"I didn't know Sphere was still on Ethan's payroll, Anna."

"Ethan needs him, what can I say."

"That lying son of a bit..."

"Ah! Ah! Ah! Clint. My virgin ears," she teased.

"I'm sorry, Anna. It's just he promised me..." He stopped talking.

"I know, Clint, but you know Ethan. He only does what he wants to do."

"Yeah, I know only too well. Tell me, Anna, is Ethan mixed up with Steven Li again?" He sighed.

"Is that what you think, Clint?"

"In a word, yes." He shook his head in disbelief.

"You know by me telling you that, I could get into a lot of trouble with Ethan."

"Never mind, Anna. You just gave me my answer."

"But you didn't hear it from me. Right?"

"Anna, my love. Have I ever..."

She interrupted him. "I'm sorry, Clint. You're right. I should know after all this time that you would never say anything about what I've told you. After all, we aren't just friends, we were just lovers once. Right?" She sighed longingly.

"Yes, we are friends, Anna. Even if we had never made love, I would never deliberately get you in trouble. You know that."

"You're right. Forgive me, Clint."

"What's to forgive."

"So when do I get to see you again?" she asked lustfully.

"Soon, Anna, I promise," he lied.

"Okay, Clint. I'm going to hold you to that promise.."

"I've got to run, Anna. Thanks."

"Anytime, Clint. See ya."

"Bye, Anna."

As Clint continued to sit on the side of the bed, lost in thought, anger swiftly swept through his veins. But it was gone as quickly as it came.

"Damn you, Ethan," he muttered silently, replacing the phone on its stand and rising to his feet. Suddenly, he remembered that Becka might return at any moment. He grabbed his two suitcases and ran down stairs, glad to be getting away from at least one of his current problems.

On his way out of the house, he glanced one final time around the old Victorian House that he loved so much. He had spent a lot of time and money attempting to return the mansion back into its original intended stature.

"Such a grand old house." He sadly sighed and shook his head. He hesitantly closed the door behind him.

Clint jumped into his Mercedes and hurried straight to the freeway. He was more than anxious to be returning to his old apartment downtown, the one that held so many wonderful memories of his beloved Nouri. After entering the on ramp to the freeway, he reached for his cell phone. He wanted to check in with his office and have his private secretary, Violet Smith, clear his calendar for the day. He had more important things on his mind than mere work.

"Good morning Peg. This is Mr. Chamberlain. How are you today?"

"Oh, hi, Mr. Chamberlain. I'm fine, thanks."

"Peg, I'm in a bit of a hurry today, and I need to speak with my beautiful Malaysian secretary. Is she in yet, please?" he asked.

"Yes, sir. Ms. Smith is in. I'll put you right through. Have a nice day," she said as she connected his call.

"*Selamat pagi* (Good morning), Clint."

"*Selamet pagi*, Violet. *Apa khabar* (How are you today)?"

"*Khabar baik* (I'm fine) and you?"

"I couldn't be any better if I wanted to." He beamed.

"Wow, boss. Its been a long time since you've sounded so...so, perky." She remarked with surprise in her voice.

"You have no idea, Violet! I've left that whacko *isteri* (wife) of mine. I'm getting a divorce, thank God!" He sighed and shook his head in relief.

"Wow, you are full of surprises today." She smiled, then added, " So what happened Clint?"

"I'm sorry, Violet. I don't have time to get into it right now. I'm in a bit of a rush, and I need you to do a few things for me. But I'll tell you all about it later, okay." He smiled.

"I hate it when you do that to me, Clint."

"What's that Violet?"

"You know exactly what I'm talking about, Clint Chamberlain." She teased.

"I promise I'll tell you everything when I come into the office tomorrow, okay."

"Okay, so what do you need me to do?" She sighed.

"First of all, Violet, call my *peguam* (attorney), Peter Toliver and tell him I want a divorce from Becka, as soon as possible. I don't care what it costs me! I want it like yesterday. Got it?" He shook his head with dread. "Next, call the Dolly Maid Cleaning Service for me. I need the works at my downtown apartment. The address is in my rolodex. Groceries. Booze. Cleaning. Just tell them I'm starting from scratch. They'll know what I mean, I've used them before. Also call my tailor. I'll need an entire new wardrobe. Have someone from the office go shopping for all my other needs. Sizes and etc., you should know by now, right?" He laughed.

"Only too well, Clint." She laughed.

"When I get home tonight, I want it to be as though I've lived there all my life. Got it?"

"Not a problem. I'll handle everything myself."

"Good. Now, Violet, there's just one thing left to take care of for me. If Becka comes to the office and tries to start anything, have her ass thrown in jail. Think you can handle all of that for me?" He smiled, knowing she was more than capable.

"Like I said, Clint, not a problem," she boasted.

"Fine. I'll check with you later, Violet. *Selamet tinggal* (Good bye)."

"*Selamet tinggal*, Clint."

Clint turned off his cell phone and stepped down a little harder on the pedal. He was anxious to stop by his old apartment, and even more excited to share the news of his divorce with the woman of his dreams. He could hardly wait to see the expression on her face, or Ethan's.

"If you are sleeping with my wife, old friend, more power to you," he mumbled to himself, as he took the downtown exit ramp off of the freeway.

The old place is just up the street, he thought, as he glanced around the old neighborhood.

"A lot of memories around here," he whispered fondly, pulling his car to a stop in front of his old apartment. He smiled affectionately, as though the old apartment building were an old friend.

After opening the door to his old apartment, he was immediately flooded with memories. He had to quickly stop his mind before it once again took him on a trip to the past. He quietly whispered to himself, "Not now ol' boy. You don't have the time." He dropped his suitcases off and quickly exited his apartment.

THIEF OF HEARTS

    His telephone conversations with Anna McCall and his secretary, Violet Smith already had him running late as it was. He glanced at his watch.
    "Oh damn!" he complained after noticing the time. He quickly put the pedal to the metal and headed for the other side of downtown.

Chapter 8

Fredrick pulled the limo up in front of the Sommers' condo and swiftly exited the car. He opened the door to the limo to assist Nouri out of the back seat.

"Thank you, Fredrick." She smiled.

"You're welcome, madam," he replied. Nouri smiled fondly at Heidi, the condo maid, and James, the condo chauffeur, as they stood patiently in front of the building. They both returned her smile.

"Hello, Mrs. Sommers," Heidi said, as James accepted a small make-up case from Fredrick's hands. Heidi added, " Mai Li phoned and said for you to phone her when you had an opportunity." She smiled.

"Good morning. I mean good afternoon," Nouri responded, glancing at her watch. "I'll phone Mai Li later, thank you. I was hoping to get here earlier, but there was a four car pile up on the freeway that we managed to stuck in." She shook her head in disbelief.

"It was unavoidable, madam," Fredrick responded.

"Oh, I know, Fredrick. I'm certainly not blaming you." She warmly smiled.

"Yes, madam." He nodded and then added, "I'd better get started back madam. If there isn't anything else." He smiled.

"No thank you, Fredrick." She smiled again. Nouri turned to face Heidi.

"Has Mr. Sommers left yet, Heidi?" She said and quickly added, "Oh, where's my mind! Of course he has. After all, it's lunch time." She smiled and shook her head. Heidi and James glanced at each other and shrugged their shoulders.

Heidi spoke, "Excuse me. Mrs. Sommers." A puzzled looked crossed her face.

"Yes, Heidi."

"Mr. Sommers hasn't been at the condo since he gave it to you a year ago."

"I see. I guess I must have misunderstood him." She forced a smile, then added, "I'm in a hurry. I'd better run upstairs and change. Heidi will you bring some coffee in the bedroom." She smiled again and quickly walked inside the building. She went straight for the elevators.

"Miss."

"Yes, James." She turned to face him, as she waited for the elevator.

"Shall I bring the Bentley or the rolls around?"

"Neither, James. I'll drive myself. Bring my Viper around. I'll be down in a few minutes. I have to change and make a few phone calls." She smiled and stepped inside the elevator with Heidi.

79

THIEF OF HEARTS

Nouri went immediately to her bedroom, closing the door behind her.

"Damn you, Ethan!" she angrily snapped, while reaching for the telephone.

"Hello operator, would you look up the telephone number for Mr. Charles Mason, private investigator. Thank you. I'll hold." A slight pause of silence crossed her ear and then the operator told her the number. "Thank you," Nouri responded. She quickly dialed the number.

"Hello, Charles Mason Investigations. How may I direct your call please?" the young receptionist asked.

"Yes. I'd like to speak with Mr. Mason, please." She sighed.

"Who shall I say is calling?"

"Just tell him Nouri...Nouri...uh...uh, St. Charles." She nervously responded.

"One moment please, I'll connect you, Ms. St. Charles." Charles broke his neck answering the call.

"My god! Sugar, is it really you?" he asked in a stunned tone of voice.

"Yes, big guy. It's me." She smiled nervously, using her pet name for him.

"Wow, I can't believe it's you, sugar!" He used his pet name for her again.

"Charles, I need to see you. I need a favor."

"Anything, sugar. When?"

"Today. How about today?" Her tone was anxious.

"Oh, damn sugar. Today is a bad day for me." He shook his head regretfully.

"Please Charles, it's important." She begged.

"I could never deny you anything, sugar."

"Then you'll meet me?"

"I'll clear my calendar, just for you. But it will cost you." He teased.

"I was afraid of that." She laughed then added, "What do I have to do big guy?"

"Buy me an early dinner at our old spot." He toyed.

"God, that old place. I can't believe it's still in business." She laughed fondly, shaking her head.

"Pompillio's. Are you kidding? It's the best Italian Restaurant in the city." He laughed.

"Pompillio's it is, Charles. I can't make it until three o' clock though. I was supposed to meet my husband for lunch, but I doubt he will show. I haven't been confirmed by his secretary yet."

"Wait a minute! Back up to the husband part!" He was absolutely stunned.

THIEF OF HEARTS

"It's a long story, Charles. I'll explain when I see you." Her tone rushed.

"Husband. Secretary. Confirmed yet... I don't understand, sugar." He shook his head.

"Please, Charles. I'm in a rush." She sighed.

"All right, sugar. But you have a lot of explaining to do." He shook his head, disappointed to learn that she was married.

"Thank you, Charles. I'll see you soon. Bye."

"Bye, sugar."

She quickly placed the receiver back on its hook and jumped to her feet, taking her cup of coffee with her to the large walk in closet. She rapidly selected an outfit and quickly dressed. She glanced at her watch just as the telephone rang. It was her husband's secretary, Anna McCall, with the time and location of her lunch date with Ethan. Anna explained that she realized that she was late phoning, but not to worry. Mr. Sommers was running late, as well.

Nouri shook her head in disbelief and rapidly ran out of the condo. Nouri quickly jumped into her canary-yellow Viper, speeding the moment she put her foot on the gas pedal. She peeled rubber for almost a mile. James smiled and shook his head, as he watched her fade out of sight.

Nouri's mind was racing in several directions at once. She didn't know whether she should run into her husband's arms or slap him in the face for lying to her. One thing she did know for sure, they definitely had to talk. She was hurt. Bored. Neglected. And if that wasn't enough for her to have to endure, what about the broken dates and now the lies!

Her heart didn't want to believe that he would have the nerve to stand her up again. But her mind knew that he probably would. It was actually more of a gut feeling. Something was definitely up with her husband. Something was definitely up with her husband and Clint Chamberlain. And something was definitely wrong with her marriage.

That's the reason she had phoned her friend, Charles Mason. He was the best private investigator in the country. The best money could buy. He was world renown for solving cases that no one else could. His clients were usually mega buck high profile cases. Mostly movie stars and huge corporations.

His handsome face was always posted somewhere on one of many newspapers or magazines, and even TV. He was very popular and always in demand. If Nouri Sommers wasn't so dear to him, she probably would have had to take a number and wait in a very long line of people to see him.

Nouri was somewhat surprised that Charles had agreed to meet with her so quickly. After all, it had been seven long years since she had last seen him. That was the very same day she had broken his heart by turning down his offer of marriage. Charles never got over the pain of losing her. And he never married. Though many women would have jumped at the chance to become his famous wife, especially the District Attorney of Boston, Ms. Tonya Lee Daughtery, or the famous movie actress Millie Renee.

He became quite the international ladies' man, but his heart has never belonged to anyone other than the heart-stopping, beautiful, Ms. Nouri St. Charles of Boston.

She had met Charles Mason while she was still attending the Fine Arts Academy of Boston. Charles had been an arranged date that turned out to be just perfect for her at the time. He was ruggedly handsome, funny, and extremely well-put-together! It was lust at first sight for her. And love at first sight for him. He was everything she seemed to need in a lover, at the time. Mature. Exciting. Passionate. Authoritative. A real take charge kind of guy. And most of all very experienced. He was her first real man.

Charles was an undercover police officer on the verge of going into business for himself. Nouri was incredibly beautiful. Very young. Deeply passionate. And eager to learn. She couldn't wait to go out and conquer the world, and everything in it. Charles, however, had very different plans for the flighty, but spicy, Nouri St. Charles, from Boston.

When she turned down his offer of a cozy little cottage by the bay, as Mrs. Charles Mason, she and Charles soon parted, leaving him agonizingly heart broken. A heart break that he never recovered from. Even today, he's still desperately in love with her. He never really understood why she left him, but he blamed it on the fact that he was fourteen years older than her. At the time, she was only nineteen.

After his phone call from Nouri Sommers, Charles Mason literally had to pinch himself to make sure that he wasn't day dreaming about her again, like he had done so many times in the past. Just seeing her, even after all this time, was more than he could have hoped for. Just the thought of her beautiful face made his excitement hard to control. He smiled anxiously, as he glanced at his watch. He quickly reached for the telephone and summonsed his private secretary. He needed to have her clear his calendar for the rest of the day. He was anxious to leave. He wanted to rush home, shower, and find something suitable to wear for his dinner date with the woman of his dreams. But first, he wanted to find out who she had married.

As Nouri continued to fly her Viper across town, she suddenly smiled unconsciously when the image of Charles Mason popped into her head.

"God, it will be good to see him again," she silently whispered, as she began to reflect. It was seven years ago. She and her best friend Genna Thomas, now Genna Matthews, were attending the Fine Arts Academy. Genna was hopelessly in love with a police officer, whose name was Michael Jones. She smiled and shook her head fondly. Michael was boyishly handsome for his age. He was tall with a muscular build. He had sky blue eyes and sandy blond hair, a real cute guy. Michael had a friend, who was also a police officer. His name was Charles Mason. He was perfect! He was all man in every way!

Nouri suddenly turned her attention back to the present, when she accidentally flew past Le Massionette's.

"Whoops," she mumbled, as she quickly made a U-turn in the middle of the street. She usually didn't have a heavy foot, but she just couldn't seem to resist going fast in her shiny new Viper. She loved the way her new toy felt when she was behind the wheel. Of course, it was only her second time driving the car. She quickly pulled the car in front of the restaurant, leaving the motor running, so the valet could park the car. She nodded a friendly hello, as he helped her out.

"Great car!" the young valet said, anxious to get behind the wheel. She smiled and thanked him and swiftly darted inside the restaurant.

Once inside, Nouri introduced herself and asked to be seated at her husband's table, instead of waiting in the cocktail lounge. She was still suffering miserably with a hang over from the night before. The last thing she needed for lunch was another cocktail.

She was seated at an elegant, but cozy table with a view of the beautiful fountain of water. The many different layers of water reminded her of a water fountain she had once seen in China. It was set in a botanical atmosphere, really quite breath taking to look at.

She declined a suggestion offering her a cocktail. Instead, she opted for a glass of Pierrier with a slice of lemon. As she nervously glanced at her watch, that gut feeling of her's came back again. She seemed to know before the host handed her the cordless phone that her husband wasn't going to make lunch.

"A phone call for you, Mrs. Sommers," the French host said, nodding a friendly smile, as he handed her the telephone. Nouri nodded appreciatively and accepted the receiver. She returned the smile to the handsome host, the same moment she responded to the caller.

"Yes, this is Nouri Sommers." The caller was once again her husband's secretary, Anna McCall, delivering yet another disappointing message from Ethan. Once again, he was *unavoidably* detained and couldn't make lunch. But he would phone her later.

"I see," Nouri coolly responded, shaking her head in utter amazement.

"Oh, Mrs. Sommers, I had almost forgotten," Ms. McCall sighed then added, "He also said to tell you not to forget to meet him in Lambert this weekend."

Nouri cut in sharply, "Meet him! I...I thought we were going to Lambert together." Her voice went from a high shrill tone to almost a whisper.

"I'm sorry, Mrs. Sommers, I'm just the messenger." Her tone was sympathetic.

"I'm sorry, Ms. McCall, I'm just rather disappointed. I certainly didn't mean to..."

Anna interrupted her, " "Oh, there was one more thing, Mr. Sommers said for me to tell you."

"Yes, and what was that, Ms. McCall." She sighed.

"He said for you to go out after lunch and buy yourself something extremely expensive, to make up for his tardiness, as of late." She released an envious sigh.

"You mean absenteeism, don't you?" Her voice filled with hurt.

"Like I said, Mrs. Sommers, I'm just the messenger," Ms. McCall replied, shaking her head understandingly.

"Yes, of course. I apologize. Thank you, Ms. McCall, good bye," she responded, as she handed the telephone back to the host, who was standing near by.

A fallen tear drop leaked down her cheek. She quickly blotted it away with her table napkin. The handsome French host noticed. He replied, *"qu'est-ce qu'llya*, mademoiselle?" A compassionate smile followed. He then added in English, realizing she may have not understood him, "What's the matter, miss? Is everything all right?"

She faked a smile and responded in his native tongue, *"oui merci. Bien sur. Je regrette."* (yes, thank you. Of course. I'm sorry).

He nodded politely, saying, *"dans ceca-ia je vous laisse."* (in that case, I'll leave you). He smiled again and turned to walk away.

Nouri quickly called out to him, *"excusez-moi, monsieur.* May I have a double, extra dry Russian martini, straight up, with an extra olive, please." She lowered her arm, realizing it was still lifted in the air from signaling the host.

He answered her from where he was standing, *"oui, bien sur, mademoiselle."* He nodded and continued walking. Nouri sat motionless, as the blood seemed to slowly drain the life from her body, which was now numb. She rubbed her now cold hands together as she continued to be lost in thought.

"Damn you, Ethan," she whispered unconsciously, thinking about her mysterious husband. I don't know who you really are Ethan Sommers, what you're up to, or even what your about, as far as that goes, but I intend to find out, mister! Her mind began to race.

She glanced at her watch, realizing that she had just consumed two double martinis in a matter of only several minutes.

"Oh, my!" she mumbled pushing the empty cocktail glass away from herself. She unconsciously began to tap her fingers on top of the table, nervously wondering what she should do next.

Nouri gestured to the waiter for her tab. She swiftly signed it, leaving a huge tip. On her way to the front of the restaurant, she asked the host to have her car brought around and if she could use the phone.

THIEF OF HEARTS

She phoned Charles Mason's office, hoping he would be in. She was hoping he could pull himself away to meet her earlier than they had agreed on. But he wasn't in the office. Not bothering to leave a message, she decided to go to their prearranged meeting place ahead of schedule anyway, secretly hoping that he would be there early, as well. But no matter, she could use the extra time to freshen her make-up and have a drink or two, and try to calm herself down a bit before Charles arrived.

She tipped the valet and jumped into her Viper, angrily putting the pedal to the metal. Flying straight down sixth street, she sharply turned at the following corner, not bothering to even stop for the stop sign.

Clint Chamberlain was pulling into the restaurant's parking area, when he suddenly spotted Nouri's unusual automobile flying around the corner, just past sixth street. He swiftly turned his car around and went chasing after her.

Curious about where she was going in such a rush, Clint deliberately stayed several car lengths behind her. His eyes stayed glued to her shiny canary-yellow Viper. He followed her to the east side of town. Clint was more than curious as to why she would be in that part of town. He shook his head and sighed. What is she up to? He silently thought, as he watched her park her car across the street from an old Italian Restaurant named Pompillio's. He slowed down and quickly slid his car into an empty slot five cars behind hers.

He sat in his car and watched her gracefully cross the street. Her thin layered skirt slightly blowing in sync to the breeze. Her hair was swaying ever so slightly to the same wind song. He smiled at her incredible beauty, as she entered the restaurant.

Clint stepped out of the car and walked across the street. He put his face up to the large front window of the restaurant and looked inside, using his hand as a visor to halt the sunshine glaring from the glass to his eyes. He immediately spotted her being motioned by a man already seated at a cozy table for two. The stranger stood to his feet, as she rushed to greet his open arm embrace intended for her. Clint's heart fell to the ground. He blinked several times hoping the female wasn't his beloved Nouri after all.

He walked inside the restaurant for a better look. Going directly to the cocktail lounge, he sat at the bar. Facing an extra large mirror, he could not have picked a better seat to spy on her with, if he had planned it. He had a perfect view of her, but she couldn't see him. Perfect, he thought to himself, before ordering a Manhattan on the rocks, with a dash of bitters. He began to watch her every move.

After realizing that it was, in fact, Nouri, Clint became content with his arrangement between he and the large antique mirror. A sneaky smile crossed his handsome face, as he continued to watch the woman of his dreams with this unknown mystery man. Who the hell is that muscle bound jerk! He jealously thought, as he waited for the bar tender to bring another drink.

"Wow, Charles. You look great!" Nouri said, as she slowly released herself from his tight embrace. She continued, "Just the way I remembered." She smiled fondly.

"Ya think so, sugar," he responded, using his pet name for her.

"Yeah, I do. Really great, big guy." She beamed, also using his pet name for him.

"And you. Spin around and let me take a look-see," he replied, gesturing with his index finger to whirl around in a circle. He smiled lustfully. Clint Chamberlain response to their apparent closeness was, "Give me a fucking break," he whispered under his breath, shaking his head jealously.

"So, you like big guy?" Her smile was inviting him to respond. He nodded his head with approval, saying, "Hey sugar, what's not to like."

Clint ordered another Manhattan on the rocks and squirmed uneasily on his bar stool.

"I filled out, huh?" Her smile reminded Charles of a child asking for approval.

"Yeah sugar, you sure did. And in all the right places. I see..." He smiled, then added, "Still the same little heart stopper, huh, sugar." Nouri blushed, but still pleased that he seemed to approve of her seven year growing spurt.

She responded, "Oh please, Charles." He pulled Nouri's chair out. After she sat down, Charles pulled her closer to him. She blushed again. "Now behave yourself, Charles," she said, smiling seductively.

His cool response, "Who me, sugar? You've got to be kidding. That's like asking me to stop breathing when I'm around you!" His eyes met hers. She squirmed uncomfortably. So did Clint. He changed his drink order to a double scotch on the rocks.

Nouri responded, "I see your point." She laughed, while Clint cringed. His face turned an angry shade of crimson. He grinded his teeth in jealously.

As Clint sat at the bar getting angrier and angrier, Nouri and Charles sat at their cozy table for two, drinking and reminiscing about their past together.

Meanwhile, Becka Chamberlain sat inside her car, now parked inside her own garage. She was trying to figure out a way to make up with her husband, just long enough to trick him into taking her to Lambert for the weekend. There, she planned to kill him and frame Nouri Sommers for the murder. She knew it was too late to pretend that she hadn't been angry at him. She thought he must have seen the broken antique glass on the front door by now. Plus, surely Nouri would have told him about their argument on the telephone the night before. So all she could hope for at that point would be to pretend that she was over her angry spell with him.

If he isn't home, I'll phone his office and tell him how much I love him and can't wait for him to get home tonight. That works every time, she thought to

THIEF OF HEARTS

herself, as she got out of her car and walked to the garage door that lead to the inside of the old Victorian Mansion. She sighed deeply, as she put the key into the lock. She pushed the door open and called out his name. When he didn't respond, she called out again.

She quickly walked into the living room, glancing around the room. She noticed that her husband had apparently been there. She could tell by the things he must have either knocked over or kicked out of his way while he was angry. Probably over his precious antique glass front door, she mused to herself silently. Heading upstairs to the bedroom, she once again shouted out to him. Still no response. "Honey...are you here?" Becka said in a loving tone of voice. Still no response. She entered the bedroom, quickly noticing the a note beside the telephone on the night stand. She let out a violent scream after reading Clint's 'Dear John' note. "You bastard! A divorce! You fuck! I'll show you divorce!" She raved out of control.

Becka quickly stormed back downstairs and poured herself a double shot of gin. She angrily paced back and forth, sipping on her drink. Lost in thought, she wondered what her next game plan should entail. The more she thought, the angrier she became. Completely consumed in rage. She downed her drink and threw her empty drink against the wall. It splattered into a million tiny pieces. She grabbed her purse and set of keys and heatedly stormed out of the house.

She jumped back into her car and quickly headed into the direction of her husband's office.

"You rotten bastard! I'm going to cut your goddamn heart out!" She wailed shaking her fist in mid-air.

Once inside her husband's office, she became so violent with the staff that Violet Smith had to threaten to have her arrested before she would finally leave. On her way out of the building, she slammed the front door so violently, that once again, she shattered another front door pane of antique glass in its entirety. The blast sent tiny pieces of glass in every direction.

She stormed back to her car and headed back home. While driving, she realized that Nouri would be in Lambert the weekend. That meant Clint wouldn't be far away. Yes, he will be there! I just know it, was her final thought on the matter, as she raced home to pack.

Chapter 9

The soft white sand felt good between young Kirsten Kamel's toes.

"I wish we could stay here forever, just the two of us. No one else on this beautiful island, honey," Kirt Jarett said, as he turned Kirsten to face him. They passionately kissed.

"Me too baby." She lovingly responded, still wiggling her toes in the sand.

"Do you think we'll ever get enough money out of these rich bastards to disappear?" He sighed wishfully.

"Sure baby, look what Ethan gave me for my birthday," she boasted, handing him the diamond necklace.

"Wow! That ought to bring a pretty penny." He smiled as he began to play with it.

"I just hope he doesn't find out about us, Kirt." She sighed nervously.

"It won't be long honey. We'll just have to be careful, that's all." Kirt pulled her into his arms.

"Yeah, but sometimes he scares me. Ethan has a terrible temper." Kirsten clung to Kirt.

"Don't worry, Kirsten. I've been getting a lot of stuff on tape," he boasted.

"What do you mean, baby?" She glared at him with a confused expression on her face.

"Ethan Sommers and Otto Lambert are into a lot of illegal shit together. I intend to get all that I can on them. Then I'll bargain for our freedom. For once and for all." Kirt said in a protective tone of voice.

"Lambert won't let us go that easily." Kirsten shook her pretty head and sighed.

"Honey, don't you worry that pretty little head of yours. I'll take care of everything. I promise, okay." He smiled and kissed her again.

"Honey, I... Should be getting back. Ethan will be wondering what's taking me so long. I told him I had to go to my room and get some of my girlie stuff. The man's a real animal." She sighed again.

"You think he's bad. You haven't made love to Becka Chamberlain. Talk about sick!" Kirt shook his head in disgust.

"Yeah, I heard Thomas talking about her. I think she's been doing Ethan Sommers too. She was leaving his suite the other day as I was coming around the corner. She looked kind of out there, rough."

"I bet. That's the way she like it." He laughed.

"Well so do you, Kirt." She glanced at him.

"Yeah, but not with you baby. I love you, Kirsten. You're the only woman I've ever loved." He kissed her again, then said, "Just hang in there honey. We will be able to put this place and everything else behind us real soon. I promise." He hugged her tightly.

"Baby, there's something I want to tell you. But I don't want you to be mad, okay." She wiggled her toes in the sand again.

"What is it honey?" He smiled.

"I...I...I think I might be pregnant," she said and began to nervously bite her finger nails.

He looked at her lovingly and responded, "Mine?" He smiled proudly.

"Yes, Otto and Ethan always use protection."

"Oh honey, that is great! Don't worry about it. We'll be out of here before you know it. I promise." He kissed her again.

"Then you're not mad at me baby?" she asked nervously.

"No! Hell no. I love you, Kirsten. Somehow everything will work out for us, I promise. Now be a good girl and go make us some money. I'll do the same." Kirt said as he kissed her good bye. She smiled and quickly headed back to Ethan Sommers suite. "Oh damn!" She mumbled after remembering she had forgotten to stop by her room for her girlie supplies. Kirsten quickly changed her direction and went to her room instead. Throwing together a few needed items, she then headed back to Ethan's suite.

She sharply knocked on the door. "Baby, it's me!" She shouted, as she knocked again. Ethan answered the door, holding the telephone between his ear and his neck. He put his finger to his lips, gesturing for her to be quiet. She walked inside and headed for the bar to pour them a drink.

She could sense Ethan was upset. She brought his drink to him, but he waved her away. Almost as though he dismissed her. A frown crossed her face, as she walked back to the bar.

Ethan slammed the receiver down, but quickly reached for it again, rapidly redialing.

"Yes. Mai Li, it's me again. Did she make it home yet?" His tone was sharp and angry.

"No sir. Not home yet. Maybe still at condo," she answered nervously.

"Okay, Mai Li, you tell her I got tired of phoning. I don't have time for her silly tantrums, and I expect her to be in Lambert this weekend when I get there! Have Fredrick drive her. She might want to stop in that cute little town that she likes so well. She enjoys shopping there. And...and tell her I said to get in a good mood for chrissakes. The last thing I want to be dealing with this weekend is one of her little hissy-fits." He arrogantly demanded.

"Yes, sir. I tell her."

THIEF OF HEARTS

"Fine. Bye, Mai Li." Ethan returned the receiver to its hook, not waiting for her to respond. Kirsten studied Ethan's expression.

She quickly went to him. "Why so pissed, baby?" She smiled and gently rubbed his strong, broad back, trying to comfort him. Ethan angrily pulled himself free from Kirsten's gentle touches.

"It's that damn wife of mine. She's trying to drive me nuts again with her silly games." He quickly downed his drink and walked to the bar for a refill. He downed another.

"So now you're gonna pout all night long over that spoiled wife of yours?" she asked in a jealous tone of voice. Ethan slammed his glass sharply down on the top of the bar.

He glared at her with an icy cold stare. He responded heatedly, "Knock it off, Kirsten. I told you before, don't talk about my wife like that. I won't stand for it!" A hurt expression crossed Kirsten's face but was gone as quickly as it came.

She replied, " So baby, if you're so worried about that spoiled wife of yours, why aren't ya home with her right now instead of here with me?" She seductively smiled and began to erotically run her hands across her breasts. Their eyes locked onto one another's.

Young Kirsten Kamel knew exactly how to handle the lustful side of Ethan Sommers. He bit his lower lip and continued to watch her run her hands up and down her young body. He licked his lips again and sat his drink down on top of the bar. He lustfully ordered, "You know why, Kirsten, now shut up and bring that young, bouncy body over here." He stood to his feet and quickly removed his robe.

Kirsten responded seductively, quickly removing her cloths, "Whew! Angry sex. I'm starting to like that baby. Hot and rough. Is that what you want, baby?" She licked her lips seductively, again.

His vulgar reply: "Stop wasting that beautiful mouth of yours with idle chit chat. I've got a better use for it."

"Is this what you had in mind, baby?" young Kirsten said in a wicked tone of voice, as she fell to her knees and began to shower Ethan's erection with her hot thirsty kisses.

Chapter 10

Pompillio's Italian Restaurant was established in the early 1900's. It was a family owned and operated business. currently being ran by a grand niece, Michelle and her husband, Anthony. Seven years earlier it was Charles Mason's favorite place to hang out. The restaurant was noted for having the best value for your buck, and the food was second to none. The house wine was cheap, but really quite good. And their dart team was almost always number one among all the other restaurants in tournament play. Charles Mason and a few of his police friends were some of the better players on the weekly dart team.

Every Friday and Saturday night, like clock work, Nouri and Charles could be found at Pompillios eating pasta, drinking house wine, and throwing darts with their many friends.

Nouri and Charles continued to reminisce:

"So tell me, Charles, do you still come here as often as you used too?"

"No, I'm afraid not. I stay pretty busy these days. I'm out of town a lot. Not to mention out of the country, and, well...to tell you the truth, sugar," he paused and reached for his drink, "After you left me, it just wasn't the same." He forced a smile.

"I'm sorry, Charles. I never meant to hurt you." She patted his hand affectionately. Their eyes met. She swallowed hard and squirmed uneasily in her chair. So did Clint, who was still watching attentively at the bar. He ordered another drink.

"I know, sugar, but you did." A hurt look crossed his face. He quickly changed the subject. "So tell me sugar, what is it that has you slumming down here on this side of town."

I...I need a favor." She picked up her drink nervously and downed it.

"What kind of a favor, sugar?" He smiled, as he motioned for the waiter to bring them two more drinks. He held up two fingers and nodded.

"I want to hire you."

"I see. Here I was hoping that you had finally came to you senses. Missed me and..." Nouri interrupted him in mid-sentence.

"Charles, I'm serious. I need you." She leveled her eyes to his.

"Does this have anything to do with your marriage to the billionaire tycoon, Ethan Sommers?"

"Oh, so you do know?" She sounded surprised.

"I do now. I didn't before you called. After your call, I did a little research. I was apparently out of the country when your high society marriage hit the front pages, a year after your marriage." He sighed.

"I was wondering why you had sounded so surprised when I mentioned being married on the telephone earlier today."

"You couldn't wait to go out and conquer the world and every thing in it. That's exactly what you've done." He shook his head in dismay. Nouri laughed light heartedly.

"I guess you could say that, Charles. But I never really thought of it that way." She sighed and picked up her drink, then added, "You know Charles, I really shouldn't be drinking this. I'm still nursing a hangover from last night." She shook her head and then took a sip of her drink.

"Hell sugar, I have just the cure that you need." He teased.

"I bet you do." She teased back before adding, "What's that, big guy, some of that cheap wine you used to feed me all the time?" They both laughed.

"No, sugar. I was thinking maybe you'd like a bottle of that sissy stuff you used to like so well, or don't you drink that anymore," he said and then downed his drink.

"That so called sissy stuff, as you put it, is the reason I'm suffering today." She shook her head playfully.

"From the sound of it, maybe you should've been drinking that old cheap wine instead of that sissy stuff. One thing's for sure about that old cheap wine," he teased, " it will either cure you or kill you." They both laughed.

"Thanks, Charles."

"For what, sugar?"

"For making me laugh. I needed that. It's been a long time since a smile had crossed my face."

"I'm sorry to hear that, sugar," he said sadly. "Well, what about it. Do you want a bottle of Asti-Spumanti?" His eyes found hers again.

"I'm impressed, Charles. You remembered the name of my favorite wine."

"Oh, yeah. I remember everything about you, sugar. By the way, still writing in those damn journals of yours?" He teased.

Charles Mason was the reason that Nouri had started writing in her journals to begin with. He was away from home a lot of the time on all-night stakeouts when he was an undercover officer with the Boston Police Department. On the nights that he was away, she would write in her journal.

She responded, "Well, Charles, a girl needs something to do when she's left alone at night, doesn't' she?" She smiled.

"So are you still writing in those damn things, huh?" He chuckled and shook his head playfully.

"Of course. It's my true passion." She smiled again and reached for her drink. She downed it nervously.

THIEF OF HEARTS

His simple response, "And you are mine." He looked into her beautiful hazel-colored eyes.

"Oh, Charles," she said softly. She blushed and swallowed hard.

Clint ordered another drink, as he continued to sit and watch the two ex-lovers toy with each other.

"Well, would you like to eat first or tell me what's on that beautiful mind of yours, first?"

"Charles. I'm not quite ready to talk about it yet. Let's eat first."

Charles waved the waiter over and ordered a bottle of her favorite wine. He turned to face her, "Shall I order for the both of us?" He smiled.

"I've missed that," she responded.

"Missed what, sugar?"

"Your take charge attitude."

"Shall I dazzle you with my suggestions of Italian Gourmet delights?" He teased.

"Oh yes, Charles, dazzle me. It's been at least seven years since I've been dazzled." She mused backed.

"We'll just have to fix that. Won't we, sugar?" His smile was lustful.

"Behave, Charles," she said knowingly.

"How the hell can I behave when you look at me like that?" He shook his head longingly.

"Charles, don't keep our server waiting. Order for us and I'll visit the little girl's room, okay?" She smiled and stood to her feet. Charles jumped up, pulling her chair out for her.

Clint Chamberlain didn't much care for what he was witnessing with his woman and her apparent mystery man. He wanted to run into the ladies' room and confront her in private. But, on the other hand, he wanted to see what her meeting with him was really about. So he opted for another drink at the bar and continued to spy on her.

Nouri returned from the ladies room where she had gone to secretly scold herself. She needed to put a little distance between herself and Charles. For a few moments, his sexiness was driving her to distraction. She was finding it harder and harder for her to concentrate on what he was saying to her. He looked incredible. So handsome. So sexy. So manly. God how she wanted to make love to him. He was after all, her first real man. It was he, and he alone, that taught her how wonderful it was to be a woman. He took her to heights of ecstasy that she had never known existed before. He was all man in every way. Her emotions were becoming harder for her to control. She deliberately brushed up against his sexy body, as she approached their table to see how he would react.

"God, sugar, you still give me goose bumps," he said, responding to her touch.

"Excuse me, Charles." She toyed, knowing exactly what he meant.

"When you brushed up against me just then, I became instantly aroused. See." Charles heatedly responded and smiled wickedly, as he gestured toward the lower part of his seated body. Nouri turned a cute shade of pink, as she glanced lustfully at his arousal. She was glad to know she still had that effect on him.

"Why Charles Mason, behave yourself!" She playfully responded. He could tell by the look on her face and the tone of her voice, that she still wanted him as much as he wanted her. But he decided to let her make the next move.

He responded, "Behave. Who me? Well...If you insist." His eyes twinkled with desire. Nouri swallowed hard and used her hand as a fan to cool herself. He chuckled knowingly.

"What's so funny, big guy?" Nouri responded coolly.

"You are sugar." Charles toyed.

"What do you mean, Charles?"

"Getting a little warm, sugar?" He smiled lustfully.

"Oh yeah!" She responded heatedly as she glanced at his still hardened arousal. She bit her lower lip lustfully.

Clint angrily grabbed the padded edge of the bar railing, holding it tightly with both hands. "Bring me another double, bartender," he sharply ordered.

"I still turn you on, don't I sugar." He smiled excitedly. Holding her eyes captive with his incredible emerald-green eyes.

Nouri surprised herself with her lustful response, "Yes, Charles, you do."

"We'll have to do something about that. Now. Won't we, sugar?" His eyes never left hers.

"Charles, please. I...I can't." She downed a glass of her cool sweet wine, blushing the whole time.

"So, you're saying what. That we're going to just sit here driving each other crazy with desire?" His voice filled with disappointment.

"Charles, God knows that I would give anything right this very moment if we could just..." She stopped talking.

"All right, sugar, let's just have another drink, and you tell me what exactly it is that you do want from me, okay?" He reached for his drink.

"I'm sorry, Charles. I don't know what I expected today, but it certainly wasn't this."

"Expected what? To still have feelings of desire for me. Is that it, Nouri?"

"Yes, Charles. That's it," she admitted shyly.

"What are you afraid of? Ethan Sommers, is that it? Your Husband?" She felt his stare burning into her flesh.

"No. It isn't because of Ethan. It's because of Cli..." She stopped talking again, and stared blankly at her drink.

"Nouri, if there is someone other than your husband, just say so."

"Charles, I'm confused right now. I don't want to talk about it, okay?" She smiled nervously.

"So there is someone else."

"Charles, please. Let's have another drink...I've never cheated on my husband if that's what you mean."

"So there isn't anyone else?" His tone was insistent.

"Charles, please." She nervously reached for her glass.

"Fine, sugar. Have it your way. Here, let me fill your glass."

"Charles, I'm getting tipsy. I can hardly feel my toes," she childishly giggled. He sat her wine glass down.

"I'm getting a little drunk myself, sugar." He laughed.

"Oh, Charles," she whispered softly. Her voice was filled with confusion.

"God, sugar. How I want you." He sighed lustfully, as he caressed her forearm.

"I want you too, Charles," she hungrily responded. Goose bumps ran up her spine caused by his touch. Charles leaned over and pulled Nouri into a passionate embrace. He pressed his lips sensually to hers. Clint Chamberlain once again fought with himself to stay in his seat and just watch. He desperately wanted to jump to his feet and knock the mystery man on his behind. A tear fell down his cheek. He quickly wiped it away, cleared his throat, and ordered another drink. He sat back on his stool and stared back into the large mirror.

Nouri didn't pull away from Charles' heated embrace. She didn't want to pull away. Finally, Charles gently lifted his lips from hers and hoarsely whispered, "Let's go make love, sugar."

Once again, Nouri surprised herself with her eager response. "All right Charles."

Charles quickly stood to his feet, pulling Nouri up with him. He hungrily pulled her into another passionate embrace, sensually molding her body snugly to his. He kissed her passionately.

Angrily Clint Chamberlain jumped to his feet.

"To hell with this!" He heatedly snapped before he stormed into the dining room, impulsively grabbing Nouri around her right arm, whirling her around so hard and so fast that she almost fell on top of him.

"What the hell are you doing, Nouri?" he shouted angrily, as she stood staring wide eyed at him, to shocked to speak.

Charles Mason quickly reached for Clint's arm with one hand and his fist doubled in the other. Nouri instinctively stepped between them.

"It's all right, Charles. I'll take care of this," she said, still in shock. Charles lowered his hands to his side with a great deal of reluctance.

"Clint Chamberlain. How dare you! Just what the hell do you think you're doing?" She finally managed to shout.

"Me, hell! Mrs. Sommers. What the hell are you doing here swapping spit with this muscle bound jerk?" Hurt and jealously in his tone. Charles and Clint shot daggers at each other.

"He's a...a what the hell business of yours is it, Clint Chamberlain?" she heatedly snapped still trying to pull her emotions back under control.

"Cut the bullshit, Nouri. Who the hell is he?" Clint demanded.

"He's a friend of mine. His name is Char..." She suddenly stopped talking for a moment, and then angrily added, "His name is none of your damn business, Bucko! That's what his name is," she said, still half dazed from that shock of almost getting caught making love to her first real man.

"An old friend huh, Nouri? Couldn't be that old flame of yours, could it? What's his name?" He paused for a moment as if in deep thought. He continued, "Oh yeah, I remember now. Charles Mason! That's his name, isn't it, Nouri?" He raged angrily, "Well thank God! I'm glad that you at least know the clown. I'd hate to think you would be acting like a tramp in public with a complete stranger." He threw his hands up into the air, letting them fall, slapping the sides of his muscular legs.

"Stop it, Clint. Just stop it!" she responded sharply. Suddenly, Charles Mason gently pulled Nouri behind him and stepped closer to Clint and got in his face.

"Ya wanna lighten up a little bud?" His tone was crisp. His eyes glared into Clint's.

With an expression that needed no words, Clint didn't bat an eye. "You want to stay the hell out of this Mason!" he said sharply.

Nouri quickly stepped between them again. "Hey guys, come on! Let's just calm down, okay." She forced a smile.

"Yeah, sure miss thing. We can all calm down, but you're not leaving this restaurant with mister smooth. Do I make myself clear?" His expression was dead serious.

"For chrissakes, Clint Chamberlain, you're not my father!" she snapped heatedly.

"You're damn right. I'm not your father. If I were, I'd turn you over my knee and bust you a good one for acting like a tramp in public. You're a married woman for godsakes, or have you forgotten, Mrs. Sommers?" He looked at her with his hurt puppy dog eyes and shook his head in disbelief. Nouri began to fume. Her eyes widened. The muscle in her jaw jerked, and her face turned an amazing shade of red.

She responded, "Clint Chamberlain if you call me a tramp one more time I'll...I'll...Just don't do it! And no, I haven't forgotten that I'm married. However,

THIEF OF HEARTS

I seriously believe that my husband may have!" A tear fell to her cheek. Her voice mellowed. She swallowed hard, trying to stop the tears that were beginning to form in her eyes.

Clint took a step back and glanced hurtfully. He also looked at Charles Mason, as he responded, "Would you excuse us a minute, Mason?" He leveled his eyes to Mason's, letting him know, without words that he should back off. It was obviously personal between he and Nouri. Charles glanced over to Nouri for approval. She nodded in agreement.

"I'll be at the bar if you need me, sugar," Charles said. She smiled and watched him disappear into the cocktail lounge.

Clint gently took her by the arm and led her to the side of the room for more privacy.

"Nouri," he finally said with hurt in his tone.

"Clint, I'm sorry. You just don't understand," she said softly, glancing up at him.

"Nouri tell mister muscles good bye. I'm driving you home. You're in no condition to drive tonight."

"Clint, I don't want to go home tonight," she stubbornly replied. He glanced down at her, once again staring at her in disbelief, with his puppy dog eyes.

"So you were planning to leave here and what Nouri? Spend the night with doctor feel good?"

Nouri leaned against the wall and inhaled deeply. She suddenly felt flushed and needed some air. "Can we go outside?" She used her hand as a fan.

"Sure," he said, removing his hands from his waist. "I'll tell whats his face at the bar...That is if your sure you want to leave with me." He looked at her as though a knife were still stuck into his heart.

"Please, Clint. Not now. I need to get some air."

"All right. Let's go," he said, taking her by the arm and leading her to the front door of the restaurant. "Wait here a minute. I'll be right back." Clint quickly went into the bar area looking for Charles, but he was no where to be found. Clint shrugged his shoulders and went back to join Nouri. "Come on sweetness, Mason's not in there. Let's go," he said as he held the door open for her. "Give me your keys, Nouri. I'll drive the car. I'll have mine picked up later." He held out his hand for her keys.

"They're in here somewhere," she said, as she tossed her purse to him. Clint shook his head as he caught the flying hand bag.

"Nouri, what the hell is wrong with you tonight?" he remarked, glancing down at her as they walked across the street. Charles Mason sat inside his car watching Clint, Nouri, and several men in a black sedan, that also appeared to be watching Clint and Nouri.

"Oh nothing...And everything. Does that answer you question, mister question man?" She inhaled the air deeply, releasing it slowly.

"Nouri, is it Ethan again?"

"Yes. I...I'm so confused. He's making me crazy." She closed her eyes and sighed. Clint walked around to the passenger side of the car, unlocked the door, and opened it. He suddenly spotted Charles sitting in his car on the opposite side of the street. He cringed with jealously, causing him to get mad all over again.

As Clint looked down at Nouri, she noticed his angry expression. She suddenly realized how much pain he must be feeling caused by her impulsive behavior with Charles Mason. She wanted to pull him into her arms and explain that it had meant nothing. That she had only gotten caught up in the moment. She was upset. She needed to be held, but she knew he wouldn't understand. After all, men were different than women. He'd never be able to understand what she was going through with her mixed emotions.

"You were mad at Ethan. So that's why you were meeting with your number one daddy of sex," he said sharply.

"Clint, please. I don't want to argue with you." She inhaled deeply again.

"Just get in the damn car, Nouri!" he angrily responded.

With hurt in her eyes, and her famous temper suddenly popping back to life, she spat, "Maybe I don't want to get in the damn car, especially with you, Clint Chamberlain!" A pout of stubbornness crossed her face.

He shouted back, "Get in the goddamn car, Nouri, or I'll pick your ass up and put you in myself!"

"Hah! Mister bully man. Now that would certainly be something to see," she snapped back, folding her arms stubbornly.

"Nouri, you've got to the count of three before I..." Nouri recognized the determined look on his face and quickly obeyed by jumping into the car.

She shouted back, "There, mister macho man, are you happy now?" Her lips puckered into another childish pout. Clint released a sigh of frustration and slammed the car door closed behind her.

"Women!" he muttered under his breath, as he shook his head in frustration.

He walked around to the driver's side of the car still shaking his head. He glanced back over at Charles Mason, who was still sitting inside his car. This time, however, his attention seemed to be focused on the three people sitting inside of a black sedan. Clint shrugged his shoulders, while he opened the car door to the Viper, and jumped inside. He glanced over at Nouri, who was still pouting, and shook his head. He started up the engine and quickly took off.

"Where are you going to take me, mister excitement?" Nouri asked coolly. He shook his head again and released a sigh.

"I'm taking your drunk ass home, miss thing."

Nouri leveled her eyes to his and snapped back, "I told you; I don't want to go home, bucko!"

"Nouri, just what the hell is going on between you and Ethan for chrissakes?"

"I just don't want to go home. I'm mad at Ethan, and I'm sick and tired of being alone!" she replied heatedly. A hurt expression crossed his face again when the image of Nouri and Charles tightly embraced popped back into his brain. He responded hurtfully, "So that's why you called your old boy friend, doctor strange love? You got pissed off at Ethan and instead of phoning me, you decided to go running back into the arms of your number one daddy of sex. The master of your universe!"

"Give me a break, Clint Chamberlain!" She shook her head and rolled her eyes while rolling down the window.

"Break. I'll give you a break! I'd like to break your goddamn..."

"Enough, mister tough guy." She turned away to hide her smile.

"So why did you phone Mason instead of me?" he hurtfully insisted.

"Oh yeah, right. Like Becka is going to let you accept a phone call from me!" She shook her head in dismay, and continued to speak, "Especially after our fight over the phone last night." She looked over at his handsome face.

"What do you mean?"

"Forget it. It was only Becka being Becka." She shook her head and threw her hands up in the air.

"So why did you call Mason? I want an answer, Nouri."

"For chrissakes Clint. If you must know...never mind Clint. It's not important now." She turned to look out the window.

"So Ethan is neglecting you. Your journals got boring. You wanted a real man...so you called Mason. That's rich Nouri, really! Why didn't you just get a hormone shot or something?" he said in a jealous tone of voice. Nouri's jaw muscles began to jerk and her face turned red. She swallowed hard.

"My hormones are just fine. Thank you very much!" She coldly stared at him.

"Well, it didn't look that way inside the restaurant, miss thing."

"What the hell are you mumbling about, mister?"

"You looked like a dog in heat. That's what I'm talking about Mrs. Sommers!" he snapped.

"A dog in heat!" She laughed. "Honestly." She shook her head amusingly.

"Well, miss hot box, what would you call it then?" He leveled his eyes to hers.

"I'd call it two old friends getting swept up in the moment, mister smart ass!" She lowered her eyes.

"Swept up in the moment! Give me a break!" He shook his head unbelievingly.

"Well, you asked me what I would have called it, and that's what I would have called it," she said smugly.

"Well, miss thing, you're just lucky that your actions didn't make the front page of the newspaper tomorrow morning, or one of those rag magazines or tabloids!"

"I wouldn't have cared if it did!" she snapped hurtfully.

"Nouri, you just don't get it, do ya? You have no idea of the type of man you're married to. If Ethan would have gotten word of your behavior tonight..." He suddenly stopped talking and shook his head.

"Well, mister enlightenment! Don't stop now. Please continue to tell me about the man I obviously know nothing about."

"Nouri, you just have no idea what he is capable of. That's all." He released a sigh of utter concern.

"So, tell me what don't ya."

"Where the hell am I taking you, Nouri?"

"Anywhere you like. As long as it has a hot tub, lots of Asti Spumanti, and no Ethan Sommers!"

"Nouri, what the hell is with you tonight? You're not even acting like yourself for chrissakes!"

"Clint, I want to spend the night with you." She paused, then added, "Please. I need to be held." She looked at him needlingly.

"Oh, so now it's me you want to make love with tonight. What happened to mister wonderful?" he asked sarcastically.

"Clint, please. You just don't understand. I didn't plan on sleeping with Charles. We just got caught up in a moment. I...I was pissed at Ethan. I couldn't call you. And well, I just needed to be held. Do you understand?"

He glared at her and heatedly shook his head in utter amazement. "And this is supposed to make me feel better about catching you sucking popeye's brains out in public!"

Nouri slid herself closer to him. She put her hand suggestively on his leg and responded, "Please Clint, don't be mad at me. I'm sorry. It wasn't like I planned on getting swept up by Charles. I told you, I just needed to be held." She laid her head on his shoulder and moved her touches up to his broad, strong chest and seductively began to rub it.

Clint melted but tried not to show it. His heart was broken and his pride was hurt. He responded, "Please, just slid back to your side of the car. I'll drop you off where ever you like, but I can't be with you tonight. I'm too hurt at you, Nouri." She refused to budge. She squirmed closer to him.

"Please, I'm sorry. I didn't mean to hurt you." She whispered in his ear with her warm breath. "You don't have to make love to me tonight. I...I just need to be held, that's all. She sighed and laid her head back down on his shoulder, as she continued to seductively rub his chest with her soft touches. He became instantly aroused.

Thank goodness her hand had moved from my upper leg to my chest, he thought, as he tried to calm his desire for her.

"Nouri, please stop. Move back to your side of the car," he half heartedly ordered.

Nouri lifted her head and looked at him lovingly. "Clint I, can't believe you're so unforgiving." She paused, "I've always forgiven you in the past."

"What the hell are you talking about?" He coolly responded.

"You know damn good and well what I'm talking about, Clint Chamberlain!" she snapped. "Did you really think I didn't know?" She removed her hand from his chest and slid back to her side of the car.

"So you did know." He looked at her with a stunned expression.

"Clint, just because I was young, didn't mean that I was blind or stupid!" She leveled her hurt eyes to his.

"Why didn't you say anything?" He continued to look into her incredible eyes.

"I had my reasons, and anyway, I stayed mostly because I loved you."

"Yeah right, and then you jumped into marriage with Ethan!" Jealously returned in his tone.

"Clint, you drove me away from you, and you know it!"

"What do you mean? Just because I wouldn't set a date."

"No, because you stormed out that night and made love to someone else before coming home to me!" She glanced at him hurtfully.

"Oh my God! You knew, and yet you let me make love to you anyway."

"It was my way of saying goodbye to you. I knew you were never going to change My staying would have been pointless. By you not wanting to set a date meant only one thing to me. That you didn't want to be tied down for the rest of your life with just one woman." She forced a smile.

"Sweetness. I...I'm sorry. The women. All of them never meant anything to me. I love you. Only you! I don't know why I did what I did. It's no excuse. I haven't any..." He suddenly stopped talking, and a tear fell from his eye. He swallowed hard, trying to stop them from streaming down his face. Nouri glanced out the window.

With her head still turned away from him, she responded, "For what its worth Clint, even though you never told me that you loved me, I knew that you did.

I could feel it. That's why I stayed as long as I did." She confessed as she squirmed uneasily in her seat.

"Please slide back over here, sweetness. I'm sorry." He reached his arm out for her.

She glanced at him and responded, " I don't think so, Clint. All I want to do tonight is to be held. And all you want to do is argue." She glanced back out the window with a hurt expression on her face. He released a deep sigh of mixed emotions.

"Oh, so now you don't want me after all. What are you going to do, call Mason to come over and keep you company again tonight?"

"There's no telling what I might do tonight! I haven't really decided yet," she snapped, still angry at her remembered image of him making love to other women.

"Well you listen to me, miss hot to trot! I'm not leaving you alone tonight. You'll thank me in the morning," he snapped back, and then steered straight ahead at the road. There's no way in hell Charles Mason is going to make love with my woman tonight or any other night! Clint thought to himself, as he pulled the Viper up in front of the Fantasy Suite Hotel.

"Well here we are. Remember this place? It's been a long time," he said, as he turned off the engine. He stretched his arms out across the seat, gently rubbing her shoulder. She glanced at him coolly with her eyes and forced a small grin. She sighed.

"God! The Fantasy Suite Hotel. It's been ages," she responded, as her eyes glanced around the out side of the old hotel.

"We sure had a lot of fun times here, didn't we sweetness?" He smiled fondly and slid over to her side of the car. She heavily sighed again, as she continued to coolly glance around the odd shaped hotel.

She softly replied, "Yes, Clint we did."

"Well, sweetness, shall we go inside and check in?" He gently turned her face to his. He smiled lovingly at her. She looked into his sexy brown eyes, desperately wanting to pull her into his arms. But she wasn't going to be the one to make the first move. After all, she had already tried that and it didn't work. She was not going to be rejected again because of his jealous pride.

"This will be fine, Clint. Thanks for the lift. I think I can manage on my own now." She looked at him without batting an eye lash. Her tone was distant and cool. A stunned look crossed Clint face.

He responded, "Nouri, if you think I'm going to leave you alone here tonight, you're sadly mistaken!"

"I thought you said you were too hurt to be with me tonight?" she responded smugly.

"Forget what I said. I didn't mean it. I...I want to hold you tonight," he said, as he lowered his head to kiss her.

Nouri quickly turned her head, stopping the kiss. "And you're sure we won't fuss anymore tonight?" She asked, as she continued to glance out of the window.

"For chrissakes! How can I promise that, with us you never know. Just answer me this one question, Nouri. Have you been secretly seeing Mason all along?" he asked jealously and then heatedly slid back over to his side of the car.

She ignored his question to her and opened the passenger side of the car door. She glanced at him hurtfully and jumped out of the car. He quickly followed.

"For chrissakes, Nouri, wait up!" he said loudly, as he began to run to catch up to her. He grabbed her by the arm and gently whirled her to face him. He pulled her snugly into his heated embrace and passionately kissed her. When he finally pulled his lips from hers he whispered, "Please sweetness. Don't walk away from me like that."

"Can we just hold each other without arguing, Clint?" she said softly.

"I'll try. God knows I need to hold you." He kissed her again. As he released her from his passionate embrace, he suddenly spotted the same black sedan that he had seen earlier at Pompillios. He quickly glanced around the parking area for Charles Mason's car. Where the hell are you? You nosy bastard! Clint thought to himself, as he escorted Nouri to the front door of the hotel.

They walked inside. Clint glanced back over his shoulder. He turned Nouri to face him. "Which suite would you like?" He smiled lustfully.

She returned the smile and then replied, "I don't care as long as it's not your old favorite suite."

"I thought you liked the Harem Suite, sweetness." A puzzled look crossed his face. A frown crossed her beautiful face.

She replied, "I just don't feel like being reminded of all your old flames tonight, Clint." She lowered her eyes to the floor.

"For chrissakes!" He threw his hands up in the air and nervously paced in a half circle. He shook his head and sighed. "Fine. How about the Movie Star Suite? You always liked the hot tub shaped like a champagne glass." He smiled as he pulled her chin up to meet his face. He kissed her before adding, "Or we could get the Tarzan Suite. I could throw you over my shoulder and carry you to the room." He playfully mused.

"Ha! Ha! Mister funny man. The movie star suite will be fine."

After checking in, Clint asked the hotel clerk to send them a case of chilled Asti Spumanti, a bottle of imported Scotch, and a large tray of assorted fruit and whipped cream.

THIEF OF HEARTS

Once inside the elevator, Clint pulled Nouri into his arms. He passionately kissed her as he seductively slid his hands inside her satin blouse. He expertly unfastened her bra and gently caressed her perfectly shaped breasts. She moaned softly. He removed his lips from hers and lowered his mouth to her breasts, kissing one nipple and then the other. Nouri moaned again as she continued to run her fingers threw his thick, dark brown hair. He reluctantly lifted his head when the elevator door slid open. Nouri quickly caught her breath and clutched her open blouse at the same time.

Chapter 11

After stepping out of the elevator, Clint Chamberlain lifted Nouri Sommers up into his arms. She snuggly wrapped her legs around his manly waist. They passionately kissed, as he playfully zig-zagged his way down the hallway toward the Movie Star Suite.

Someone had left a tray outside the door by their suite, and Clint was much too busy to notice it. He stumbled, losing his balance. Both he and Nouri fell to the carpeted floor, laughing hysterically. Clint pulled Nouri back into his arms and showered her face with wet passionate kisses, as they laid on the floor in the hallway. Finally stopping for air, Clint stood to his feet and helped the playfully intoxicated lady to her unsteady feet.

"Come on, sweetness. Our suite is just down the hallway. They raced each other to the door. Nouri won the race because Clint had his mind on more important issues, like ravishing her magnificent body.

As he fumbled with the lock on the door, Nouri refused to keep her hands to herself, caressing Clint's perfectly shaped, manly body, driving him to total distraction.

"Sweetness, please behave, or I'll never get this damn door unlocked," he said teasingly, but still grateful that she hadn't stopped sexually toying with him. After several fumbled attempts, the lock finally clicked, and the door flew open.

She jumped into his arms, and he teasingly staggered backwards, not stopping until he reached the large sofa. He suddenly collapsed on top of it, with her still locked inside his arms. They kissed and kissed. Clint wanting her more than ever. Nouri wanting him more than ever.

"Let's go make love," she whispered anxiously into his ear with her hot breath. Just at the same moment, room service knocked on the all ready opened door to the suite.

"Oh damn!" Clint moaned, quickly trying to hide his noticeable arousal from the waiter.

"Just put the tray anywhere." He motioned away from the sofa, which was sitting next to the bar.

"Yes sir." The waiter grinned knowingly. "But I still need your signature, sir." He nodded with a blush.

"For the love of..." Nouri quickly interrupted.

"Clint, I'll sign it," she offered, jumping to her feet. She straightened her skirt with one hand and clutched her blouse closed with the other. She signed the tab swiftly and closed the door behind the waiter, laughing. Clint jumped to his feet laughing.

"It just isn't our day, sweetness."

Nouri smiled, responding, "I don't know about that!" She seductively glanced up at his handsome face. He returned her lustful smile.

He walked over and joined Nouri at the bar where she was busy struggling with the colored foil that was wrapped around the neck of the Asti Spumanti bottle.

"Here, give it to me, sweetness. I'll do it," he offered.

"Thanks," she said, handing over the wine. "It would have probably taken me all night to unwrap that damn thing." She said watching him quickly removing the foil and popping the cork.

"Ummm! You're a handy man to have around, Clint Chamberlain," she said, playfully arching her eyebrows.

He looked thoughtful for a moment before responding: "Now where have I heard that line before?" He smiled then poured himself a shot of imported scotch. "Whew, I needed that," he said after downing his shot of strong brownish liquor. He poured them both another drink and then walked over to the patio door. He slid the glass panel open and walked outside. A man with a lot on his mind. Clint breathed in the clean, crisp air, as he stood in silence, glancing around the odd design of the old hotel. He suddenly spotted the black sedan still parked outside. Who the hell can they be? He thought to himself before realizing it had to be someone spying on Nouri for Ethan. He released a deep sigh and shook his head, not wanting to tell Nouri about his suspicions.

Nouri watched him as he stood in continued silence on the patio. She smiled fondly at the remembered thought of him standing on the patio, in the same stance she had seen, at least a hundred times before. He was lost in thought.

She walked out to the patio to join him. "It's a beautiful night," she said softly, wrapping her arms lovingly around his waist. She laid her head on his strong back. Clint tenderly patted her folded hands, before reaching gently around her and drawing her around to face him.

"Yes, sweetness. It is a beautiful night." He sighed and pulled her even closer. She laid her head across his muscular chest.

"I wish we could stay here forever, darling," she said glancing up at his handsome face.

"Me too." He sighed again, secretly glancing back down at the parked sedan. Clint was too far away to notice any movement inside the car.

"What are you so lost in thought about darling?" she asked, tightening her embrace on him.

"You, sweetness. I've been so lost without you." He confessed and then kissed her on top of her head softly.

"I've missed you too," she whispered hoarsely. Suddenly, Clint noticed the back door open on the black sedan, and a tall man stepped out. He was holding what appeared to be a video camera. Clint couldn't decide if he suspected Ethan of spying on Nouri. Or, if it was someone from the newspaper, or tabloid magazine. It could even be paparazzi for all he knew. No matter. He wasn't going to take any chances. The last thing he wanted was to wake up to and find a photograph of himself and Nouri on the front page of the newspaper. After all, Nouri Sommers was front page news. She is married to one of the wealthiest men in the world. Ethan Sommers' estimated net worth made him one of the three wealthiest men of all time.

He quickly ushered Nouri inside. "Let's go inside, sweetness," he said, as he placed her hand inside of his. He quickly closed the sliding door and locked it behind them.

"What's the matter, Clint?" You look like you just seen a ghost or something."

"Don't be silly, sweetness. I just wanted to refill our drinks...Oh the hell with our drinks. Come here sweetness, I'd rather have you!" He smiled lustfully, holding his arms open for her to enter. She returned his smile and excitedly ran into his embrace. He lifted her into his arms and she wrapped her legs tightly behind him, showering his face with kisses.

Clint walked to the bedroom and gently sat Nouri down on top of the bed. Her arms clung tightly to his neck, pulling him down on the bed with her. He chuckled at her urgent need to have him make love to her. He always loved her lack of shyness when it came to showing her love for him. Not to mention her sizzling, hot blooded nature.

"Oh, darling! I've missed you so much," she whispered lovingly.

"I've missed you more," he whispered back with his warm breath across her full, moist lips. Nouri released her arms from around his neck at his urging. Clint gently slid his warm hands along her delicate arms. "Ummm, sweetness, you're so soft," he whispered, as he moved his touches to outline her beautiful face, throat, and breasts.

"Oh God, Nouri. I want you so bad," he heatedly moaned, quickly removing her blouse, skirt, and panties. He continued to whisper sweet words of love in her ear while nibbling on her ear- lobe and neck. His gentle, warm caresses sent shivers up her spine.

"Please Clint, make love to me now!" She heatedly begged. Her need for him-urgent! He chuckled with delight once again at her eagerness to have him inside her.

He responded with another whisper, "I intend to." She moaned with need again. "Please baby, now." He smiled knowingly.

"Soon, sweetness," he whispered, as he continued to caress her magnificent naked body. "You're so beautiful." He continued to travel the length of her supple body with his masculine hands. His thirsty wet kisses trailed slowly behind.

His hands roamed across the hot flesh of her smooth, flat stomach...Down to her inner shapely thighs. His chin parted her legs, as his hot, wet tongue sensually invaded her. She eagerly arched her back wanting him deeper inside. She began to pant with heated desire, as he slowly continued to drive her orally out of her mind. He tightened his hold on her perfectly shaped bottom, at her urging. Her erotic movements silently begging for more!

"Oh God, Clint. That feels so good," she whimpered breathlessly. "Oh, please Clint. I...I need to feel you inside of me!" Her body movements growing more and more rapid. "Baby, please! Let's go there together." She excitedly begged one final time. "Oh! Ohh! Ohhh!" She moaned with heated passion, as Clint brought her to her first and second oral climax.

He slowly lifted his head, and pulled himself up to her breathless embrace. He passionately kissed her again and again. Finally, he released himself from her exhausted tight hold. "I love you, Nouri," he said, as he gazed into her incredible hazel colored eyes.

She returned his loving smile and responded, "God, help me, Clint. I love you too." She paused momentarily. "And probably always will." She pulled him back down on top of her for another wet, passionate kiss, but quickly objected after realizing that he was still fully clothed.

"I can't believe you're still dressed," she complained, quickly sitting up in protest. She went to remove his shirt, but he stopped her by gently removing her hand, and kissing it romantically. He gazed into her eyes.

"I don't want to rush this sweetness. I want our love making to last forever. First I need to hold you. To taste you. To remember how wonderful you are. I...I need you Nouri. I was so stupid to ever let you go." He kissed her hand again.

"Oh Clinton Jerome Chamberlain! I was the stupid one. I should have never left you." She cried, as she pulled him into her arms. She kissed him deeply and passionately. It was a kiss that lasted an eternity. Finally, they were both forced to come up for air.

"Please darling. Take those damn things off!" She seductively begged, as she gestured to his clothing. He returned her seductive smile, but declined.

"Not just yet, sweetness. I'm not finished playing. I'm saving the good stuff for last." He playfully teased. Nouri began to laugh, amusingly toying with him like she used to do, so long ago.

"Good stuff. Ha! You big tease! Mister thing. You ain't all that!" She said teasingly as she stood to her feet. She put her hands on her hips and began to playfully giggle. She turned and began to walk toward the bedroom door.

With his voice low and sexy, he responded, ""No, maybe not now, but I will be. By morning I promise you, miss thing, you'll never have the desire to be with another man, except for me, for as long as you live!"

THIEF OF HEARTS

Nouri circled the bar area and glanced over her shoulder. "Ummm. Been eating the breakfast of champions again, I see." Her tone was playful, but smug. He walked up to her and gently lifted her chin to meet his face.

"What we just did in the bedroom was only the appetizer!" he said, smiling lustfully. "Now why don't you bring me that can of whipped cream and bowl of fruit. All of a sudden, I'm beginning to feel very hungry. I think I'm about ready for my first course, of about an eight course meal." He softly brushed his lips across hers. She inhaled excitedly, as goose bumps ran up her spine.

"Whew! I'm scared of you, mister studdly!" she responded, using her hand to playfully fan herself. She smiled longingly.

He arched his eyebrow seductively, put one hand on his hip, and said, "You should be!" He returned the smile and walked to the bar. After freshening their drinks, he glanced at her saying, "I've got the drinks, you bring the whipped cream and fruit. I'll run some water in the hot tub." Her heart began to race wildly with anticipation. She eagerly obeyed his playful request of her. She quickly joined him in the hot tub.

After the first, second, third, and fourth course of his lustful meal, Clint Chamberlain was more than ready to get down to some serious love making with the woman of his dreams.

When Clint finished licking off the last drop of Asti From Nouri's luscious body, they had course number five in the shower. The remaining three courses of his heated meal were for the bedroom. He gently towel dried her soft body and carried her to the bedroom.

"I told you I was saving the best for last," he whispered romantically, as he laid her down on the bed. He excitedly joined her. He was more than ready to join his body to hers.

In the next moment, his arms were around her, and his lips were pressed against hers. She returned his passionate kiss with a longing of her own, seductively molding her body to his. The feel of her beneath him was so compelling, so magical, he lifted his head momentarily to make sure she wasn't just another dream.

In the past several years, he had often relived, in great detail, moments such as this one: of the breathtaking beauty who had stolen his heart.

"God, baby! I love you," he whispered against the nape of her neck, as he continued to be hopelessly caught up in a surge of uncontrollable desire. She was too moved to speak. She could only listen to the beautiful words of love she so desperately longed to hear from the man who had captured her heart so long ago.

She finally managed to speak. "Oh Clint, darling, I'll never leave you again," she said in her moment of passion; reeling from the glow of his new found ways to finally express his love for her. Both unexpectedly caught up in a remembered moment of passion and love.

THIEF OF HEARTS

His mouth moved from her sensuous lips to the nape of her delicate neck. He hungrily showered her throat, earlobes, and shoulders with hundreds of tiny sensual kisses. He eventually made his way down her perfectly proportioned breasts, where he kissed, sucked, and teased her nipples to taughtness. First one, then the other. She began to moan with delight.

After showering each breast with equal affection, he slowly carried his kisses down the rest of her delicious body, stopping to tease and excite the tender spot between her shapely thighs.

When she began to beg for more intimate contact, he used his muscular leg to separate hers. He slowly entered her trembling body. Slowly gliding his body movements to equal hers. He groaned against her throat and shoulder, as her body movement became more needy, more demanding, more rapid. He gently brushed the fallen hair from her face, as she urgently clutched the back of his shoulder, silently begging him to enter her even deeper. He obeyed her silent command by plunging one lone stroke and slowly withdrawing, over and over again, allowing her to have two instant completions, one right after the other.

For his final course, the dessert on his erotic menu, he gently rolled her onto her stomach for deeper penetration. Where erotic thrust for erotic thrust, she eagerly met his each and every time, driving each other into utter sexual bliss.

He finally plunged one final time, sending her and himself into complete and total ecstasy. He breathlessly collapsed on top of her hot, damp, exhausted body. Too weak to move, he finally managed to roll off of her and onto his side. Where he pulled her almost lifeless body closer to his. "I passionately love you, Nouri," he panted breathlessly.

Her breathless response, "Ya better call 911, Superman!" They both began to laugh hysterically.

Chapter 12

A dreamy, thick, white cloud of fog lay heavy over the small town bridge of Mason, as Becka Chamberlain zoomed her way past the posted warning signs on the bridge. Suddenly, Becka slammed on her brakes when she noticed a pair of headlights almost upon her in apparently the same lane. She quickly sounded her horn, cursing profoundly and shaking her hands in the air, as she leaned her trembling body halfway out of her car. "You Goddamn idiot!" she whaled, as the other car zoomed past her. "Some people, I swear!" She continued to gripe, as she attempted to regain control of herself, as well as her car. She finally exited the dangerous bridge of Mason. She released a sigh of relief and returned her attention back to the more important issue at hand. Which, of course, was revenge.

Becka glanced at her watch. She had left Boston several hours earlier in a fit of rage. She was headed for the beautiful Island of Lambert. But instead of a weekend of pleasure on the island of paradise, she had murder on her mind. *Who's sorry now*, was not the only song that was playing loudly on her radio, but were also the words raving over and over inside her sick mind. "I told you both, didn't I? But you just wouldn't listen, would you? Well, we will certainly see just who's sorry now! Won't we?" she manically muttered to herself, as she glanced into the rear view mirror.

She suddenly spotted an all night diner and quickly pulled her Mercedes into the parking area. She was starving and desperately needed some coffee. She wasted no time in going inside. Once inside, she stood out like a sore thumb. A real beauty and the beast scenario. Wall to wall truck drivers. Every size, shape and color, and they were all quite manly. Ummm, this could prove to be very interesting, she lustfully thought to herself, as she ordered a cup of coffee and a B.L.T. on whole wheat.

The late night sky had turned into a much lighter predawn illumination, as Becka Chambrelain bid a fond adieu to her three flavored dessert from her late night stop. Lou Kirtedes, originally from Greece. Raoul Decarlos, originally from Mexico, and just plain Demarco from everywhere, USA. She smiled wickedly, as she jumped inside her car, waving goodbye to the three strangers she had just spent several lustful hours with.

"Today will reach well up into the eighties, with a slight chance of a late evening shower, especially for those who live in the South-Eastern Bay area."

"Thank you, Simon. Well ladies and gentleman that was from our National Weather Station affiliate W.B.E.R.T. in Lambert. Looks like another spectacular day is heading our way. This is Kitty Doyle, and your listening to 106.9 F.M..."

"Shut the hell up!" Becka angrily snapped, as she turned her car radio off. She quickly pulled her Mercedes in front of the Lambert Hotel. She glanced down at her gold Rolex watch, as Veda, the valet, escorted her out of the car.

"Good morning, Mrs. Chamberlain," Veda said smiling.

"What's so damn good about it!" Becka rudely snapped, turned, and huffed away.

What a bitch! Veda thought to himself, as he shook his head in amazement, jumped into her Mercedes, and pulled off.

Becka wasn't aware of how wind blown her hair had become while driving the past few hours with her convertible top down. And with the wide, crazed look in her eyes, Otto Lambert came running out from behind the front desk to check on her.

"Why, Mrs. Chamberlain, are you all right?" he inquired with concern.

Becka's mouth flew open, and she gave him a look laced with the boiling blood from her veins. "Well, of course I'm all right Lambert. Why the hell wouldn't I be?"

Otto's face turned a bright shade of pink. His eyes turned from the normal shade of dark blue to an icy shade of black. He glared a look at her that would terrify most people, but not Becka Chamberlain. He responded sharply, "Madam!" He pointed to the mirror in the hallway to the right of where she was standing.

After glancing into the mirror, she shouted, "Oh my God! I look a fright! No wonder you seemed so concerned Otto." She smiled faintly and continued to speak. "I'm sorry. I didn't mean to snap, it's just...well...I decided to drive to Lambert instead of taking a plane. I thought the long drive would do me good," she said, and then shrugged her shoulders. "I guess I'm just tired."

"I see," he replied coolly, turning to walk away from her. He headed back behind the front desk. "So you say your alone, Mrs. Chamberlain?" He asked with an edge.

"Yes." She sighed, as she quickly brushed her hair.

"Will you be requiring any special services today, madam?" He leveled his eyes to meet hers. She looked at him with a lustful expression and remarked with uncertainly, "Maybe later. Is Thomas working?" She smiled hopefully.

"Yes, madam."

"Good." She smiled wickedly.

"Shall I schedule him for a visit to your suite later?"

"I don't know yet. Where is Kirt Jarett?" Her look was urgent.

"He's off today," Otto lied. He glared at her again with his cold eyes.

"I see." She responded disappointedly. "Well keep Thomas' schedule open. I'll probably need him later." Her tone was arrogant and smug.

"Anything else madam?" he asked coolly.

"Any new faces, Otto?" She anxiously awaited his response.

"You met three of them on your last visit the other day, madam." Otto rolled his eyes.

"Yes, Otto. But they didn't please me, especially the young girl. She was too inexperienced."

"Sorry, Mrs. Chamberlain. I'll dismiss them right away." He stared into her cold eyes again.

"Good." She smiled triumphantly.

In an appeasing tone of voice, Otto Lambert responded, "Here, at Lambert we aim to please, madam." He averted his eyes to her icy stare.

She reached over to pick up the plastic key to her suite, and in a deliberate, sharp tone, she remarked, "Of course you do, Otto. That's why we pay a quarter of a million dollars each year in membership fees." She leveled her eyes to his.

"Yes, madam." He lowered his head in anger and slowly bit his tongue. He was stunned that Becka had the nerve to speak to him in such a rude manner.

Becka turned to leave the front desk, when she suddenly decided to ask Otto another question. She glanced over her shoulder.

"Otto, is Ethan Sommers still here in the hotel?"

Otto's jaw muscle jerked and his face turned from pink to red. He responded, "I realize Mrs. Chamberlain that you have only been a member here at Lambert for only nine months, unlike your husband, who has been a member for almost twenty years, but even at only nine months, you should know by now that we would never give out that type of information on our guest-elite. Our no ask-no answer policy is only one of many reasons why we get by with charging such exuberant membership fees!" He smiled wickedly at her with his back at you bitch smile.

Becka saw red. Her mouth flew open as she turned stubbornly to face him. She placed her hands on her hips and arrogantly snapped, "Well, I never! I'll just have to speak to my husband over your rudeness Mr. Lambert!" She jerked her body sharply around and stormed toward the guarded side of the elevators.

"What a bitch," Otto muttered under his breath as she walked away.

She suddenly realized that Otto had given her the key to their regular suite instead of her special services one. "That moron!" she barked as she quickly stepped back off the elevator. She stormed back to the front desk. She heatedly requested the other key. Otto fought back a smug grin as he exchanged suite keys for her.

"Send Kiki to my suite. I've decided that I'll need a little assistance with my bubble bath."

"As you wish, madam," he responded, shaking his head in disbelief.

When Becka passed by the small cocktail lounge to the right of the guarded elevators, she spotted Ethan Sommers sitting at an intimate table beside the small stage. She quickly went into the lounge. But she stopped after only several short steps when she recognized who he was sitting with.

Rage once again surged through her body. She quickly turned to leave before he spotted her. As she glanced over her shoulder on the way out of the lounge, she watched Ethan lick a melted ice cube off of young Kirsten Kamel's half exposed breasts.

"That young whore!" she whispered jealously. Becka suddenly shifted her hatred from her husband and Nouri Sommers, to young Kirsten Kamel.

"I'll get even with all of you bastards!" She angrily muttered before stepping inside the elevator. "The thirty-second floor," she barked to the guard.

Young Kiki was excitedly waiting for Becka as she entered her suite. She was sitting at the bar where she had Becka's double shot of brandy waiting for her. Kiki smiled, reached for Becka's drink, and walked over to her.

"Hi," Kiki said sweetly, as she brushed her lips across Becka's, handing her the drink.

"Let's forget all the small talk, Kiki!" Becka snapped sharply, still in her angry mood. A hurt expression crossed young Kiki's face.

"Yes, Mrs. Chamberlain."

Becka took a sip of her drink. "For Godsakes, get that stupid look off of your face. I'm in a pissed off mood at the moment, and the last thing I need to see now is..." She stopped talking and downed her drink. "Here, get me another drink!" She rudely ordered. Kiki accepted Becka's empty glass.

"Shall I send for Thomas?" Kiki knew that when Becka was in a foul mood, she liked to play rough, and rough was, after all, Thomas' specialty.

Becka spoke to her from across the room. "No Kiki. I'm pissed at men right now. You'll do just fine...Well, at least for starters," she snapped and then began to laugh wickedly. After several moments of uncontrollable laughing, she added, "Now be a good girl and bring me my drink before you run my bath water. And don't forget to bring my favorite bath toy. My little rubber dickey!" She arched her eyebrow and laughed again.

Kiki handed Becka the double shot of brandy and turned to retrieve her little pink bag of sexual play toys. Just as she bent over to pick up the bag, Becka roughly pushed her onto the plush shagged carpet where she quickly joined her.

"Undress me!" she ordered. Young Kiki swiftly obeyed.

"Yes, Mrs.Chamberlain," she said softly, as she gently began to unbutton her silk blouse. Becka's face suddenly turned flush and her jaw tightened.

She remarked cruelly, "No, you moron! Tear my blouse off. You know I like it rough!" Kiki quickly ripped Becka's beautiful blouse from her body and tossed it across the floor.

Becka reached over the top of Kiki to retrieve the pink bag. As Kiki continued to kiss Becka's large breasts, one at a time, Becka quickly emptied the contents onto the floor, anxiously locating her favorite twelve inch rubber play mate. She eagerly squirmed loose of Kiki's sucking hold and playfully pushed her away.

"Here...strap it on!" Becka eagerly ordered, tossing the toy to Kiki. She anxiously obeyed. Becka excitedly positioned herself on all fours for deeper results. She was more than anxious to experience the feelings of pain mixed with pleasure that her play toy would bring. Soon she began to scream cries of utter ecstasy as the gifted play toy manned by Kiki came to life, pleasuring her tremendously with each thrust.

After four exhausting climaxes, Becka grew tired of her rubber play toy. She and Kiki moved the action to the bathroom, where they shared another hour or so of oral bliss together in a hot bubble bath. When Becka finally bored of her young female play toy, she sent her away, but not before ordering her to send Thomas to her suite next.

"Enough foreplay! I'm ready for some serious pleasure!" She scoffed wickedly, as she anxiously waited for Thomas to arrive. He was her second favorite human play toy. Kirt Jarett was her first.

Becka walked over to the balcony entrance and slid the double door open. She walked outside and inhaled the crisp salty air. She walked closer to the railing to view the scenic sight of the ocean, but instead she noticed people walking along the shoreline. Their arms were snugly wrapped around each other's waists.

"You idiots! You all make me sick!" She scoffed jealously, suddenly whirling herself around when she heard Thomas enter the suite. She excitedly walked back inside. "Well, Thomas! I almost got tired of waiting!" She barked, crossing the room to meet him. "What the hell took so damn long?" She snapped, as she rudely jerked the little black bag of sex toys from out of his hand. Thomas didn't respond. He just stood inside the closed doorway and continued to watch her eagerly empty the contents of the goody bag.

"Where the hell is it, Thomas?" Becka shouted, tossing the black bag at him. She glared at him with her famous icy stare. Thomas dodged the flying toy bag. He shook his head as though he didn't know what she was talking about, shrugging his muscular shoulders, and stared back at her with his own icy stare.

"What toy would that be, Mrs. Chamberlain?"

Becka turned red in the face, and with her hand on her shapely hip, she barked heatedly, " Thomas you jerk! You know damn good and well what toy I'm talking about!" Thomas continued to stand in his same spot just inside the doorway. He smiled wickedly, meeting her angry gaze.

"Oh, you mean the whip, Becka. Is that the toy you're so hot about?"

She angrily threw her hand into the air and screamed, "listen to me you little shit! Don't you ever address me by my first name again! Do I make myself perfectly clear?"

Thomas chuckled at her idol threat and repeated her first name slowly. "Like I said, Becka, is this what has you so hot?" He quickly pulled the whip out from behind his back where it was tucked inside the waist band of his slacks. He slapped the whip sharply against the floor and smiled lustfully. Becka's expression of anger didn't change.

"Thomas, you fuck!" she shouted, walking closer to him. Thomas slapped the whip angrily against the floor again and met her wild-eyed stare. His tone of voice was as threatening as hers. "Knock it off, bitch!" he ordered.

She continued to rant and rave. "Don't you dare fuck with me. Not tonight, Thomas!" She stubbornly put her face up to his face, silently begging to be spanked.

Thomas watched her expression change from anger to rage. He arrogantly laughed. "Whew! You need it really bad tonight huh, Becka," he said before rolling the loose end of the whip up into his hands. His eyes never left hers.

"Fuck you Thomas!" she angrily shouted. Thomas violently ripped the towel from her body and shoved her roughly across the room.

"Now you've gone and done it bitch! I'm going to hurt you real bad!" He slowly walked across the room to where she had fallen.

Becka threw her arms up to protect her face and began to beg with sick delight as he grew nearer to her. He slapped the whip hard against the carpeted floor. "Are you ready bitch?" He smiled wickedly nasty.

Becka dropped her arms from around her face and shouted heatedly, "That's what the hell I'm paying you for, isn't it? You simpleton!" She rolled her eyes impatiently.

"Ouch Becka! You really need it bad tonight!" He shook his head in disgust. Becka began to tremble.

She responded, "Real bad, Thomas! You have no idea how very badly I need it." She begged with a whine. Thomas laughed coldly again, as he playfully teased Becka with his whip. He wiggled the whip across her beautiful face, breasts, and back. She began to get excited by just the feel of the whip touching her flesh.

"Here doggie-doggie, come to your master. You'll have to beg for it first!" She eagerly accepted her doggie treat in her hot, thirsty mouth. After she gave him what he wanted, he rewarded her for her obedience by slapping her across her very sexy bottom with his whip. Becka, still on all fours, began to beg once again. "Please Thomas, will you hurt me now! I need it baby. Please!"

Thomas laughed wickedly before responding. "Not just yet Becka. That hot swollen mouth of yours felt so good, I think we need to try that again.

"Please Thomas. Don't make me wait for it." She continued to beg.

"Soon Becka. Now be a good doggie and come fetch your bone." She once again obeyed her master like a good doggie should.

THIEF OF HEARTS

After Thomas' third oral completion, he violently grabbed Becka by the head of her beautiful honey-blond hair and aggressively shoved her on top of the bed. He excitedly hand cuffed her to the bedposts. "I'm really going to enjoy this Becka!" He whispered in her ear with his hot, sizzling breath. He eagerly began to devour the flesh of her trembling body with his hot, hungry mouth, tongue, and teeth. "You taste so good Becka." He savagely panted, as he continued to journey down her hot, sexy body. After completely satisfying her time and time again orally, he reached for his bag of play toys.

"You're a very naughty girl, Becka. You're turning into a real nasty nymph," he whispered wickedly, as he continued to get Becka off with his many talented toys.

"Just shut the fuck up! And do what I pay you to do Thomas!" She heatedly ordered. He grinned and continued to play. Finally, Thomas released her from her bedded torture chamber, but she angrily protested.

He laughed at her again with a vulgar laugh and said, "Don't worry, doggie. I've saved the best pain for last." He savagely entered her from behind, bringing her to heights of pain mixed with pleasure. The kind that she only experiences with her rubber play toy, him, and of course Kirt Jarett. She soon began to breathlessly beg him to stop, after she could no longer move a single muscle.

But Thomas didn't want to stop. "No baby. I'm far from finished." He cruelly whispered in her ear, as he once again savagely entered her tight shapely rear. She screamed and screamed, as he continued to have his way with her lifeless body. Finally, completely exhausted, he collapsed on top of her. He hoarsely panted, "You sure you had enough my sick little doggie?"

"Fuck you, Thomas!" she angrily replied, as she continued to lay motionless in the bed, but still silently begging for more. He knew the more she protested and cursed, the more she wanted. That's the way she liked to play. Thomas shook his head unbelievingly.

"I don't fucking believe you. You sure are one sick bitch, Becka! I fuck your goddamn brains out, and you still want more! Okay bitch, that's what your paying me for." He shook his head again.

"Let's have a few drinks and a little coke." He sighed, then continued to speak. "And then I'll really make you suffer, if that's what you really want. Well...is it bitch?"

"I'll get the coke and the drinks, Thomas. You go run the bath water. And after our bath you can stop with the goddamn foreplay and get serious!" She cold heartedly remarked before adding, "I only wish Kirt Jarett was here tonight. He'd show you how to do it right, you little wimp!"

Thomas began to fume. In a fit of rage, he jumped to his feet and pulled Becka out of bed by the hair of her head. He made her stand to her wobbly feet.

He doubled his fist and sent her flying across the bedroom floor. Her head hit the side of a dresser. You could actually hear the impact. She began to laugh hysterically. After catching her breathe, she sarcastically responded, "Now that's more like it! First you're supposed to beat me. Hurt me real bad, but never in the face. Got it? And then you're supposed to fuck me! Think you can remember that this time, Thomas?"

Once again, Thomas shook his head in disgust and stormed into the living room. He went to the bar and poured himself a half of a glass of bourbon and quickly downed it. He anxiously poured himself another. He released a sigh of frustration before shouting to Becka in the other room. "Where's the goddamn coke, bitch?" Becka picked herself up from the floor and walked into the living room after retrieving the cocaine from her suitcase.

Dangling the plastic bag of drugs in one hand, she slowly walked into the room. "Is this what you want?" She seductively toyed. Thomas eagerly jerked the coke out of her trembling hands.

"Just give it to me bitch!" he angrily remarked, quickly opening the bag.

Becka swayed over to the bar and poured them both a drink. "Here, Thomas, down this. I'll get the whip," she remarked excitedly. Thomas quickly grabbed her tightly by the arm to stop her. He pulled her down between his legs. "Not before dinner, doggie!" he heatedly said, pushing her face down on her lap. "Now be a good doggie and open wide." He ordered as he quickly grabbed a handful of her hair to help guide her head rhythemetically to his body movements.

She eagerly went at it. Once again driving him insane with her deep oral kisses. After another long hour or so of painful, kinky sex, and several through spankings, Thomas finally departed her suite, leaving behind a very satisfied Becka Chamberlain. She went to the bar and poured herself a night cap before surrendering herself to exhaustion. She soon passed out on top of her bedded torture chamber.

Becka Chamberlain jerked herself from the depths of slumber, when she fell out of bed onto the floor, hitting her head on the side of the nightstand. She glanced at the clock beside the radio. It was midnight. "Oh damn it!" She moaned, reaching for her head. She rubbed the spot that was currently hurting due to her self-inflicted pain. She pulled herself up off the floor and went to pour herself a strong shot of brandy. She wanted to try and calm her nerves after waking from a disturbing and painful sleep. The terrible nightmare that had caused her to fall out of bed was still heavy on her mind. After pulling herself together somewhat, she went to the bathroom for a long hot shower. She needed to soothe the terrible pain her entire body was experiencing brought on by the brutal hand of Thomas. "Thomas," she whispered longingly, as she began to recall the heights of pleasure that he had given her just a few short hours before.

THIEF OF HEARTS

Becka stepped inside the steamy hot shower, still basking in the glow of it all. She began to day dream, needing to recall as much as she possibly could about the unique sensations Thomas so masterly made her feel.

After her daydreaming was completed, she stepped out of the shower, glancing at her image in the mirror. She was anxious to admire the new red marks and bruises that Thomas had so graciously bestowed upon her body. She smiled lustfully again just thinking about Thomas and his powerful whip. She enjoyed rubbing the welts and bruises, as she continued to stare at herself. Suddenly, the image of Ethan Sommers and young Kirsten Kamel shoved her own image out of view. Ethan was seductively toying with Kirsten over and over inside Becka's sick brain. In an attempt to stop the horrible image, she reached for her hairbrush and angrily threw it at the mirror. She quickly ran out of the bathroom, the images were still crystal clear inside her mind.

"You young whore!" she heatedly shouted, as she stumbled her way to the bar. She quickly poured herself a shot of strong liquor and immediately began to plan young Kirsten Kamel's untimely demise. "When will you stupid people learn not to fuck with me?" she angrily shouted, as she walked over to the closet to get her suitcase. After setting the suitcase down on the bed, she unzipped it and took out a needle, heroin, and her .32 millimeter automatic. "Bye, bye young Kirsten!" she wickedly said, as she put the bullets into her gun.

Chapter 13

It was daybreak before Clint Chamberlain would let Nouri Sommers finally go to sleep. "I love you darling," were the last four words she said before falling into a deep, contented sleep. My woman is back where she belongs was Clint's final thought as he nodded off shortly after her.

Not long after, they were stirred from their sleep by the bothersome ringing of the telephone. It was just past noon. "Who the hell could that be?" Clint complained, as he reached across Nouri's naked body to answer the phone. "Yes, what is it?" Clint hoarsely mumbled into the receiver. It was the front desk wanting to know if they had planned on spending another day in the hotel. If not, it was check out time. "Yeah, sure...we're staying," he muttered, quickly dropping the phone onto the floor. Clint laid his head down on Nouri's back side. She gently stirred. "Oh, sweetness, " he whispered, as he began to nibble up and down her sexy spine with sweet little kisses of affection. Nouri was still half asleep, but still wanting to respond to his longing for her, slowly rolled over to invite him aboard. "Good morning, sweetness," he responded, before he lowered his head to meet her kiss.

After an hour of sweet, gentle love making, they both fell back asleep wrapped inside each other's tight embrace. Both breathlessly happy. Both childishly content. Both very much in love, all over again. It was just what Clint was hoping for.

It was late afternoon before Clint finally woke up from a very satisfying sleep. He longingly rolled over to cuddle with the woman of his dreams, when panic suddenly surged through his body. He wanted to make love to his woman again, but she wasn't there. He quickly jumped to his feet and ran to the bathroom. He felt rather silly when he saw her standing in the shower. He slowly opened the door and stepped inside to join her. The worried expression was still obvious on his face. He quickly pulled Nouri into his arms and tightly hugged her.

"What is it, darling? What's wrong?" she asked in a concerned tone of voice.

Clint tightened his hold on her and whispered against her throat, "Oh God, Nouri. When I rolled over in bed and you weren't there, I almost lost it! I can't loose you again! My heart can't take it!" He continued to hold her tightly against his trembling body.

Nouri responded softly, "I know, Clint, darling." She gently loosened herself from his tight embrace and slowly began to kiss her way down his incredibly sexy body.

Clint soon began to moan words of delight as Nouri's hot, wet mouth began to respond to his rapid body movements. His moans began to grow deeper and deeper, as she tightened her grip on his body. Her mouth and his body were solidly joined. She continued to pleasure him, as she moved to the rhythm of his silent demands of her.

He held her head, firmly guiding her to his moves. "Oh God, don't stop. Please baby, don't stop...Ah...Ahh...Ahhh!" He groaned heatedly, as she brought him to heights of oral completion. She erotically kissed her way back up his fantastic body, into his open arms.

"God! How I've missed you doing that to my body." He panted into her ear with his hot breath.

After several passionate kisses, Clint was eager to take her to the heights of oral ecstasy that she had just shown him. He slowly began to move his hot, wet kisses down her slippery wet body. He was anxious to kiss the sensitive area between her luscious, shapely thighs. She soon began to shout moans of pleasure, as Clint continued to seduce her with his thirsty kisses.

Clint eventually made his way back up into her arms and after several deep, passionate kisses, he pinned her against the wall, where he continued to seduce her with his loving caresses and well-built body. "Oh God, darling," he heatedly whispered against the nape of her sexy neck. They soon reached sexual harmony together, as their bodies melted into one.

After their explosive climax, they both collapsed on the shower floor. Too weak to move, they both sat on the floor with the water running full force on their hot, steamy bodies, laughing uncontrollably.

Once they finally caught their breath, Clint helped Nouri out of the shower, towel dried her, and carried her back to bed, where he quickly joined her under the sheets. They snuggled together once again, falling asleep inside each other's embrace.

Chapter 14

Nouri gently loosened Clint's muscular arm from around her body and slipped out of bed. The last thing she wanted to do was leave the man she wanted to spend the rest of her life with. She knew she would first have to find a way to get out of her marriage to Ethan.

Nouri walked into the living room, quietly closing the bedroom door behind her. She walked over to the bar and made herself a mild bloody Mary. She needed a little time alone to think about the many things that Clint had said. And also, the things that he couldn't say in their conversation a few short hours earlier.

She walked to the sofa, sipping on her drink. After sitting down, she immediately began to recall Clint's words:

"Nouri, you have no idea what you have gotten yourself into by marrying Ethan Sommers. He's not the man you think he is at all. You haven't a clue what he's capable of. It wouldn't surprise me if he hadn't deliberately arranged to meet you. To steal you away from me, for what ever his sick reasoning... Sweetness, there's a lot I can't tell you about Ethan or his business affairs. But I will tell you this, he will not let you go that easily. Please let me handle it... Now I know why you wanted to meet Charles Mason. I guess I can even understand it to a degree, but damn it, Nouri, you can't get Mason involved. If he goes sticking his nose into Ethan's business affairs, he will live to regret it! Ethan will have his big nose cut right off his face. Do you understand what I'm trying to tell you?"

Nouri, I don't want you meeting with Charles Mason. I don't trust him. I've seen you two together. Sure I trust you, Nouri,, but I've seen the way he looks at you. The man is still in love with you. I see it. Hell woman, I know it! I don't want you to go near him anymore, at least not without me. Is that understood? Okay sweetness, have it your way! Hire him if you want to, but when he gets hurt or worse, don't say I didn't warn you. But you call Mason and hire him. Don't go in person. I don't want you to be alone with him, and I mean it! Sweetness whatever you do, watch your back, and be careful. I promise I'll work something out with Ethan. Just give me a little time. Meet him in Lambert, like I said. Fake a headache, your period, something, just use any excuse not to make love to him again...I can't tell you that Nouri...I can't tell you that...I can't tell you that either, sweetness...Nouri we will find a way to see each other everyday. I swear! We'll just have to be careful for a while, do you understand? Please baby, don't let that pervert touch you again. I couldn't bare it! Trust me, Nouri. We belong together. It was meant to be...I swear I'll never cheat on you again as long as I live. I completely and totally love you and no other...Forget about the past Nouri. Let's concentrate on our future today. Darling, will you marry me the very instant your divorce becomes final? I swear I won't let you down again. Trust me okay!..I'd almost forgotten to tell you. I've left Becka for good. I've already started the divorce yesterday morning. Yes, I said yesterday. Sweetness, you're the only woman for me. Baby, you don't even have to say that to me. I know. I wouldn't expect you to stay if I ever cheat on you again. I won't, so let's just don't go there, okay. How could I even think such a thing, Nouri? I've changed. I swear it! I love you more than life itself!"

After Nouri's second bloody Mary, she went back into the bedroom and quietly opened the nightstand drawer. She took out a sheet of stationary with the hotel's logo on it and an ink pen. She quickly scribbled a note to the man of her dreams, asking him to trust her and that she was off to meet Charles Mason for breakfast, if he could fit her in. She promised not to have one drink with him and that it would be a meeting of a business nature only. She had to find out about the mystery man that she impulsively married, and she understood that Clint couldn't help her with the facts that she so desperately needed to know.

She reassured him of her undying love for him and asked him to phone her later at the estate. She sealed her note to him with a lipstick kiss. Copper colored, of course, her favorite shade.

After she showered and put her clothes back on, she gently kissed her man good-bye and quickly left the Fantasy Suite Hotel. She was anxious to go back to her downtown condo, change clothes, and phone Charles Mason. She had her fingers crossed, hoping that he wasn't too angry with her because of her actions from the two nights before.

Chapter 15

It was such a beautiful late spring morning. The trees were in full bloom. Everywhere Nouri looked was a beautiful shade of green and the birds were all singing to be fed. Nouri felt more alive that morning than she had in the past two years. For no apparent reason, she suddenly began to laugh. She was happy to be alive. "I love you so very much, Clint Chamberlain," she whispered to herself, as she pulled in front of her downtown condo. James came running out to meet her.

"Good morning, Mrs. Sommers," he said as he opened the car door.

"Hello James, and how are you on this magnificently beautiful morning?" she said with a sparkle in her eyes. She smiled warmly.

"Fine, thank you. Shall I clean the car and put it away, madam?" He smiled fondly.

"Yes, thank you, James. You can clean it later. I'll need you to bring the Bentley around. I'm hoping to meet a friend for breakfast. I'll have to phone my friend first, and of course, I'll have to change. But I'll make it fast. I'm in a bit of a rush today. When we get finished with breakfast, I'll need you to drive me back to the estate. Oh, one more thing, James, I'll need to stop by the bank before I meet my friend for breakfast, okay." She smiled again.

"Yes, madam. Shall I escort you upstairs?"

"No thanks, James. I can manage on my own. I'll be down in a few minutes." Nouri rushed into the building, jumped inside the elevator, and pressed the button, taking her up stairs to her penthouse condo in the sky.

After stepping off the elevator so rapidly, she almost knocked her housemaid, Heidi, over.

"Oh Heidi! I'm so sorry. I hope you're all right," she asked in a concerned manner.

Heidi smiled and responded, "I'm fine. Nothing to worry about. Good morning, Mrs. Sommers."

"Good morning Heidi. I'm in a bit of a rush, and I need to make a few phone calls and change clothes. But I would appreciate a cup of coffee if you have some made. If not, don't worry about it." She continued to walk toward the front door of her condo. Heidi followed with a stack of phone messages in her hand, several of which, were from her husband.

Nouri thanked Heidi for the messages and quickly went to her bedroom to phone Charles Mason, Mai Li, and her best friend for the past seven years, Genna Matthews.

She was relieved that Charles agreed to meet with her for breakfast at a wonderful restaurant downtown called Hathaway's International Coffee House, located on fourth street. They had the best coffee in town. Not to mention their fantastic strawberry and whip cream waffles.

Mai Li informed Nouri about her husband's apparent anger with her, but forgot to mention Beck's odd behavior two days earlier. Nouri thanked her for the message and asked her to have Fredrick get the limo ready. She wanted him to drive her to Lambert a day early. She wanted to surprise her husband, who was apparently already there. Nouri also asked Mai Li to have her bags packed. She wanted everything to be ready to go just as soon as she arrived home. Nouri also told Mai Li not to tell her husband, if he should phone, about her surprise for him.

Nouri then thanked Heidi for the coffee and took a quick sip before phoning Genna Matthews.

"Hello, Jeanette. This is Nouri Sommers. Is Genna awake yet?" she asked, as she glanced at her watch.

"No madam. But I'll wake her if it's important." she offered, knowing they were both best friends and were also going to Lambert together, the following morning.

"Thank you, Jeanette. If you're sure it's no trouble." She reached for her cup of coffee.

"It will take a few minutes. Would you rather me have her phone you back Mrs. Sommers?"

"Yes. Why don't you have her phone me back. Oh, Jeanette, by the way, I'm at the downtown condo. Do you need my number?"

"No, Mrs. Sommers, I have it right in front of me."

"I didn't know Genna had this phone number. I'm never here." Nouri stated in a puzzled tone.

"I have it on the caller ID machine, Mrs. Sommers."

Nouri laughed and shook her head at herself. "How silly of me. I should have known." She said amusingly, realizing how often she used her own caller ID machine.

"It will be a few minutes, okay, Mrs. Sommers."

"Yes, Jeanette, that will be fine. But I'm leaving here in fifteen minutes. I have to meet someone for breakfast."

"Yes, Mrs. Sommers. I'll hurry upstairs to wake her, bye," she said politely.

Nouri walked over to the dresser and quickly pulled out her clean undees, pantyhose, and bra. She then walked into her large walk-in closet and selected a casual outfit with matching shoes and handbag. By the time she changed into her late spring outfit, Genna Matthews returned her call.

"Hello, girlfriend," she said in a sleepy tone of voice.

"Hi, Genna. I'm glad you called back so quickly. I've got tons to tell you."

THIEF OF HEARTS

Genna yawned, stretched, and rubbed her eyes, as she responded, "You sound excited. What is it, Nouri?"

"I don't have time to tell you right now. I'm getting ready to...Are you ready for this?" she said excitedly.

"What? Am I ready for what, Nouri." Genna shook her head.

"I'm on my way to meet Charles Mason for breakfast." Genna suddenly sat straight up in bed giving Nouri her complete attention. "You what!" she exclaimed excitedly.

"I told you, I can't get into it right now, but I'll tell you all about it later. I have other news to share with you about Clint Chamberlain too. But again, I don't have time to get into it right now." She glanced at her watch.

"For godsakes Nouri, you're driving me crazy with curiosity!" She sighed.

"Sorry Genna. The reason I'm calling is because I've decided to drive to Lambert instead of flying there tomorrow. I'm leaving this afternoon. I was hoping that Guy would let you ride with me. We would arrive in Lambert sort of late, but then who's on a time schedule, right? Or better yet, maybe we could spend the night in that cute little town along the way. You remember. The one that has the male strip club that you..."

Genna interrupted her. "Oh yeah. The club in Mason."

"Yes, that's it, Mason. I love to stop there. They have the cutest hand made..." Genna interrupted her again.

"I'm sorry, Nouri, I don't think Guy will let me go without him. I'm being punished again. He caught me for the umpthteenth time." She laughed.

"Oh really, Genna. Since when have you ever really listened to Guy anyway?" Nouri laughed and shook her head amusingly.

"Yeah, well he got real mad this time. He told me if he ever caught me again, I had blown my last wad of his money." She laughed again.

After Nouri finished laughing, she responded, "Oh, I would've love to seen that. What did you say to his remark?"

"I told him that if he didn't lighten up, that it would be him that had blown his last wad!"

"You are too crazy girl!" Nouri shook her head.

"So tell me where are you having breakfast with Charles Mason?" Genna's tone of voice suddenly seemed anxious.

"I'm sorry Genna, I don't have time to get into it all, but I want to tell you everything, that's why I want you to ride to Lambert with me."

"Can I at least have a hint on what you're going to tell me?" She nervously stood to her feet and began to pace back and forth.

"Okay, what I have to tell you is HOT! Very, very hot. That's all I have time to say Genna. I gotta run. I'll phone you this afternoon to see if Guy will let you ride with me, okay." Nouri nervously glanced at her watch again.

"But, Nouri..."

"I don't have time for this, Genna."

"Wait, Nouri. Just answer me this one question. Is what you're going to tell me have anything to do with your two day disappearance?" Her curiosity was getting the better of her.

"Okay Genna, I've only got two words to say to you to answer that question, but after I say them I'm going to hang up without even a good bye. And I'll phone you this afternoon. The answer to your last question is...Oh y e a h!" Her tone of voice was seductive and hot!

Nouri could still hear Genna shouting words of curious protest, as she put down the receiver. "Sorry girl friend," she whispered to herself, as she quickly exited the bedroom.

Nouri said goodbye to Heidi and quickly ran out of her penthouse condo. As Nouri stepped off the elevator, James was waiting for her. "Are you ready, Mrs. Sommers?" he asked politely, walking her toward the Bentley.

"Yes, I think so, James," she said, as her mind flashed the image of Genna with a curious look on her face. She laughed to herself knowing just how nosy her friend was by nature.

James looked at her with a puzzled expression on his face. Nouri noticed and responded, "I'm sorry, James, Something funny just popped inside my mind. James opened the car door for her, and she quickly told him where they were going.

Chapter 16

Clint Chamberlain rolled over on his side to pull Nouri into his arms. He had planned on waking her with a morning kiss. But instead of pulling her into his arms, he found a note instead. His heart suddenly fell to his feet, as he quickly fought off a panic attack. He sat up in bed, almost afraid to read the note she had left behind. He inhaled deeply and began to nervously read her message.

After reading the note, he released a deep sigh of relief and quickly jumped out of bed and ran to the shower, singing a happy tune. His heart was soaring like an eagle. He had so much to look forward to. He was so very much in love.

He quickly showered and dressed. He only stopped for one virgin Mary before departing the Fantasy Suite Hotel. As he walked outside to hail a taxi, he quickly glanced around the parking area of the hotel to see if anyone seemed to be watching him. He released another sigh of relief, as he quickly jumped inside the taxi, anxious to go back to his old apartment and see how it looked after the Dolly Maid Cleaning Service had performed their magic on it.

After Clint gave the taxi driver the address to his downtown apartment, he began to think about all of the obstacles he and Nouri would have to deal with before they could truly be together again.

Oh God. He silently thought, as he tried to make a mental list. There were the problems with the Medallion Corporation. The problems with his whacko wife Becka and their super ugly divorce he would have to deal with sooner or later. And, of course, the problems surrounding Nouri's husband, Ethan, which also happens to be his best friend. There were other issues he would have to deal with, like dumping his current squeeze, Brenda Joyce, that neither Becka or Nouri knew about. And if all those problems weren't bad enough, he had to find the courage to tell Nouri the problems associated with the secrets from his past. "The dreaded sins of our youth," he whispered to himself.

Clint released a deep sigh of frustration. "Ahh, the list of things I need to do goes on and on," he whispered again, as he cracked the window inside the taxi. He suddenly needed some extra air. He laid his head back on the seat of the taxi and closed his eyes.

Even with the screeching brakes on the taxi and the blasting horns from outside, not to mention the loud blaring car radios and the three car pile-up just ahead, Clint somehow managed to drift away from the problems of his past, as well as the problems of the present. His mind swiftly shifted back to a more pleasurable time of just a few short hours before. Where he was embracing the beautiful woman of his dreams. "Nouri," he lovingly whispered, as he was being urged to open his eyes by the taxi driver.

"Well, here we are sir." The taxi driver repeated in a louder tone of voice.

"Oh sorry cabbie. I must have been day dreaming," he confessed with a grin.

As Clint was paying the cab fare, he glanced around the area of town that he once lived. He smiled when he recognized the familiar German mom and pop carryout restaurant, a block down the street. He suddenly felt very hungry, when it dawned on him that he hadn't eaten anything except an erotic meal with the woman of his dreams covered in whipped cream and fruit. He smiled at the lustful memory and quickly made his way to the familiar eatery for one of its famous hot Ruben sandwiches on dark rye pumpernickel bread.

Clint quickly thanked the old German couple of The Hauf Brau Haus restaurant, grabbed his hot-boxed lunch, and swiftly headed to his apartment. He could hardly wait to sink his teeth into the thick slices of hot-spiced corned beef, hot German potato salad, and kosher dill pickle. A smile of anticipation crossed his incredibly handsome face.

After almost dropping his boxed lunch while trying to open his apartment with only one hand, he finally made it inside. With his food still reasonably intact, he quickly headed for the bar and sat the sandwich down on top of it. He was hoping the Dolly Maid Cleaning Service hadn't forgotten to restock the bar.

He jerked the small refrigerator door behind the bar open, crossing his fingers, silently praying that the icy, cold beer would be there, staring back at him when he looked inside.

"Thank God!" he muttered, as he reached for a cold bottle of imported beer. "Nothing like an icy cold beer to go along with a German corned beef sandwich!" he eagerly whispered, as he popped off the cap. "Ahh...That's great," he said after drinking almost a half the bottle. He reached for the now warm sandwich and was grateful the corned beef was still as delicious as he had remembered. After he ate his lunch and opened another cold beer, Clint reached for his telephone. He needed to check in with his office.

"Clint Chamberlain and Associates, how may I direct your call please?" said the young voice of Peggy O' Malley, Clint's receptionist.

"Hi Peg, this is Mr. Chamberlain. How are you today?"

"I'm great, sir. Thanks. I'm so glad you called." She sighed in relief.

"Is Mrs. Smith all right, Peg?"

"Oh, yes Mr. Chamberlain. Everything is fine. It's just we haven't heard from you in a few days, and well sir, we were just worried about you. That's all."

"I see. Well thanks for your concern, but I'm fine. It really wasn't necessary, Peg. Is Mrs. Smith in?"

"Yes, Mr. Chamberlain, I'll put your call right through. Have a nice day, sir."

"Thanks, Peg, you too."

THIEF OF HEARTS

"Clinton Jerome Chamberlain! Where in the Sam hell have you been for the past two days! We've been worried sick about you. The least you could've done was phone in, answer your cell phone, pager, or answering service. Something for chrissakes!" Violet Smith finally stopped shouting to come up for air.

"Hello, Violet. I've missed you too. Are you finished shouting yet?" If you haven't, I can wait." He chuckled.

"Very funny, Clint. I've been worried sick about you, especially after the visit from that nutty wife of yours! Whew! I had no idea about her. You poor man!" She shook her head in disbelief.

"What did she do, Violet?" No, wait...Let me guess...Something to do with breaking something very expensive. Am I close?" He laughed and shook his head before cringing.

"Right on brother! She broke the entire antique glass out of the front door. Crazy bitch!"

Clint laughed again before responding. "Scary isn't she. Hell, Violet, you don't know what that woman is capable of. We got off cheap!"

"You call that cheap! Do you know how much that damn thing cost to replace!" she shouted.

"Of course I do. It's my office, remember?" Clint mused.

"Oh, sorry boss. It's been so long since we've seen you around here. I'd almost forgotten," she playfully snapped.

"Very funny, Violet."

"All joking aside, Clint, where have you been? Ethan Sommers has been driving us nuts around here. He's pretty hot that he hasn't been able to reach you. I have some pretty angry messages for you." She cringed playfully.

"Violet, I'll take care of Ethan myself. Don't worry about it. Anything else?" He walked over to the refrigerator and opened another beer.

"You're not going to tell me are you, Clint Chamberlain?"

"Tell you, what miss snoop?" He laughed, knowing what she meant.

Violet rolled her eyes and responded, "Give me a break!"

"Violet, my pet, if you must know. I've been with the woman of my dreams. I'm hopelessly in love." He sighed.

"In love! Are you insane! Why, you're not even divorced yet for chrissakes. Who is she?"

"I can't say yet. She's still married too."

"Oh, my lord!"

"Calm down, Violet. She was mine to begin with. She was stolen from me, and well...I've decided to take her back. We belong together."

"I see. Well does this mystery lady at least have a first name?" she asked in a curious tone of voice.

133

"Well of course she does, but I can't tell you until I break some old ties." He downed half of his beer.

"Clint Chamberlain! I hate it when you do that to me. Now you really have my curiosity peeked," she huffed.

"Violet, love...I promise you'll be the first one that I introduce her to, just as soon as I possibly can. I swear, okay." He chuckled.

"All right, Clint. Have you called your attorney yet?"

"No, but I will. Anything else?"

"No, I don't think so. I took the liberty of clearing your schedule today, but I sure could use your autograph on a few things. It's pretty important, Clint."

"I'll try to at least pop in today, okay."

"Sure. Was everything at your apartment to your liking? I picked out your undees myself." She giggled .

"To tell you the truth, I just walked in the door, Violet. But you know my taste, I'm sure everything is just fine."

"How does the apartment look?"

"Great. It feels just like home, thanks."

"You're welcome, Clint."

"Well Violet, I'd better go now. I have a few more calls to make. I'll stop by later." He glanced at his watch.

"Okay, Clint, see ya later. Bye."

Clint finished his bottle of beer, as he looked around his apartment. He smiled approving, glancing down at his watch. After getting over the dread of phoning Ethan, he reached for the telephone.

"Now what hell is that damn number to Lambert again," he muttered to himself, after dialing the phone number incorrectly twice. On his third effort, he finally managed to get it right. "The private island of Lambert. What a paradise! If you're with a woman that you love," he whispered to himself, as he patiently waited for someone to answer his call.

After several minutes of continuous ringing in his ear someone finally answered, "Lambert. Your pass code please," the young voice of the hotel operator said. He rubbed his chin trying to remember the numbers he needed to transfer from alphabet form to number form. He finally answered after a few moments of silence, 19-23-5-5-20-14-5-19-19, which in their alphabet form spelled sweetness. The operator responded after a short pause. "Hello, Mr. Chamberlain. How may I direct your phone call, sir?" Knowing the membership rules of Lambert, he was aware that the operator wasn't allowed to confirm or deny any member even being at the island resort. Much less, any phone calls to the guest elite to be sent through, so he asked to speak to Olivia or Otto Lambert.

"Yes, operator. I'd like to speak to Olivia or Otto Lambert, please." He reached inside the refrigerator for another ice cold beer and popped the cap.

THIEF OF HEARTS

"One moment please, Mr. Chamberlain." After a few moments of silence, Olivia Lambert answered the call. "Hello, Mr. Chamberlain, how may I be of service to today?" Her tone of voice was flirtatious.

"Olivia, I know that it is against the membership rules, but I need a huge favor. I need to speak with Ethan Sommers. I know that he is there. He has been trying to reach me for the past two days. It's very important that I speak with him. Believe me Olivia, he wants this call. Can you help me?" He sighed hopefully.

"You realize, Mr. Chamberlain, that I can neither confirm nor deny that he is here. However, since you are one of my favorite members, I'll check to see if he is here. If he is, I will inquire to see if he is available or not. If he is here, and if he is available, is there a phone number that I could give to him for you, Clint?"

"Thank you, Olivia. I owe you one. Just have him phone me on my cell phone. He has the number."

"Very well, Clint, I'll see what I can do. You know, Clint, one of these days I'm going to have to cash in on all of the IOU's that you have promised to me through the years," she stated lustfully.

"Olivia, my pet, I will anxiously look forward to that day," he lied, humoring her.

"Goodbye, Clint."

"Goodbye, Olivia."

Clint finished his beer and switched to drinking scotch. He was pouring his second drink when his cell phone rang. It was Ethan Sommers returning his call.

"Clint, you son-of-a-bitch! Where the hell have you been for the past two goddamn days?" He hot heatedly snapped into Clint's right ear.

"I could ask you this same damn question, Ethan," Clint barked back.

"I am serious as hell you, bastard. Where the hell have you been?" His tone was insistent.

"I'm serious as hell to. Ethan, we have major problems with the Medallion Corporation to deal with, and two days ago I couldn't find your ass anywhere!" He heatedly remarked, deliberately trying to draw the attention away from his two-day disappearance. He continued to talk, "I've found out a lot about that goddamn corporation since we last talked. I think we're better off calling the whole thing..."

Ethan rudely interrupted him. "Goddamn it, Clint, I don't want to talk about business right now! I want to know where the hell you have been for the last two damn days!" His tone was sharp and insistent.

Clint quickly downed his shot of scotch, nervously wondering if he had already found out about his two night sex-a-thon with Nouri. Screw it! I don't give a damn if he does know. It had to come out in the open some time, may as well be now, and get it over with. She's my woman. Nouri belongs with me. And the sooner she's with me, the better I'll like it. I hope the bastard does know. Clint was

135

still thinking silently when Ethan suddenly jarred his attention back to their conversation by shouting into the phone again.

"Goddamn it, Clint, I want an answer!" Ethan barked again, shoving younger Kirsten Kamel angrily away from him. She had been busy showering his hard body with her hot, juicy kisses. She jumped to her feet with a hurt expression on her face. Ethan rudely motioned her away from him with a wave of his hand. "Bring me a goddamn drink, Kirsten," he shouted into the receiver.

Clint shook his head in disgust before replying, "Who the hell is Kirsten?" Ethan hatefully jerked his drink from out of Kirsten's hand.

"Why? You wanna come over and share her, old buddy?" Another frowned crossed Kirsten's face.

"No thanks, Ethan. I haven't enjoyed your sloppy seconds since our old college days... so you're not alone, huh?" he said disappointedly.

"I thought you knew me better than that old pal. Since when have you ever known me to spend a goddamn night alone in the past nineteen years?" He laughed wickedly.

"You're back one that garbage again, aren't you?" Clint shook his head in disbelief.

"Garbage hell! It's the best shit money can buy my friend." He laughed again, slapping Kirsten across her firm, young bottom. "Come here Kirsten. No baby the other way. Shit Kirsten, spread those damn legs! That's better baby. Damn! Baby that feels nice. Ah...Ahh." He moaned into the receiver as he continued to have sex with young Kirsten, while Clint was forced to listen on the other end of the phone. Clint rolled his eyes and shook his head in total disbelief.

He responded angrily. "Ethan, you're one sick fuck! Stop doing that! Leave that slut alone while you're talking to me on phone. Do you hear me?" He shouted angrily.

"Ahh. Oh shit! That's it baby. I'm almost there. Don't quit on me now, god damn it, Kirsten. Oh...Ohh...Ohhh! Damn that tight little ass on this young bitch drives me crazy Clint, you sure you don't want to come over and have a taste?" He laughed coldly and then shouted into the receiver again, "Get your ass up. I need another drink, and then go take a bath. And goddamn it! Stop looking at me like that!" His tone was demanding and cruel.

"Ethan, you're out of control. I'll fly to Lambert first thing tomorrow morning and get you. I'll call France and make all the arrangements. All right?" he said in a concerned manner. Ethan laughed into the receiver.

"I don't think so! I'm having too much fun with young Kirsten here. She's my newest. Wait until meet her Clint, she's really something, and that young goddamn bouncy body, and tight little..."

"Stop it, Ethan. Leave that young girl alone before you hurt her. Have you forgotten what happened last time you got hooked on that nasty shit?"

THIEF OF HEARTS

"You know I don't like to talk about that, Clint. And anyway, I still don't believe I was one that actually hurt that young bitch. I still believe it was Stephen," he remarked sharply.

"Ethan! Hurt? You mean killed. Go ahead say the word. Killed, Ethan! Not hurt. The poor girl was only sixteen." He sighed, suddenly remembering Ethan and Steven's sex game with a young girl several years earlier that had gotten out of hand and caused her death.

"Well, what ever. I still don't think it was me." He quickly downed his Vodka and snorted two lines Coke.

"It was you, Ethan! And Otto Lambert was paid to make your little problem disappear."

"Well like I said old buddy, whatever." He poured himself another drink. Clint also poured himself another shot of Scotch and took a drink.

"Ethan, do you want to tell me why you're behaving this way again?" Ethan began to pace back and forth across his hotel suite. "It's that goddam wife of mine. I can't find her sexy ass anywhere. She's making me crazy. I've been trying to track her down for the past two days. That's odd old pal, don't you think?" His tone accusing.

Clint shook his head, released a deep sigh of dread, thinking to himself, "Here it comes."

"What's that, Ethan?" He responded nervously.

"Both my goddamn best friend and my hot natured wife, missing for two goddamn days. Pretty strange, huh?" Clint tried to change the subject on his strung out friend.

"I thought she was supposed to meet you this weekend in Lambert? He impulsively said then quickly bit his tongue after realizing Nouri had given him that information, and not Ethan. All he could hope for now was that his friend was too out of it to pick up on his mistake. Ethan continued to pace back and forth across the room, trying to piece things together in his confused mine.

He finally responded, "Maybe you're right. I should try to calm down, hell! She'll probably be here first thing tomorrow afternoon. And anyway, it's not like I won't eventually find out what she's been up to, or where she's been." He paused briefly, took a hit off his joint and then continued to speak. "Or who she's been with!" He downed the rest of his drink.

Oh shit! The rotten bastard does know, and even if he doesn't right this second, whoever was in that black sedan was probably hired by him to spy on her. So it's only a matter of a day or two before he finds out anyway. I should have known. He's probably always had her followed and spied on from day one, knowing him. That would be right up his alley. Should I confess our love for one another now or wait in do it face-to-face tomorrow. Clint continued to think himself when Ethan suddenly shouted back into his ear, jarring his attention back to the present.

"Goddamn it, Clint! Are you listening to me?"

"Yeah, sure, Ethan. I was just pouring myself a shot of Scotch. What were you just saying?" he remarked, deciding to wait until he arrived in Lambert to confess his undying love for Nouri.

"I was talking about that goddamn wife of mine. I was telling you about how she was making me crazy." He lit another joint that was laced with several exotic drugs.

"Okay Ethan, so she's making you crazy. How for chrissakes?" he asked, trying to humor his drunken friend.

"She makes me feel inadequate for one thing. And hell, she's too old to me for another thing, you know what I mean?" He inhaled his joint deeply, then slowly releasing it.

"What the hell are you talking about! Nouri is only twenty-six, Ethan, you moron!"

"Like I said, old pal, she's too old. You know I like them young. The younger the better. They get past twenty-one, Chow baby, they're history. You know what I mean?" He laughed wickedly.

"Oh, yeah! I remember. You once told me that you like to raise them to suit yourself. I believe that's what you said. Wasn't it? Old buddy." His tone noticeably disgusted

"You're damn straight, Clint. When they're young, they're so tight. So delicious. So... yummy..." he slapped his lips together.

"Ethan, you are a very disturbed person. Hell man, you're almost forty years old, when are you going to start acting like it for chrissakes! You go through women like..." He suddenly stopped talking and shook his head.

"I bet you're wondering why I married my lovely, antique eighth bride, huh?" He walked back to the bed and began to caress young Kirsten's soft body.

"That has crossed my mind a time or two I must confess, Ethan. After all, she was so old already when you married her, what? About twenty four?" He rolled his eyes, suspecting that he already knew why he married her.

"She was twenty-three. I believe we were married about six months before her twenty fourth birthday."

"Yeah, so. Why did you marry her?"

"I have two reasons old pal. One reason is that I love to collect beautiful, old antiques. She's magnificent, isn't she? I truly enjoy looking at her. She's probably one of the most beautiful possessions I've ever owned. Her price was a touch high, but if I really want something, I'll go the price, no matter what the cost." He pushed Kirsten's head down between his legs. Anxious for her to orally satisfy him again.

"What the hell do you mean, her price was a touch high?" Clint asked defensively.

"Her price was marriage. The bitch was still hung up and so hot over that old boyfriend of hers. She moped over his two timing, non-committal ass for what seemed like forever. I think she still does. Anyway, the goddamn prick teaser wouldn't give me any until I married her, so I did. She's bought and paid for! I own the bitch!" Ethan said arrogantly.

Clint turned red in the face with anger. "Ethan, you are unbelievable!" He shook his head angrily.

"What was your other reason for marrying her?" Ethan's laugh was cruel and spiteful.

"That, my friend, is something that I don't care to share with you right at this moment. But I intend to. Not to worry Clint... get the hell up off me, Kirsten, and get me another goddamn drink."

"Ethan, if she makes you so unhappy why don't you just give her a divorce and be done with?" Clint crossed his fingers, hoping.

"Yeah, that, of course, would be one way to end the bullshit she seems to enjoy putting me through, and I'm sure that would solve a lot of problems for her and that ex-boyfriend of hers, don't you think? But of course, I'd never give her a divorce. That's out of the question. The only way she would get out of her marriage to me would be in a body bag." He laughed coldly.

"Ethan, you need help. I'm calling Ms.Schaffer in France. I was going to fly to Lambert tomorrow, but maybe it would be better if I take a flight out as soon as I can get one. I want you to..."

Ethan interrupted him. "Hey, Clint, old boy, slow down. In the first place, I'm not going anywhere, especially to France. And secondly, Steven is supposed to phone me here tonight. I have to be here. He has some demands from the red Devil himself for me." He laughed uncontrollably again.

"Ethan, what the hell are you doing? I thought all this nonsense was behind us once and for all. You told me a year after you got married, this time you're going to go completely legitimate. You promise me if I stayed with you, that you were going to change. What happened, for chrissakes?" Clint sighed.

"Relax, my lily white friend. I wouldn't dream of asking you to get your hands dirty again. I've already asked Thomas Sphere to come back aboard. He'll help me get everything taken care of. Don't worry about it. I won't involve you in it. You know, Clint, I really hated that you have changed on me so. There was a time I could count on you for just about everything. Hell, you been acting sort of funny since the unveiling of my beautiful bride a year ago, odd isn't it?" All of a sudden you're no fun anymore. No more women. No more parties. No more drugs. Hell, I'm surprised you still drink, for chrissakes, my old college chum.

You're turning out to be a major disappointment to me, not to mention a real bore lately."

"Ethan, I haven't really changed. I've just grown-up. I just don't enjoy the things from my youth anymore, that's all. And as far as cleaning up your dirty work with all of your many business enterprises, I've got you straightened out for the last time. So if you insist on continuing to let the Chinese Mafia be a your part of your life, then my old friend, I guess it's time for us to say goodbye. I'll turn all of your..."

Ethan interrupted him in mid-sentence, "Whoa! Backup there, slick! It's not over until I say it's over old pal. Who the hell do you think you're talking to! You've made millions off of me, and you think I'm going to let you get away from me that easily. Think again, sweetheart! You're bought and paid for too." Ethan heatedly shouted as he stormed over to the bar and poured himself another drink.

Clint angrily downed his shot of Scotch, wondering what he should say or do next. When Ethan was strung out like this, he knew that it didn't matter what he would say or do, he couldn't help him, unless he was actually there. That was the only way his friend would listen and let him take him to France for the help that he so desperately needed again.

"Ethan, we will discuss this tomorrow when I get to Lambert. So, tell me, Ethan, what time do you expect your wife to arrive tomorrow? You better make sure Kirsten is out of your suite before Nouri arrives." He laughed. It was his way of trying to change the subject to lighten the mood.

"Oh, shit! You've got that right!" He playfully cringed. "She once told me that was the only thing she wouldn't put up with in our marriage, you know old pal, I believe her. She would die if she could see me now." He laughed sounding like a naughty little boy. He added, "You know Clint, that woman is really something else! I was telling you how she drives me nuts, remember?"

Clint shook his head trying a clear his thoughts. He responded, "Yes. Yes, you were telling me that, Ethan, please continue, why don't you." He sighed.

Chapter 17

Ethan began to pace back and forth across the floor again "Did I ever tell you that my wife writes in a fantasy journal when she gets pissed at me. Can you believe that? I think she's writing what a bad fuck I am. I swear! Gives me a goddamn complex. One night, I tried to sneak a quick look in one of those damn things. She got so upset with me; she's been keeping the stupid things under lock and key ever since! Can you imagine a grown woman acting like that?" he scoffed.

Clint had to fight back his laughter. "Imagine that," he mused.

"Between her goddamn fantasy journals and not being able to track the bitch down the past two days, I'm about to go nuts! You know she makes me nuts whether I'm home or not. That damn hot nature of hers, combined with getting worked up with those goddamn fantasy men of hers in those damn journals, makes me not want to go home anymore. But then I think to myself, if she ain't doing me, that can only mean one goddamn thing. She's got to be getting it somewhere. You know what really pisses me off? I haven't made love to her but maybe seven or eight times since we've been married, and you want to know why? Well let me tell you. She just doesn't want to be screwed. No. Not that hot natured bitch! She wants to be romanced. To be wined. And yes, even dined! Too much bullshit for me. Fuck it! I say shut the hell up! Spread those goddamn legs. Take care of business, roll over, and go to sleep, goddamn it! Am I right or what?" Ethan stopped long enough to let Clint respond.

"Ethan, you vulgar bastard! What you don't know about women is apparently plenty. No wonder you prefer young, stupid teenagers. What the hell have they got to compare animals like you with?" He shook his head in sick disgust.

"So what are you saying, Clint? That you're on her side, mister Don Juan?"

"Your damn straight, you simple bastard! You know, Ethan, you should take some of your billions, and invest some of that money in a little class for yourself." He walked back to the bar and poured himself another shot of scotch.

"Ouch, old pal of mine, that really hurt. So you want to play. And rough at that, huh? Okay, let's party."

"What the hell are you talking about now, Ethan?" He rolled his eyes and sighed.

"I wasn't going to do this just yet, but what the hell, you talked me into it. I'm tired of talking about my boring prim and ever so proper wife. Let's talk about the sick bitch you're married to. Want to?" Ethan laughed wickedly.

"Not really." Clint sighed and took a sip of his scotch.

"Come on, Clint, it's my turn to hurt you. You drew first blood so to speak, it's only fair." He downed his shot of vodka and poured himself another.

"Okay, Ethan, have it your way. Go for it! But I have to tell you, I already know that you have been having an affair with Becka, and it's okay with me. I don't give a shit." Clint walked into his bedroom and stretched out on top of his bed.

"Well damn! I have to admit I honestly didn't think you were that sharp. And the fact you already know about me fucking your wife takes a little of the fun stuff away, but I'd hardly call what we've been doing an affair. That is one sick bitch you're married to, Clint, old boy. Hell, I get hard thinking about that sexy little nymphomaniac. Damn!" He shook his head and walked back to the bed, motioning for young Kirsten to come joined him again.

"I'd really rather not hear about it, if you don't mind." He closed his tired eyes.

"Oh, but I was still looking forward to sharing the whole sick story with you, Clint." He paused and continued to aggravate him with the unwanted details of his sexual encounters with his wife Becka. "You know, Clint, when I saw how hot you seemed to be for Becka the night I introduced her to you, on my first wedding anniversary party with Nouri, I just had to try her out for you first. Damn that was thrilling! My wife and you right in the very next room with what was it... about several hundred other people. No matter. Anyway, I was standing up at the bar talking to Guy and Stuart. You and Nouri were still busy being uncomfortable with each other still at the table. Becka walked up to me and told me to go out on the terrace, she had something she wanted to give me in private. My mother didn't raise no dummy. I knew immediately what she had for me. She wanted to fuck me, but certainly no more than I wanted to fuck her. I walked outside and lit up a joint, and like a dog in heat the bitch pulled up her evening gown and dropped her panties down to her ankles, stuck her finger into herself, and then put her finger into her own goddamn mouth. My hard on was instant." He shook his head in awe of the remembered thought. "You know what that sick bitch said after she finished sucking the juice off of her finger? I'll tell you what she said. She said, 'umm... I taste so good.'" He laughed and then continued talking, "She then stuck her finger back into herself, walked up to me, took the joint out of my mouth, and traded me her nasty finger for my smoke. She was right about one thing. She did taste pretty damn good. Next, she had it out of my slacks, and well, let's just say, that woman could suck a flea off of a tick. Damn she was good. I was so damn excited by then I couldn't stop. I had to have more and lots of it. I made her bend over and grab hold of her ankles, and I lost all control. I tore that bitch up! She was begging me for more when I finally stopped to catch my breath. Shit! I've never seen anything like it before or since! After I fucked that tight ass of hers, I told her to seek upstairs and go to one of the guest rooms. I'd joined her there as soon as I could. I pulled myself back together, went back to join my lovely wife and my best friend, who were still apparently trying hard to avoid each other. I left unnoticed and broke my damn neck running up the stairs to find the bitch, and I'm here to tell you, that for an old broad that apparently had more pricks poked inside her than a porcupine, she was the best goddamn fuck I'd ever had in my entire life. And you know as well as I do, I've certainly had my fair share of ass." He paused for moment, lit a joint, then continued to speak. "After I couldn't get it up anymore she asked me to send up a few friends to finish the job. So I sent up Stuart and Guy. When they finally rejoined the party, I was ready for one more go at it. I almost had to crawl out of that goddamn room. Whew! That was a party to remember. Hell, I was too worn out to give Nouri any that night." He stopped talking, walked to the bar, and poured himself another drink.

"So you've been screwing Becka ever since the night I met her. I should've known." He sighed, shaking his head in utter disbelief.

"Screwing! Hardly Clint. You mean fucking! I am talking hard core shit! Whew! That damn bitch is worse then a dog in heat. The more the merrier. Men, women, boys, girls, hell, I'm surprised she doesn't do animals. She seems like everything else. Becka likes it raw. A girl after my own heart! She pissed me off so badly the other day, I beat the hell out of her, and she was begging me for more when I stormed out of the room. I'm telling you old buddy, she's one sick puppy. Her and that goddamn kid she's always sucking on around here, Thomas, I think is his name. I watched him beat her half to death with a whip a few weeks ago. I thought for sure he had killed her, but when I left, she was still begging him for more." He laughed wickedly and then added, "Now, Becka is the bitch I should've married this time." Ethan motioned for Kirsten to join him at the bar.

Clint suddenly felt sick at his stomach. He got up off of the bed and walked over to the patio and opened the door. He walked outside and inhaled deeply. He finally responded. "Well, Ethan, you're right. That certainly was some kind of story. You know it does sound like she would've been a better choice for you than Nouri. Why don't we trade? You take Becka, and I'll take Nouri. Sounds like a fair change don't you think?" he said sharply, a his hot temper started to come to life.

Ethan suddenly jumped to his feet, almost knocking young Kirsten off of her barstool. He shouted, "Fat chance slick! You had your god- damn chance with my wife, and you blew it! Did you honestly think I didn't know about you two all along? Why do you think I married her to begin with. Well let me tell you old buddy, to hurt you. That's right. Did you really think I was that stupid? And yes, I do know that you two spent the last two nights together. You should know me by now. I know everything about everyone that is affiliated with me in anyway, shape, or form.

"So why the games, Ethan?" Clint sighed a sigh of relief. Glad, at least, it was out in the open. Now Nouri could come back to him, where she rightfully belonged.

"Because it was my way of getting even with you after all of these years. I really do know you better than you know yourself, Clint." Ethan sighed.

"I don't understand. You say it was your way of getting even with me. Even with me for what?" Clint couldn't understand what the hell he could have done to make Ethan want to get even with him for any reason. As far as he was concerned, up until Ethan married Nouri, Clint thought that he and Ethan were the best of friends.

"I'll tell you that, my friend, at a later date. I can't give it all to you at once. Now can I?"

"Ethan, knock it off. It's the combination of drugs and alcohol talking. I'll meet you first thing tomorrow morning, and we will work everything out."

"It's not that easy, slick! You've done broke our bond of friendship for the second and final time."

"What the hell you talking about, Ethan," he asked sharply.

"I'll tell you my old college chum when I'm damn good and ready. And right now, I'm just not ready. But I will tell you this much, if you ever go near my wife again, first I'll have her killed, and then I'll have you killed. Do I make myself clear?" he shouted angrily into the phone.

"Now you understand this, Ethan, you sick bastard. If you touch a hair on Nouri's beautiful head, I won't have you killed. I will kill you myself with my own two bare hands. Do you understand?" he heatedly responded.

"Whew, I'm scared of you," he arrogantly cackled.

"By God you better be. If I can't get you one way, you sick son-of-a-bitch, I'll get you another. You're a spineless prick and always have been. You've always had poor, unsuspecting bastards like me to do your lousy cleanup work. I've become so good at it you would be impressed. And to me, getting rid of your rotten ass would be just another dirty little job that I had to do deal with! If you think I haven't got my own means of protection from a sick fuck like you, then you are crazier than I thought you were. I don't give a damn about dying. Do you hear me? If something happens to me, believe me, they will come after you. I've got my ways of dealing with your ass whether I'm alive or dead. It doesn't mean shit to me. But if you so much as lay a hand on Nouri, believe me you pervert, you will pray for death by the time I'm finished with you, Ethan!" Clint shouted, as he stormed back inside.

"Well, ol' boy. I've got to go. It's time for Steven to call. It's far from over between us. Hell Clint, I've just gotten started toying with you. I intend to make you suffer before we're finished. I've looked forward to this for the past fifteen years. I'll be in touch!" The next thing Clint heard on his telephone line was the angry click of Ethan slamming down the receiver in his ear.

"That crazy son-of-a-bitch! I have to warn Nouri, but I need to phone my office first. I'd better have Violet hide some of his goddamn assets, just in case I need a little insurance to cover my ass. Shit! I knew it would get crazy like this if he got mixed up with Steven again. Damn, I can't believe Steven is back. I'd better call France and have Ms.Schaeffer send someone to Lambert to help me get that goddamn sick bastard out of there before he hurts someone again. Maybe young Kirsten, maybe Nouri. Damn, I guess I better fly out tonight to be on the safe side. Clint continued to be lost in thought, as he sat on the sofa with his head inside his hands. "Damn it, Ethan, you crazy bastard!" he muttered, as he reached for the telephone, silently wondering what he had done in their past fifteen years together to make Ethan hate him so.

Chapter 18

"We're here, Mrs. Sommers." James said, as he opened the door of the Bentley. Nouri glanced around her unfamiliar surroundings, then let out a soft sigh of dread. She was still very nervous about hiring Charles Mason to spy on her husband and his business affairs, but it was something she knew she had to do. She had obviously married a man that she knew nothing about. It was time that she found out just who Ethan Sommers really was.

For her to be able to get out of her marriage to this mystery man and allow her to finally marry the real man of her dreams, she would need the help of her friend Charles Mason. With his help, she knew he would be able to help her find a way.

She quickly turned and entered Hathaway's International Restaurant and immediately spotted Charles Mason before he had a chance to see her. She managed to sneak up behind him without him noticing her. She put her hand on her hip, and quickly pulled the chair next to him out, startling him. "Excuse me, sir. Is this seat taken?" she teased.

"Shit! Sugar, you startled me." He chuckled, quickly standing to his feet to push in her chair.

"Charles, thanks for meeting me." She smiled nervously then continued to talk. "I'm sorry about the other night. I'm so embarrassed. I hope you weren't angry at me." She blushed.

"Ah, forget it sugar. I want you to know, Nouri, that you never have to apologize to me for anything." He returned her smile. She lowered her eyes to her empty coffee cup. Charles noticed. "Sorry, sugar. Here, let knew pour you some coffee," he said, reaching for the stainless steel coffeepot already sitting on top of the table.

"Thanks, big guy." I needed that," she answered quickly, reaching for the cup. Charles met her searching gaze. He smiled.

"Well?" he impatiently asked.

"All right, Charles," she responded. Already aware of what he had meant by just that one very descriptive word. She released a nervous sigh and began to speak. "His name is Clint Chamberlain. He is my husband's high-powered attorney and best friend. He's also my ex-fiancee." She offered with a blush.

"And?"

"And, we're still very much in love," she confessed.

"No wonder the poor son-of-a-bitch was so damn upset the other night." He shook his head understandingly.

"Yeah, well he was pretty hot!" She playfully cringed.

"I can understand that. I would have been too." He smiled, adding, "Nouri, you little heartbreaker!"

"I didn't mean to hurt anyone," she sighed.

"Not deliberately anyway," he said, as he glanced a look at her.

"Charles, I...I need you." She looked at him with her begging eyes.

"Yeah, I know, sugar. That's what you said the other night. That's why I'm here this morning. What can I do for you?" He leveled his eyes to hers.

"I want to hire you. I want you to find out who Ethan Sommers really is. I need to know." She sighed hopelessly.

"I don't understand, Nouri." He squirmed in his seat before adding, "Are you hungry, sugar?" He smiled.

"No thanks, Charles. I'm sort of in a rush this morning."

"Well, I'm starved. You don't mind if I..."

Nouri stopped him from finishing. "No, of course not. Please eat." She smiled, then said, "Oh, what the hell, I'll try one of their whipped cream strawberry waffles that I've heard so much about in the past." She smiled again. Charles Mason motioned for the waiter to come over. He quickly ordered for them and went immediately back to their conversation.

"Please Nouri continue." He gave her his complete attention.

"My marriage is a joke. My husband is never at home. I don't know who he is, or what type of businesses he has. Quite frankly, I've apparently married a man who doesn't really exist," she said, as she reached nervously for her coffee cup again.

"Go on, tell me everything, starting with how you met." He nodded.

"Well, I was living with Clint at the time. We had a huge fight, and I left. I was very hurt and vulnerable. Ethan zoomed into my life and made me forget about my broken heart. And on our second straight week of dating, we impulsively married. I've slept with my husband only seven or eight times in our two years of marriage. He is not the man I thought I was marrying. He's a stranger to me. I want a divorce, but I know he won't give me one. I've become a possession to him. One that he won't part with. I need you to help me get one. But first, I need to know who it is that I did marry.

Charles listened attentively, as his heart began to secretly break into, yet once again, as the woman of his dreams continued to asked him for his help in getting out of one marriage, so she could jump into another marriage with a man other than himself. He released a sigh of disappointed frustration while he continued to learn more and more details of her past seven years away from him.

"Okay, Nouri. I understand, but I'll still need to ask you a few more questions," he said, as he gently patted the top of her hand. Nouri studied the hurt expression on his face for a few moments. It suddenly occurred to her that Charles Mason was still very much in love with her.

THIEF OF HEARTS

"Charles, I want you to know that I do love you, and I will always love you. If we would have made love the other night, I wouldn't have regretted it because of the type of love I'll always feel for you. She turned his face up to face hers. She added, "I'm... I'm just not in love with you. I'm in love with Clint Chamberlain. I can't seem to help myself. Do you understand?" She smiled.

"Yes, Nouri, perfectly. That's how I feel about you. And God help me! I probably always will. But life goes on." He sighed again, deciding to tell her a lie to keep her from pitying him. "That's why I finally married someone else after you turned me down. People just can't stop living because we can't be with the ones we really love. We somehow learn to love the ones we're forced to be with." He lied convincingly.

"Charles, you're married!" Nouri asked, as a stunned look subtly crossed her face.

"Yeah sure. I couldn't wait around forever, right?" He lied again. Suddenly, Nouri felt a surge of jealousy come over her, but she wasn't quite sure why. Charles Mason noticed the expression change on her face. He smiled knowingly. He couldn't resist the temptation to tease her. "So why the long face. You surely didn't think I'd go on forever waiting for you to come to your senses and come back to the only real man that has ever loved you. No one could ever love you more than I do, sugar." He sighed regrettably.

Nouri looked affectionately at him. "So you're still in love with me, Charles?" She smiled.

A smile came over his handsome face. "And, I always will be, sugar. But in vain. In vain." He shook his head playfully before continuing to speak. "So let's get back to the issue at hand here, shall we." She nodded in agreement. He continued to ask her question after question, many of which she had no answers for. He was nearing the end of his question-and-answer period. "So, tell me, Nouri, is Ethan Sommers a dangerous man?" He studied her beautiful face while he waited for her reply.

"I'm not sure. He's a tad on the crude side at times, but to me he has never displayed any signs of violence. Sometimes, when he's angry it seems as if he has to fight with himself to regain control." She sighed and then continued. "Clint, of course would know better than I, and he told me the other night to watch my back, and..."

"And what, Nouri?"

"He said that Ethan was capable of some pretty unthinkable acts, and yes, he is a dangerous man. Sadly, I believe him." She lowered her head in shame.

"Nouri, have you been seeing Clint Chamberlain all along?"

"You mean since I've been married?"

"Yes, that's what I mean."

"No. Of course not. I've never cheated on my husband except..."

"Except what?"

"Except in my fantasy journals." She giggled, trying to lighten the mood between them. Both she and Charles began to laugh. He slid his chair out a few inches from the table when he noticed three gentlemen dressed in business suits slowly walk past their table. He continued to avert his attention to them after he realized they seemed very interested in Nouri and who she was with. Charles didn't want to alarm her with his suspicions, so he continued to encourage her to tell him as much as she possibly could about her mysterious and elusive husband.

After Nouri finished explaining her unusual relationship with her husband to Charles, she stared at him point-blank, and asked, "Well Charles, will you help me?" She smiled nervously. Charles glanced down at his watch, took another sneak peek at the three gentlemen seated three tables across from him, and gave her a nod of agreement. She reached into her purse, pulled out an envelope, and laid it down on top of the table in front of him.

"Charles, there's a cashier's check for twenty five thousand in here," she said, touching her finger to the envelope. She added, "There's also a blank check from one of my personal accounts that Ethan doesn't know anything about. Make it out for any amount you like, Charles. I didn't know how much you charged for..." Charles smiled at her lovingly, and slid the envelope back to her.

"This one's on me, sugar," he said, quickly interrupting her. Nouri objected and tried to push the envelope back at him. But he swiftly intervened. "I mean it. It's a favor, remember? Friends don't charge friends for a favor. At least where I come from." He smiled, as he picked the envelope up and placed it into her hands. He noticed three gentlemen watching attentively.

"Charles, but you may have to travel out of the country to France or China, God only knows where else." She shrugged before adding, "And that could get expensive." She glanced into his eyes.

"Nouri, for chrissakes, I'm the wealthiest private investigator in the country. If you insist on giving your money away, give it to a charity or..."

"What was the name of that charity you sponsored years ago?" She smiled.

"Battered women and teens. When I was a cop, I used to witness some pretty ugly sites." He shook his head. "I still do what I can for the cause." He smiled again at her.

"Here, take this Charles. Give it to the cause. I suddenly remember some of the horror stories that an ex-friend and business associate used to tell me about when she was a child." She shook her head sadly.

Charles accepted the envelope Nouri once again offered to him. He smiled appreciatively and slid the envelope in the inside pocket of his suit.

"Thanks," he said, as he gently patted her arm affectionately, aware that their every move was being monitored.

"How shall we get in touch, sugar?" He looked into her eyes.

"I guess I'd better be the one to get in touch with you, Charles," she responded, as she watched Charles pull out his pen and business card. He scribbled down several phone numbers on the card and handed to her.

"The first number is my private answering service, twenty four hours a day. They can track me down any time of the day or night. The other numbers are my cell phone, my pager, the office, and my home." He smiled.

Nouri accepted the card, smiling. "Now, your wife isn't going to get all upset if I phone you at home, is she?" She arched her eyebrows and stared into his beautiful sky blue eyes. He momentarily forgot about his make believe wife.

"My what?" His tone was one of surprise.

Nouri looked at him suspiciously and responded, "Your wife. What's her name in case I have to phone your house?" She studied his face, as she waited for his answer.

"Oh, my wife. Her name is...is...uh...uhh, Talulla." He smiled again. He had just given her the name of his furry pet feline.

Nouri laughed amusingly. "Now that's a name you don't hear every day. She teased and then added, "Is she pretty?"

"She's not as beautiful as you are of course, sugar. But she's really very special. She's so soft. I just love cuddling with her. And she's quite the home body. I like that in my women, as you might remember." He teased.

"I'd like to meet this bride of yours some time," she said jealously. Charles laughed, knowing Nouri was jealous of his pretend wife.

"Oh would ya?"

"Yes. I'd like to see the woman that replaced me in your heart." The jealousy was still in her tone. Charles chuckled again, as he glanced at his watch.

"Well sugar, no one could ever take your place in my heart, but I'm sure you would just love Talulla. She's really very special."

Nouri suddenly remembered she had tons to do before leaving for Lambert, so she pushed her chair back several inches, getting ready to stand.

"Charles, I have to run. I'm leaving for Lambert this afternoon, and I have one million things to do first". She wanted to mention their mutual friend Genna Matthews, but she had forgotten all about her.

"Lambert?"

"Yes. I'm supposed to meet Ethan there tomorrow. But since I need a little time to get my courage up to ask for a divorce that I know he won't give, I decided to have my chauffeur drive me today."

"Maybe you should wait, sugar. I mean to ask him for a divorce. At least until I have a chance to check into a few things." His tone of voice was one of concern.

"Maybe you're right. I'll wait and see what kind of mood he's in. If we fight again, I'll demand a divorce." She sighed.

"Boy, you sure are hot to get back with what's his face, huh?" Charles asked jealously.

Nouri smiled, recognizing the tone. "His name is Clint Chamberlain. Remember. And God help me. Yes, I can hardly wait." The thought of his handsome face sent goose bumps up her spine.

Charles shook his head in awe after remembering the longing look in her beautiful eyes. "Lucky man! This Clint Chamberlain. Nouri, please don't rush into anything again. Give it a little time."

"What do you mean, big guy?" She leveled her eyes to his.

"You may not like some of the things I find out about Ethan Sommers, and if he and what's his face are as tight as you say they are, well... just be careful. That's all, okay?"

"I appreciate your concern, Charles, I really do. But Clint isn't anything at all like Ethan." She smiled, but her tone of voice was defensive.

"Sugar. That very well may be. But you said he was quite the ladies' man. I just don't want him stepping on that fragile heart of yours again. People don't usually change that much." He smiled caringly.

Nouri reached over and patted his arm affectionately. "Charles, I truly love you. And I am so very grateful for your help. But I am a big girl now, in case you haven't noticed. I can take care of myself. If Clint ever cheats on me again...Well, less just say he's quite aware of the outcome." She smiled nervously, suddenly remembering Clint's weaknesses and track record with beautiful women.

"Sugar. Just don't rush into anything. Also, heed the advice of what Clint Chamberlain has told you pertaining to Ethan. Don't provoke him. If the opportunity presents itself and you feel you're safe enough to ask for a divorce, then go ahead and give it a shot. But be careful! Nouri, I wasn't going to say anything to you just yet, but..." he suddenly stopped talking when the three men that had been watching them so attentively stood to their feet and walked past them. They went outside of the restaurant. Charles quickly stood his feet and asked Nouri to hold on for a second, that he'd be right back. A stunned look crossed her face, as she watched him quickly dart across the room to the front of the restaurant. He opened the door and raced outside. He wasn't fast enough to get the license number of the black sedan. But he was definitely sure of one thing. And that was, it was definitely the same car that was parked in front of Pompillio's restaurant, two nights earlier. He had just accepted a case and was already aware of the fact that his beloved Nouri might be in terrible danger. He shook his head heatedly and walked back inside the restaurant, wondering if he should fill her in on the fact that she was being followed.

THIEF OF HEARTS

Out of habit, he glanced back over shoulder as he entered the restaurant. Nouri was still sitting in the same position with the same stunned expression masked across her beautiful face. Charles decided not to fill her in on his suspicions or fears. He sat down still a little out of breath.

"What was all that about, Charles?"

"Sorry sugar. I thought I recognized someone I hadn't seen in awhile. I couldn't catch up with them." He lied.

"Well, you scared the hell out of me." She released a sighed of relief.

"Sorry, sugar. Where were we?" he asked apologetically.

"I was about ready to leave, Charles." She smiled.

"Okay, sugar. Wait until I pay the tab, and I'll walk you out to your car." He returned a smile.

"That's not necessary Charles. I have a driver waiting on me today."

"Let me guess. Your Bentley out front?"

"Mine. No. Actually it's Ethan's."

"Like I said, sugar, your Bentley." He teased.

"Okay, mister smart guy. I have to leave. I'll call you in a few days. I don't know if I'll stay the entire weekend in Lambert or not. But in any case, I'll check in with you on Monday, okay."

"Okay, sugar, but be careful and don't forget to... well you know what I'm trying to say. Right?" He smiled lovingly. She smiled, knowing he was only trying to offer her some fatherly advice.

"Yes, Pop-a-son." She teased, as she stood to her feet. She leaned down and kissed Charles on the cheek. "Thanks, big guy," she said and quickly turned to leave.

"Nouri. Make what's his face earn your love and your trust, okay?" he said rather loudly, embarrassing her a little. She blushed and glanced back at him from across her shoulder, giving him a questionable look without speaking. She rolled her eyes and waved him a goodbye, as she quickly left the restaurant.

Chapter 19

Once Nouri entered the Bentley, she quickly reached for the cell phone. "Hello Marry. Is Stacy out of bed yet? This is Nouri Sommers."

"Oh, hi Mrs. Sommers. She and Mr.Gullaume aren't here. They decided to go to Lambert a few days earlier." The house maid of the Gullaume's responded.

"I see. Okay, Mary, thanks. I'll just wait to talk to her when I get to Lambert."

"Are you sure you don't want me to give her a message when she phones me later?"

"Yes, Mary, thank you. It can wait, bye."

"Damn." Nouri whispered to herself, as she glanced at her watch again. She was anxious to share her latest news about Clint Chamberlain with her other girlfriend. I guess I'll just have to wait, she thought to herself, as she decided to phone her husband's office.

"Yes, Mrs. Sommers. How can help you?" Anna McCall said, as she answered the phone call her secretary passed through to her.

"I understand my request is highly unusual. But I insist that you have my husband phone me on my cell phone this instant. I simply won't take no for an answer. Do I make myself clear, Ms. McCall?"

"I see, Mrs. Sommers. You're right. I can't do that. I can lose my job," she replied nervously.

"Listen Ms. McCall, I'm not trying to get you in trouble. I just need to speak with my husband. It's... it's urgent!"

"Oh, all right, Ms. McCall. Let me help you. I know that Ethan is in Lambert. I also know the Lambert's won't send personal phone calls through."

"I don't have our suite number. But Ethan doesn't know that. I need that phone number. He'll never know that you gave it to me, I promise, Ms. McCall." Nouri sounded very upset.

"I have your solomn word on that Mrs. Sommers?" she sighed nervously.

"I swear, Ms. McCall." She crossed her fingers hopefully. After Anna McCall gave the phone number of the Sommers Suite to Nouri, she nervously dialed the phone number. She didn't know exactly what it was that she was going to say to her husband. She was mostly just curious about his mood, but she was also silently praying to herself that she would have the guts just a go ahead and ask for a divorce over the phone. She desperately wanted to spend the rest of her nights with the man of her dreams, Clint Chamberlain.

Third ring. Fourth ring. Fifth ring. Suddenly a nervous, young female voice groggily answered with a sleepy hello. Nouri couldn't respond immediately. She couldn't believe her ears. It was the same young voice that had disrupted her hot bubble bath three nights earlier. Finally she somehow managed to ask to speak with Ethan.

"Baby, wake-up for chrissakes. It's for you," the young voice said over the receiver.

"Who the fuck is it?" Ethan angrily snapped.

"I don't know. They didn't say." She responded.

"Tell the son-of-bitch to call back later, Goddamn it!" He drunkenly ordered. Nouri, completely stunned, quickly shut off her cell phone.

"That rotten bastard!" She fumed, as she quickly made the decision to go to Lambert and face him with his infidelity, ask for a divorce, and get it over with. Nouri was suddenly engulfed with mixed emotions over Ethan's obvious infidelity. She felt like such a fool. "How could I have been so blind? So stupid? So believing? Oh God!" she hurtfully whispered, fighting the tears back that were beginning to form in her eyes.

Chapter 20

Nouri rolled her window down inside the Bentley and began to stare out of it. She was wondering to herself how things in her life managed to get so far out of hand. What will I do? Does Clint really want to marry me, or is he going to break my heart again? Will Ethan finally agree to a divorce now I know he's been having an affair? What will I do if he won't let me go? He'll have to let me go, won't he? Should I take him through the ringer. Or walk away from this marriage with what I came into it with? After all, we never signed a prenuptial agreement of any type. What will I do? Where will I go? Oh, Clint I need you! She thought to herself while staring out of the window.

Suddenly, she recognized the century-old trees of the estate grounds and knew she was home. Mai Li came running out of the mansion to greet her.

"Miss...miss. Mrs. Matthews anxious to talk to you."

"I'll phone her right away, Mai Li. Thank you."

"No need miss. She waiting inside." Mai Li smiled.

"Oh good. Have Frederick bring the limo around. I want to leave immediately, okay Mai Li."

"Yes miss. Right away." She smiled and disappeared into the mansion. Nouri smiled fondly, as she watched her disappear out of sight, thinking how much she was going to miss her after her divorce from Ethan.

"Oh, Genna. I'm so glad you could make it," Nouri said, as she ran into her arms and hugged her tightly, taking Genna Matthews completely by surprise.

"Nouri, what is it? Are you all right?" she asked excitedly.

"Come on, Genna, I'm anxious to get on the road. We can talk inside the limo," she said, ushering her best friend out of the house. She turned to Mai Li, who was now standing just inside the doorway.

"Oh, Mai Li. Sorry. I was in such a rush I had almost forgotten to say goodbye," she said, as she ran back to the mansion and hugged her tightly. Mai Li was also stunned.

"Miss you okay?" she said, as she freed from Nouri's tight hold around her shoulders.

"Yes, Mai Li. I guess I'm just feeling a little overly emotional today." She shrugged her shoulders.

"You sure. You okay miss?" she asked again in a concerned tone of voice.

"Yes, Mai Li. I'm fine. I just wanted to tell you how much I appreciate all that you do for me. You're a very lovely woman, Mai Li, and I like you very much. Bye," ahe said, not waiting for Mai Li to respond.

Genna's stunned expression still remained on her face, as they entered the limo. Once Frederick shut the back door to the limo, Genna turned her friend and replied, "Nouri. Girlfriend, what the hell is with you today?" She stared at her, anxiously waiting for her to reply. Nouri's hands suddenly began to shake. She quickly reached for the plastic container of premade Bloody Mary's.

"Would you care for one, Genna?" She offered with a nervous smiled. Genna glanced at her suspiciously and nodded..

"What is it Nouri? What's got you in such a tizzy today?" she asked again. Nouri finished downing a Bloody Mary before responding.

"Genna, so much has happened these past few days. I simply don't know where to begin."

Genna laughed amusingly and then said, "I once had an old lover that told me to start at the beginning. That's always the best place to start." She smiled.

Nouri looked at her with a puzzled expression. "That's odd, I once had an old lover who said the same thing to me all the time." Genna shifted in her seat uneasily, hoping Nouri hadn't noticed.

"Yes, that is rather odd isn't it?" She quickly took the focus of the odd comparison away by saying, "So you gonna make me wait all night to hear about your so-called hot news flash concerning Clint Chamberlain and Charles Mason?"

Nouri glanced at her friend again and suddenly felt a little strange sitting next to her. *How odd.* Nouri thought to herself, as she awkwardly reached for the premade Bloody Mary container again.

"Refill, Genna?" she asked, still wondering why she suddenly felt uncomfortable about being so close to her best friend in the world.

"Yes, thanks, now would you please tell me what's going on. I'm about to go nuts with curiosity." She reached her hand out to retrieve her drink.

"Genna, the Clint and Charles story seems to fail in comparison with my latest news flash." She reached for her drink.

"Damn it, Nouri! You're driving me crazy! Spit something out for chrissakes!" She snapped heatedly.

"It's... it's Ethan. He's having an affair. I'm going to Lambert to confront him about it." She sighed sadly.

"And you just finding this out?" Genna's particular look instantly sent a surge of caution throughout Nouri's entire body, like a bolt of electricity.

"Yes.. I...I found out that he has apparently been in Lambert shacking up with some young bimbo for the past few days or so." She emptied her drink and reached for another.

"Oh, that would be Kirsten Kamel, I would imagine." She offered freely, and then shrugged her shoulders. Nouri looked at her with amazement.

"You knew, and you didn't tell me?" she remarked hurtfully.

THIEF OF HEARTS

"Give me a break, Nouri. Do you know anything about the man you're married to?" she said coolly.

Nouri was completely stunned by her friend's remark.

"Apparently not." She finally managed to say, shaking her head in disbelief.

"I'm sorry, girlfriend. I thought you knew." She shrugged her shoulders again.

"Knew what, Genna?" she asked in a surprised tone of voice.

"About your billionaire husband and his very hungry appetite for very young teenage girls." She stared coldly into Nouri's eyes. Nouri was shocked at this point. She suddenly needed something stronger to drink. She quickly reached for the brandy bottle and poured herself a double shot of the strong tasting liquor.

"Well, say something, Nouri, for chrissakes," Genna said sharply

"I can't believe you never told me about any this, Genna. I can't begin to tell you how hurt I am with you." Nouri glanced out of the window.

"Girlfriend, I'm sorry. Don't be angry with me. I...I just thought you knew that's all." She lied convincingly.

"All right, Genna. I'll forgive you this time on one condition." Nouri looked her square into the eyes.

Genna squirmed uneasily in her seat again, reached her Bloody Mary and responded, "And what condition would that be, Nouri?" She faked a smile. Nouri continued to stare into Genna's cat-green eyes.

"That you tell me everything that you know about Ethan, and I mean everything."

"I don't mind telling you, girlfriend, but it didn't come from me. Okay?" Genna smiled wickedly.

"Fine, Genna. Just tell me what you know about him and his business affairs."

"I don't really know much about his business affairs. I just know he's got some very heavy connections all over the world. Some people even say he's mixed up in the Chinese Mafia."

"Oh my God!" Nouri groaned and then released a deep side of regret.

"And, I understand that he has a weakness for very young teenage girls."

"Children?" She shook her head in discussed.

"Yes. The younger the better. He likes to break them then to suit his appetite for shall we say kinky sex." Genna giggled.

"This is far from funny, Genna. Where does he find these children?"

"I'm not sure, but I believe that Otto Lambert helps supply them in some way." She shrugged her shoulders again.

"Oh my lord. Otto Lambert?" Nouri shook her head again.

"Yeah, he ain't no angel." Genna laughed.

Nouri downed her double shot of brandy and refilled her empty glass.

"Would you like another Bloody Mary, or do you want to change, Genna?" She forced a fake smile.

"I'll switch to just a plain vodka, make it a double. I have to catch up with you girlfriend." She forced another fake smile.

"I just can't believe how stupid I am." Nouri shook her head again before adding, "So don't stop now. What else can you tell me about Ethan."

"Girlfriend, I don't want to hurt you. Isn't what I've told you enough?" Genna glanced at her face.

"I want to hear anything and everything you can tell me about my husband. And I mean everything," Nouri replied sharply

"Some of it is pretty ugly, Nouri, sure you can handle it?"

"I want to know," Nouri insisted.

"Fine. Have it your way." Genna sighed reluctantly.

"Thanks, Genna. Please continue."

"Your husband is a real sicko, especially when it comes to sex. He's been doing Becka Chamberlain since your last anniversary party. I think about nine months now. He screwed her brains out on the terrace that night and then had her sneak upstairs to one of the spare bedrooms, where he and she went at it for hours on end. Guy told me that Ethan sent him and Stuart up to Becka to finish the job he obviously couldn't handle." She shrugged her shoulders again.

"Oh God... I think I need some air," Nouri said, as she reached for her stomach.

"Oh shit! Shall I have Fredrick pull over?" Genna put her hand the buzzer.

"No. Just roll the window down for a few minutes, I'll be all right," Nouri said, quickly inhaling deeply. "Oh, I'm feeling much better now. Thanks Genna... Go ahead continue talking. I'm fascinated."

"That's funny, girlfriend. You look more sick than fascinated."

"Ha..Ha, very funny, Genna. Please go on." She smiled.

"Well, I was pissed off at Guy for a while for doing Becka with Stuart. You know how I hate the bitch! Anyway, Stacy taught me the only way to stay married to these rich sickos, was to let them do pretty much what they want to do...when they want to do it. The only way to come out on top of the game was to get even by spending lots and lots of their money. So that's what I've been doing for the past six years. I let Guy do what he has to do, and I do the same. I just have to be careful that he doesn't catch me doing it. You know his motto. What's good for the goose is not good for the gander. He's still insanely jealous of me even after six years. He's old and rich and doing young girls makes him feel young again." She shook her head and reached for her drink.

THIEF OF HEARTS

"I can't believe my ears! I could never live like that." Nouri reached over and patted her friend's hand affectionately. Genna coolly pulled her hand away and quickly reached for her drink.

"Girlfriend, we all can't be as perfect as you are." Jealousy surfaced in her tone of voice. Nouri looked at her hurtfully.

"I'm sorry, Genna. I didn't mean to sound like I was passing judgment on you or Stacy or anyone else as far as that goes. I just meant it wasn't the life for me that's all. I don't understand why a man thinks that he needs more than one woman at a time. Hell, Genna! You, Stacy, and me we're all only twenty-six years old, for chrissakes! And to our husbands we're considered old, for chrissakes! Give me a break! Hell, at sixteen, I didn't even have breasts yet. I think? Much less pubic hair." Nouri teased.

Genna laughed. "Oh Nouri, who are you kidding? I met you when we were both excited about our nineteenth birthdays just being a few weeks away. You were a knockout! Breasts, pubic hair, and all!" She laughed.

"Yeah, we were something all right. God! When you put it like that, I do feel old. Almost antique. She laughed again before adding, "But we're only twenty-six, and if I do say so myself, we look pretty damn good. No drooping behinds or boobs. Hell, were almost half our old men's ages. We're the ones that should be looking at the younger sex, don't ya think?" She teased again, trying to put Genna back into a playful mood

Genna smiled. "Why do you think I spend so much time sneaking out to go to those male strip shows. My one true weakness." She sighed lustfully.

"Yeah, that's true enough. But Genna, male strippers have always been your weakness, even before you married Guy, remember? I never knew what flavor you were going to sneak into my apartment so Mike Jones wouldn't catch you. Remember?" She chuckled.

"Oh shit! I'd almost forgotten about that and Mike, as far as that goes." She laughed amusingly.

"You used to crack me up girl. One minute you would tell me how hopelessly in love with Michael you were, and the next, you wanted to borrow my spare bedroom so you could ravage some sexy male stripper. You were a mess, Genna." She chuckled again at the humorous memory.

"Speaking of old times girlfriend, what were you going to tell me about Charles Mason?" Her tone was nervous and almost insistent. Nouri couldn't explain why she kept getting this odd feeling every time Genna would ask about her meeting with Charles Mason, but the feeling was very obvious to her, so once again she declined to answer. Nouri chose to switch subjects on her friend again.

"Oh, it was nothing, Genna. I couldn't make breakfast." She lied. "So, getting back to my husband. Is there anything else you can tell me about my mysterious husband?"

"I don't know, Nouri. I guess that's pretty much it." She sounded disappointed suddenly. Nouri suspected her friend's mood change was because of her not wanting to share her news about Charles Mason. She decided to ask her a few personal questions about Charles Mason to see how Genna reacted.

"You know Genna, even though I didn't get a chance to actually see Charles Mason, I did get a chance to talk with him over the phone for a few minutes." Genna's face suddenly lit up. She squirmed uncomfortably in her seat, and then she nervously reached for her drink. No it was not Nouri's imagination. Genna's entire attitude would change whenever Charles' name was mentioned.

"Oh, really. Tell me, girlfriend, how is good ol' Charles these days?" She offered Nouri her undivided attention.

"Well apparently, he's doing just fine. I understand he's the best private investigator in the country," she said, keeping her eyes focused directly on her friend.

"Yeah, I think I may have heard that about him somewhere."

"Oh really? Why didn't you mentioned it to me?"

"I didn't see the need. He..." She suddenly stopped speaking.

"He...what, Genna?" Nouri asked curiously.

"Oh, I don't know. I guess I just didn't want to bring up any bad memories." She smiled nervously.

Nouri suddenly looked stunned. "Bad memories? Charles Mason was, I mean, is...a wonderful memory. How could you say such a thing, Genna?"

In a jealous tone of voice Genna said coldly, "Well, if he was so goddamn wonderful to you then why in the hell didn't you go ahead and marry him!" She nervously reached for her vodka.

"Genna. Why are you so upset? I was only nineteen years old at the time. I wanted to go out and conquer the world. Not stay home making babies, for chrissakes. However, I would imagine that had I had a baby by Charles Mason it certainly would have been a beautiful child." She softened her tone to her obviously upset friend.

"Huh, a child by Charles Mason. Give me a break! He didn't want children," she snapped hurtfully.

"How in the hell would you know something like that?"

Realizing her slip of the tongue, Genna nervously responded, "I don't, of course. I was just going by what Mike had said about him, that's all." She lied.

"I see. That's funny, to me all he could talk about was us getting married and starting a family." Nouri shrugged her shoulders, as she continued to watch Genna's reaction. Nouri witnessed Genna turn red in the face. Her jaw muscle tightened and her hands began to shake. Nouri pretended not to notice. Humm...Genna is acting like she's still in love with Charles. I knew she had a crush on him hell, what woman didn't at the time. But love? I would've never believed it! I wonder if she actually slept with him, Nouri thought to herself, as she continued to watch her best friend try to regain her composure.

Genna finally managed to speak. "Well, I guess Michael must have been wrong, huh?" She forced a smile.

"It doesn't matter, that was a long time ago," Nouri said, and then reached for her glass again.

That's easy for you say, you little thief! Genna silently thought to herself, downing her drink.

"So, where shall we stop for lunch?" Nouri asked, trying to lighten the mood between them once again.

"I'm not really hungry just yet, let's wait until we get to the little town of Mason. We can eat there, go to my favorite strip club, and spend the night with one of those little cuties. What do you say girlfriend?" Genna smiled wickedly.

"Well Genna, I wanted to get to Lambert as soon as..." She stopped talking when she noticed a disappointed expression on her friend's face.

"Oh, what the hell! We can spend the night in Mason. But the little cuties are all yours. It's not my thing. Remember?" Nouri smiled.

Chapter 21

"Hi, Peg, this is Mr. Chamberlain again. I need to speak with Ms. Smith."

"Right away, sir," his young receptionist said, as she swiftly connected his call to Violet Smith.

"Oh, hi boss." Violet Smith said in a surprised tone of voice.

"Hi, Violet. I'm calling because I need you to do a few things for me."

"Sure Clint. What do you want me to do."

"Clear my calendar for all next week. I've got some major problems with Ethan Summers that I have to deal with immediately." He sighed

"What kind of problems, Clint?"

"I'm sorry. I don't have time to get into it all right now, but for starters he's out of control. Back on the shit again. And as if that isn't bad enough, he's messing around with Steven Li again!" He shook his head in disgust.

"Oh God!"

"You've got that right, Violet. I need you to phone Mrs. Schaffer in France. Have her send someone to help me get Ethan out of Lambert before he hurts someone." He sighed

"Before he hurts someone? I don't understand, Clint."

"Explanations come later, Violet, okay? Anyway, tell Ms. Schaffer he's on the heavy shit again. I can't get him out of Lambert alone. He's mad at me. More so than usual. He's blaming me for something to do with our past. I have no idea what the hell he is talking about, but I am worried about a young girl that is currently with them. I'm worried for her safety. That's why I'm flying to Lambert tonight.

"Violet, make the arrangements for me. Also, I'll need you to pick me up at my downtown apartment, as soon as possible. Got that?"

"Yes, Clint."

"One more thing, before the close of business today, transfer one-billion dollars of Ethan's funds into a new account in Switzerland. I'll phone you later for the new number. Don't give it to anyone except me. That includes Ethan himself. Understand?"

"Yes. Anything else?"

"Start getting all the paperwork together that you have on the Medallion Corporation and put it into a safety deposit box. Use your own name, Violet. Again, don't tell anyone about the paperwork or the safety deposit box."

"Anything else, Clint?"

"Bring all the papers with you that you needed me to sign today. I'll sign them while you drive me to the airport."

"Is that it, Clint?"

"For the time being, Violet. Now get a move on it. I'll be waiting here for you. Just blow the horn out from my apartment. I'll run out when I hear your horn."

"You got it boss, bye."

"Bye, Violet."

Clint walked over to the bar with his cell phone still in his hand. He dialed the Sommers' residence and quickly poor himself another shot of Scotch.

"Hello, Sommers' residence. How Mai Li help, please?"

"Hi, Mai Li, I need to speak with Mrs. Sommers."

"Sorry. Mrs. Sommers not here."

"Do you know where she is, Mai Li?"

"Went to Lambert with Mrs. Matthews."

"Shit!"

"Excuse, please."

"I'm sorry, Mai Li. Forgive me, I didn't mean to swear in front of you. It's just that I'm worried about Mrs. Sommers. Ethan's apparently back on drugs again," he said sharply.

"Oh no! Mr. Chamberlain, you better go to Lambert and get her."

"Yes, I intend to Mai Li. What time will she arrive in Lambert?"

"Not know. Frederick drive her and Mrs. Matthews."

"Thank God! At least she's not alone. And I can catch the next flight out, so I'll get there before she does." Clint sounded relieved.

"Good." Mai Li also sounded relieved.

"Mai Li, he's with Steven again."

"Oh no. Steven no good! Bad seed." Her tone apologetic.

"Yes, Mai Li. A very bad seed. I'm sorry to say."

"My son, it's true. Sad to admit." She hung her head in shame.

"You can't blame yourself Mai Li. You're a wonderful person. Life is about choices. It isn't your fault he turned out the way he has."

"He's very angry. Always a very angry boy. Even when small boy in China."

"Mai Li, I'm sorry, but I have to run. I'll phone you tomorrow and let you know what's going on, okay?"

"Thank you, Mr. Chamberlain," Mai Li said softly.

"You're welcome. Bye, Mai Li."

"Bye, Mr. Chamberlain."

Clint glanced down at his watch and quickly headed to the bedroom and packed his suitcase. Just as he finished fastening his suitcase shut, his private secretary, Violet Smith, blew her car horn. He glanced at his watch again, quickly grabbing his suitcase and flew out the door. He was more anxious than ever to get the next flight out to Lambert

Chapter 22

Young Kirsten Kamel was lying across the bed sideways, whispering on the phone to her real true lover, Kirt Jarrett. Unfortunately, she wasn't aware that Ethan Summers was standing behind her listening to every single word. She thought that he was still in the shower because she could still hear the water running.

"I love you too baby." Young Kirsten said to Kirt Jarrett. "Okay, I will. I better get off here before..." Suddenly, Ethan Summers jerked the telephone out of her hands.

"You fucking whore!" he shouted heatedly, as he pulled her up out of the bed.

"No! Wait baby!" she begged with tears streaming down her face.

"Wait my ass! Who the hell are you talking to? That Goddamn Kirt Jarrett! Admit it you whore!" he shouted again.

"You misunderstood me baby. Honest! You know there isn't anyone for me except you, baby," she continued to lie and beg.

"I warned you. You should have listened you bitch!" He angrily shouted. He suddenly knocked her across the room with his fist. Poor young Kirsten went sailing across the room. Her tiny petite body finally fell to the floor. She hit her head against the glass coffee table that Ethan had carried into the bedroom just a few short hours earlier to put his huge supply of new drugs on. The glass shattered all around her, and the blood came oozing out of her head very rapidly. She didn't move.

"Get the fuck up, you whore!" Ethan continued to rave out of control.

Ethan finally stormed over to her side. He started to shout at her again, when he noticed the blood gushing out of her head. It was running into the open bags of heroin and cocaine. Broken blood stained-glass everywhere. He suddenly couldn't move. He just froze for several long moments. Finally, he fell to his knees and began to cry.

"Oh God! I didn't mean it, Kirsten. I was mad, but I didn't mean hurt you. Please baby, get up," he whined drunkenly, holding his head into his hands. "Oh God! What have I done?" he continued to whine to himself. Ethan suddenly realized he better get his drugs together and get the hell out of there. So, completely strung out on a combinations of drugs and alcohol, he swiftly packed his suitcase and quickly disappeared into the night.

Chapter 23

Becka Chamberlain walked over to the walk-in closet in her bedroom. She quickly decided on what to wear. A thin silk blouse and a thin layered, full length skirt with deep side pockets. All the better to hide her .32 automatic weapon in. She finished applying her make-up and brushed her beautiful thick honey-blond hair. Her mind was entirely tuned out to everything and everyone, except one thing. And of course, that one thing was her need to kill Kirsten Kamel. And Ethan Sommers, too, if he tried to stop her.

Her plan was to visit his suite. Knock on the door, knowing young Kirsten would most probably be the one to open the door and BANG! Bye, young Kirsten. Of course, Ethan Summers would be allowed to choose between death beside his lifeless young whore, or she would allow him to live, but only if he dumped Nouri and married her. Such a masterful plan. How could it possibly fail?

She loaded her gun, slid it into the deep side pocket of her skirt, walked back to the bar for one last drink of courage, and swiftly walked out of her suite and over to the fire steps, where she quickly ran up three exhausting flights of stairs. She stopped for only a few moments to catch her breath. She opened the fire door and slowly approached Ethan's room. She glanced her left and then to her right.

Too bad she hadn't glanced directly behind herself. She would have notice Kirt Jarrett, not far behind her, coming out of Stacy Gullaume's special service suite. If she would have spotted him, she might have changed her mind about killing Kirsten and settled for another sexual go around with her favorite human play toy.

She knocked on the door to Ethan Sommers' suite again. Still no answer, so she quietly turned the door handle. Much to her surprise, it was unlocked. Becka slowly entered the suite. She glanced around the living room, not spotting Kirsten or Ethan. She walked into the master bedroom.

As she entered the room, she immediately spotted young Kirsten trying to sit up. She was holding her head, still half dazed inside a pool of blood, moaning hysterically. Becka glanced once again around the room for Ethan, but not spotting him. She quickly walked up close to Kirsten and pulled out her weapon. Becka shot her point-blank in her heart, killing young Kirsten instantly. She suddenly got the bright idea to frame Nouri Sommers for the young woman's death. She quickly decided to rush back to her suite and retrieve Nouri's antique hairbrush and jeweled lipstick holder. She quickly left the room, making sure the door didn't lock behind her. She smiled victoriously, as she swiftly walked toward the fire doors.

Chapter 24

Clint Chamberlain, still out of breath from rushing, quickly entered one of the guarded elevators.

"Hello, Mr. Chamberlain," the security guard said, after recognizing him. "You're suite, sir?" he asked politely.

"No. Not yet. I'm supposed go to Mr. Sommers; suite first." He lied.

"Sure, jump in," he said, as she quickly pressed Ethan Sommers' floor.

"Here we are, sir." the elevator guard said, tipping his hat to Clint, as he walked off the elevator.

"Thanks," Clint responded, stepping off of the elevator. He swiftly walked to Ethan Sommers' suite. He knocked on the door. No answer. He knocked again. Still no answer. He turned the handle to the door and, surprisingly, it opened. He slowly entered the room.

"Ethan, it's me. Where are you?" he said, as he glanced around the room. He walked to the master bedroom. The door had been left open by Becka. Spotting Kirsten's lifeless body, he ran to her side. "Oh my God! Ethan, you crazy son-of-a-bitch! Clint cried, as he glanced around the room.

"Damn it! Ethan, why did you have to kill her? She's just a child for chrissakes. Poor girl. I was afraid of this. Ethan has completely lost his mind. Shit!" Clint continued to mumble to himself, as he tried to think of what he should do next.

His first instinct was to phone the police before Otto Lambert had a chance to make yet another little problem of Ethan Sommers disappear, but his next thought stopped him cold.

"Nouri," he whispered nervously. He decided he better track down Ethan before he decided to target her next. "Damn you, Ethan!" he said, as he glanced at the diamond necklace around young Kirsten neck. "I'm sure you earned that," he said to the dead girl, shaking his head sadly. He quickly mumbled a silent prayer for the young Kirsten.

Clint walked back into the living room, trying to decide if he should go to France or China first, to track down his friend. He was aware that Ethan was probably running scared to France or China. These were his friends' favorite places to hide when he didn't want to be found.

After he wiped his fingerprints off the door handle, inside and out, with his handkerchief, he suddenly left the hotel suite and quickly vanished into the night.

Chapter 25

"Come on ladies, give it up. Let's hear a round of applause for Cuddly Studdly Duddley. Your French connection right here in good old downtown Mason!"

"Oh, damn! They've already started the show." Genna pouted, as she and Nouri continued to wait in line to be seated.

"Calm down, Genna, we have all night for chrissakes." She amusingly shook her head at her anxious friend. Several moments later, they were approached by their host for the evening.

"*Vous eses combien de personnes*? he asked politely.

"What the hell did he just say?" Genna giggled.

"He asked how many are you." Nouri laughed and then held up two fingers to him.

"Boy, this place sure has changed since my last visit," Genna remarked, as she continued to glance around male strip club, while they were waiting to be escorted to their table.

"Tonight is a special treat or so the posted signs say. They have apparently flown in the famous French stripper Pierre Lemonnier for tonight's lead performance. "Have you ever heard of him?" Nouri asked Genna, as they continued their long walked to the front of the strip club. Their tickets were for a front row table.

"*Par ici, s'il vous plait.*" The young handsome host gestured to the table directly in front of them.

"*Merci,*" Nouri responded, as she glanced at Genna's puzzled expression.

"For goodness sake, Genna, all he said was this way please." She shook her head at her silly friend

"*Et comme boissin*?" He smiled.

"Genna what would you like to drink?"

"I'd like a Margarita with extra salt around the rim," she responded.

"Make that two Margaritas please." Nouri smiled

"*Bien sur*. Of course." He nodded. After five extra large Margaritas, Nouri was ready to call it a night. But not her feisty best friend, who appeared to be just getting started.

"Listen, Genna, I want to get an early start tomorrow, and I'm tired, so I'm going to go back to the hotel. Are you coming or would you rather stay and kick it with Pierre Lemonnier?" She smiled, already knowing her friends answer.

"Now what the hell do you think girlfriend?" she laughed wickedly.

"That's what I thought," Nouri teased, standing to her feet.

"Oh, Genna, do you need some extra cash to shove down Pierre's thing-a-ma-bob?" She laughed amusingly.

Genna smiled at her friend and responded with a shake no of her head.

"I still have a couple of grand in cash, but thanks. Buzz my room tomorrow to wake me when you're ready to leave, okay?"

"*Au revoir* Madam," Nouri teased, as she turned to leave.

"Oh, I know that one, Nouri. You said goodbye, huh?" Genna eagerly shouted, as Nouri continued to push her way past a crowd of sexually excited women. Nouri turned to glance at her friend from over her shoulder. She nodded her head yes and waved goodbye. She was anxious to get back to her room. She wanted desperately to track down Clint Chamberlain and share her newly discovered news about Ethan with him. Plus, she just wanted to hear his voice. But most of all his words of love for her.

"Darling," she whispered to herself, thinking of Clint, as Frederick opened the limo door for her.

"Where to Madam?" he asked, as his eyes met hers in the rear view mirror.

"To the hotel please. I want to get an early start tomorrow morning." She smiled again.

After several unsuccessful attempts of trying to reach Clint Chamberlain, Nouri disappointingly decided to take a quick shower and call it a night. She could hardly wait to get to Lambert and confront Ethan about his affair. Correction, affairs!

"Young teenage children. How sick. You're a horrible person Ethan Sommers!" she angrily muttered to herself, as her mind continually insisted on aggravating her about the man she married. She tossed and turned. And then turned and tossed, finally slipping into an uneasy sleep. In her sleep, she was frightened. Someone was chasing her, and though this person seemed familiar to her, she had never seen this person before. Panic instantly surge throughout her entire body. She began to tremble with fear. "No please stop!" she was shouting. She suddenly jarred herself awake from her terrifying dream.

She jumped out of bed and quickly turned on her bedroom light. Her hands were still trembling, as she sat back down on the side of her bed. "Whew!" she sighed in relief, after realizing that she had only been dreaming. She glanced at the clock. It was six a.m.

I'm too upset to sleep, she thought to herself, as she decided to take a shower, get dressed, and get an earlier start than she had intended. She picked up the telephone to give Genna her earlier than planned wake-up call. She dialed her room number and patiently waited for her to pick up the phone

After ten consecutive rings, she decided to walk across the hallway to knock or her friend's door. As she opened the door to her suite, she quickly stepped back inside her room and quickly shut the door. She had seen an Asian man nervously leaving her friend's room and didn't want to embarrass him.

"She's so damn fickle," Nouri mused to herself, remembering Genna was going to spend the night with the French male stripper, Pierre something or another. But she obviously changed her mind, as well as her desert menu.

"That woman!" Nouri whispered, shaking her head, as she walked back to the telephone to call her friend again.

"Good morning sleepy head."

"Don't tell me we're leaving already?" Genna complained, as she yawned and stretched.

"I'm afraid so, Genna. I want to get an early start, especially since we're in the limo. The last time we wanted to take the ferry across to Lambert they made us wait for an eternity, remember?"

"Oh yeah, I remember. We were stuck in bum- fuck-Egypt for most of the day. Okay, I'll be ready about twenty minutes. I'll jump into the shower right now," she said, sitting up in the bed.

"Well, let's have breakfast before we leave. I'm starving. I'll meet you downstairs in the restaurant, okay."

"Okay, Nouri," Genna remarked, quickly putting the phone down and running into the shower.

Stepping out of the shower, Nouri suddenly decided to try and reach Clint Chamberlain one final time. She quickly dressed, applied her makeup, brushed her hair and packed her suitcase.

"God, I hope he answers the phone," she said, as she dialed his cell phone number. After five rings, Nouri laid the phone down. "Damn!" she mumbled, reaching for her suitcase. She handed it to Frederick, who was now standing right outside her door.

"We're having breakfast downstairs before we leave, Frederick. Jave you eaten yet?" She smiled, as she watched him hand the suitcase to the bell boy.

"Yes, thank you, madam. I'll be out front chatting with a few of the fellows." He rolled his eyes humorously.

"Fine, Fredrick. We won't be long." She smiled, as she walked to the elevator. Fredrick pressed the lobby floor. Nouri noticed the same Asian man that was coming out of her friend's room, slouching in an overstuffed chair partially hidden behind an upside-down newspaper. She giggled to herself, thinking that her friend's overnight playmate might be trying to sneak one final look at her before she left town. She amusingly shook her head, as she quickly walked past him.

"The restaurant is this way madam." Fredrick gestured to her, as he watched her disappear inside the restaurant.

Halfway through her breakfast, Nouri glanced down at her watch. Genna, for chrissakes, where the hell are you, she thought to herself, only to glance up and see her finally walk into the restaurant.

"Thank goodness!" she silently muttered to herself, as she stood her feet to motion Genna over to the table.

"Its about time Genna Matthews," she said, as her friend sat down at the table.

"Sorry, I just couldn't seem to get it all together. It's so damn early. Has the cock's crowed yet?" she mused sarcastically.

"Very funny, Genna," she remarked back at her grumpy friend.

"I'm just not a morning people, I guess." Genna's tone was apologetic.

"So what do you feel like eating this morning, Genna?"

"You've got to be kidding! After, all the Margaritas I drank last night, I don't think I will be able to look at any food for least a month!" She put her arms around her stomach and made a funny face.

"Oh Genna. Honestly! You'll at least have some coffee, won't you?" Nouri glanced at her friend.

"I don't do coffee anymore, remember?" Genna said, glancing at her watch.

Nouri rolled her eyes impatiently at her friend and responded, "Well if you don't want breakfast, and you don't want coffee, then what do you want?"

Genna returned the rolled eye look back at Nouri and said, "I want to get the hell out of this Godforesaken town of Mason!" They both began to laugh, as they stood to their feet to leave.

"There, that ought to cover it," Nouri said, as she threw a twenty dollar bill down the table. She chuckled to herself, as Charles Mason's face suddenly popped inside her brain. She had seen him do the same thing many times in the past whenever he was in too much of a hurry to wait for his tab.

"What was that tiny chuckled for?" Genna asked, as she glanced in the direction of the Asian man, who was still slouched over in his chair reading his upside-down newspaper. Nouri noticed her friend glancing in his direction.

"Why don't you go over and tell your friend goodbye?" She smiled

"Who?" Genna asked with a stunned look on her face.

"The Asian man." Nouri looked at her curiously.

"Now why on earth would I do a dumb thing like that?" she snapped, as she quickly walked past him.

"Sorry. I just thought you knew him." Nouri suddenly got that "proceed with caution" feeling again.

"Obviously you were mistaken, girlfriend." She shook her head and opened the double glass door to the hotel.

THIEF OF HEARTS

A puzzled expression crossed Nouri's face, as she responded to Genna. "Obviously." Silently wondering to herself why her friend had denied knowing the man, when she had just seen the very same man coming out of her friend's hotel suite. Her friend's behavior was starting to become curiouser and curiouser.

After a brief conversation in the limo headed for Lambert, Genna Matthews suddenly dozed off to sleep. Nouri didn't mind in the least. That would give her time to be alone to organize her thoughts and maybe put together a plan or two in her mind.

"These past few days have been unbelievable," Nouri whispered to herself, as she began to rehash each odd thing that she has had happened to her in the past four days. "Unbelievable!" she whispered again, shaking her head, as she continued to think.

Four days ago I was anxiously waiting for my husband to come home and take me out to dinner, when suddenly my ex-fiancee shows up at my front door, from out of nowhere. My husband cancels yet another dinner date with me, leaving me all alone in the company of my ex-lover, who after arguing with me and confessing his undying love for me, offers to actually fix dinner for me... she continues to think... *before we have dinner, I go upstairs to change, where I pass out from having too much to drink. When I wake up, I have a crazy fight with my husband over the phone and my ex-lover is gone, but then his crazy wife calls me and accuses me of having an affair with him, which of course I'm not. But would not have minded at all if we would've been having one.*

The next morning, I go to the city to meet my husband for lunch. Hoping to make up with him, but instead, he stands me up again. So I call yet another ex-lover of mine to ask him for help, only to be swept up into remembered moment of heated passion, suddenly finding myself wanting to screw his brains out.

If all this isn't complicated enough, my ex-fiancee catches me in the arms of my first real lover, and, of course, they want to fight. I end the evening by sleeping with my ex-fiancee, falling back in love with him and out of love with my husband. And two days later I meet with my first real lover to ask him to help me get a divorce from my elusive and mysterious husband so thatI can marry my ex-fiancee.

I then phone my husband in Lambert only to find out that he's not only has been having an affair with a young teenager, but I also find out that my husband is some kind of Mafia pervert, whose only passion is obviously having sex with children. I end the fourth day by visiting a male strip club on the way to Lambert to ask my perverted husband for a divorce that I know he will not give me. I also find out that my husband has been screwing my so-called friends and an ex-associate.

And on top of that, after seven years of friendship with my best friend in the world, I find out that she's not only knows more about my husband and his

177

Mafia connections and business affairs than I do, but there is a very strong possibility that she's been doing my husband, as well!

And even worse, I find out this very same friend has apparently been in love with my first lover, all along, secretly, which makes me wonder if she has had sex with him, too.

Finally, I catch my best friend not only in a deliberate lie, but a stupid one at that! Over an Asian guy, I actually see sneaking out of her hotel suite after spending the night with her. She has the nerve to tell me she's never seen him before in her life!

"I can hardly wait to see what this day has in store for me," Nouri mumbled to herself, as her chauffeur rolled the middle piece of glass down to ask her if she would like to get out of the limo to look at the ocean for a breath of fresh air, while they crossed the ferry to Lambert.

"Why yes, Frederick. I would thank you," she responded, as she tried to wake her sleeping friend.

"No. Go without me," Genna Matthews replied, groggily laying her head back down on the seat of the limo.

"Madam," Frederick said, as he held his hand to assist Nouri out of the back seat of the limo.

"Thank you, Frederick," she responded, appreciating his gesture. "Oh this is beautiful, Frederick," Nouri said, as she continued to look at the incredible beauty of the blue-green ocean.

"It sort of makes you feel as though one could stay right here forever just admiring the wonder of it all, doesn't it?" She said, as she glanced over to Frederick, who was no longer standing beside her. In his place however, was an incredibly handsome man. He smiled approvingly, as he quickly sized Nouri up.

He responded, "Well, I'm not Frederick, but will I do?" He quickly added, "My name is Daniel Job Edwards." He smiled again, as he anxiously waited for her to respond.

"Hi, my name is Nouri Sommers. Nice to meet you." She returned the smile before adding, "I thought you were my chauffeur, Frederick."

Pointing into the direction of where Frederick had moved to, he said, "I believe your Frederick is over there." He smiled again.

"Oh," she said softly, as her eyes traveled into the direction Daniel was pointing.

"In answer to your question of Frederick, if you wouldn't mind my opinion, the answer is yes; it is beautiful. Quite magnificent actually, but staying here forever...well, my dear young woman, that might need a little more consideration on my part." He chuckled.

Suddenly, the ferry went into a rather large wave, causing the ferryboat to take a large dip. The swift movement made Nouri quickly feel a little seasick.

THIEF OF HEARTS

She put both arms around her stomach snugly. She glanced up a Daniel, forcing a smile.

"I see your point." She giggled, nodded, and walked back to her limo.

Frederick had his eyes on her and quickly came over to her side. "Are you all right, madam?" he asked in the concern toner voice.

"Yes, thank you, Frederick. I think I'll go back inside the limo, however." She smiled, as Frederick opened the door to help her inside. The handsome man watched as Frederick closed the door behind her. He smiled and shook his head in awe of Nouri's beauty.

"Madam, we'll be a Lambert in about ten minutes. We're pulling up to the loading dock now."

"Thank you, Frederick," she replied back, as she once again tried unsuccessfully to wake her sound asleep friend. Frederick rolled the middle piece of the glass down again to speak with Nouri.

"Madam," he said, as he glanced at her through the visual aid of the rear view mirror.

"Yes, Frederick, what is it?" she responded, glancing in the mirror.

"Apparently something is going on at the hotel, madam," he remarked excitedly.

"Oh yes. So it seems, Frederick. Wonder what it could be?"

"I don't know madam. Maybe Veda will know. I'll pull around to the side of the hotel."

"Yes, please do Frederick. I want to avoid all the TV cameras and news reporters if the possible."

"What the hell are you talking about, Nouri? TV cameras and news reporters," Genna shouted, as she suddenly sat up and quickly rolled down her window.

"What in the world?" she added, as her mouth flew open when she noticed the police cars parked all over the place.

Veda, the head valet at Lambert, came running over to the Sommers limo. He swiftly opened the back door to the car and Nouri stepped out.

"Madam," he said with a nervous smile.

"What on earth is going on here, Veda?" Nouri asked, as she watched news reporters stepping on top of one another. Television crews were setting up their podiums everywhere for live taping. Police cars parked in the strangest places. Wireless microphones being shoved into sunglassed-hidden faces. And, flash cubes going off a thousand flashes per minute, as the TV cameras suddenly began to roll.

Nouri instantly realized that something terrible must have happened. Lambert was always so quiet. So private. So perfect. No publicity. No outsiders. Everything always so hush hush. But not today!

"What did Veda say, Nouri?" Genna eagerly asked.

"Nothing yet, Genna!" she said coolly. "Give him a chance to open his mouth, for chrissakes," she added nervously.

"It's a double murder, madam," he answered with a shaky voice.

"A what!" Nouri shouted, glancing inside the limo at Genna.

"A double murder, right here in Lambert madam," he repeated.

"Oh my God! Who? Why? How did happen? Do they have the murderer or murders?" Nouri blurted out in an excited tone voice.

"One question at a time, please, Mrs. Sommers," he remarked, as he nervously scratched his head.

"You're right, of course. I'm sorry, Veda. It's just so shocking. I can't believe it." She shook her head disbelievingly, as she continued to glance around at the hotel and all of the busy activity surrounding the incident.

"Yes, it is, Mrs. Sommers. Very shocking." He shook his head sadly.

"Who was it, Veda?" Nouri glanced at Veda's face.

"One of them was a friend of yours, madam. I believe. Mrs. Chamberlain."

"What? Surely you don't mean Becka Chamberlain, Veda." Her voice began to crack and a tear fell down her cheek.

"Yes, madam. Becka Chamberlain." He nodded

"How did it happen, Veda?"

"I don't know, Mrs. Sommers. All we were told was they found her body down on the beach. She was naked, madam. That's all I know about it." He looked at her sadly.

"Who is they, Veda?"

"The Gullaumes found her."

"You mean Stacy and Stuart Gullaume?" She shook her head in disbelief.

"Yes, Miss Sommers. That's who found her."

"How terrible!" she remarked excitedly.

"Veda, who was the other murder victim? You did say there were two murders, didn't you?"

"Yes madam. I did say there were two bodies. The other person was a young employee. Her name was Kirsten Kamel. She was a barmaid here. Did you know her?" He glanced at her. Nouri shook her head know no. "I'm so sorry, Veda. Was she a friend of yours?" She patted his shoulder.

"I guess you might say that she was."

"I'm so very sorry, Veda," she said comforting.

"Thank you, Mrs. Sommers." He smiled.

"If there is anything I can do, just let me know, okay." She smiled sympathetically.

"Thanks. Poor Kirsten has only been on the island for a few short weeks." He hung his head again.

"Does she have a family close by?"

"I'm not sure. Most of us don't have anyone, I mean family, so we stick together to make our own families here."

"I see. Well Veda, remember if there is anything I can do just let me know, okay?" She smiled again.

"Thanks."

"How was your friend murdered, Veda?"

"I'm not sure. All I know is that she was murdered inside of the hotel. Apparently inside one of the secret suites."

"The secret suites. What does that mean exactly, Veda?" Veda suddenly turned red in the face.

"I'm sorry, Mrs. Sommers. I thought you knew," he said, as he suddenly glanced at Genna inside the limo. She shot him a dirty look.

"Nothing, madam. I have to go now." He turned to leave. Nouri noticed he got nervous after looking at Genna. So she decided not to push the issue with him.

"Just a second, Veda."

He turned to face her nervously, "Yes Mrs. Sommers?" he responded, as he glanced back at Genna, who was now almost hanging out of the car.

"Do you know if Mr. Sommers is still here?" she asked, as she continued to watch him fidget around Genna nervously.

"No I don't believe so, madam. I think I heard someone tell Mr. Lambert that he left for the airport last night. Maybe it was right after midnight. I'm not sure." He nodded and turned to leave again.

"Thanks, Veda," Nouri said, as she stepped back inside the limo.

"Oh my Lord! Genna, did you get all of that?" She released a sigh and shook her head.

"Poor Clint. I wonder if he knows about his wife being murdered?"

"God! I just can't believe it. Becka Chamberlain. Wow!"

"I guess you just never know," Genna said, shaking her head.

"Yeah, from one moment to the next." Nouri sighed again, as she began to wonder if Clint was here when the murder had taken place. She was wondering if maybe that's why he never returned her call at the hotel in Mason last night. Maybe someone like Mr. Lambert had phoned him before they called the police.

"I wonder if she was murdered last night or early this morning?"

"Now, how in the hell would I know something like that, for chrissakes!"

"Oh for goodness sakes, Genna, I didn't mean it like that. I just thought you might have an opinion or wild guess. Something, anything. I don't know."

"Well, I didn't like the bitch! So I really don't care," Genna said reaching for the bottle vodka.

"Shame on you, Genna. I didn't much like Becka either, but I certainly wouldn't wish her dead. I'm sorry that she's dead. I feel so sorry for poor Clint." She sighed.

"Oh God! The news media will have this plastered all over the newspapers and TV stations before the day is out."

"Yes it will be. Actually, the cameras are rolling as we speak."

"Well, I don't know about you, Nouri, but I sure as hell don't want my goddamn face plastered all over the networks for the next goddamn umpteenth months!" Genna said, as she suddenly rolled up her car window halfway.

"Not to mention having the damn news media camp outside of our homes for the next few weeks, just to keep the double murder at Lambert at the headlines for the next few months!"

"Poor Stacy and Stuart, they may as well pack a bag and disappear to another country! The Goddamn news media won't leave them alone until the murderers are solved. After all, according to Veda, they are the ones that found poor Becka's body."

"Naked on the beach! It's really quite like her if you think about it. After all, Becka spent more time taking her close off than putting them on." Genna laughed.

"For goodness sake's Genna Matthews, you are shameless!"

"Yeah, maybe so, but honest. I don't think there's a man in Lambert or Boston that hasn't tapped in on a piece of that woman. I hear she was quite a little nympho!" Genna said sarcastically.

"Oh, shame on you, Genna. Let the poor woman rest in peace; she's only been dead a few hours!" Nouri said in an agitated tone of voice.

"I can't believe you, Nouri St. Charles Sommers. You hated that woman when she was living, now you're probably the only one on the face of God's green earth that is willing to take up for her now that she's dead! Doesn't it bother you that she's been sleeping with your husband for the past nine months." Genna shook her head disgust.

"I don't care what you say, Genna. None of that matters anymore! Becka was insane. She was so out of it that she wasn't responsible for her actions. I should've been more patient with her, maybe if I had tried to help her more when we were friends, make her get the help she really needed, I don't know. But surely there is something more I could've done. She was a very sick person. Poor thing. The horror stories that Becka used to tell me about herself when she was a child. No child should have to endure such abuse." Nouri wiped a tear from her eye and reached for the brandy bottle.

THIEF OF HEARTS

"Give me a goddamn break! Next you're going to pull out a damn violin. And I'm here to tell your girlfriend, when you do, I'm going to get out of the goddamn car and walk back to Boston. Do you hear me?" Genna laughed in a mean-spirited tone of voice.

"Point well taken. But I honestly never knew that ice actually ran through your veins, Genna Matthews! So, do you want to drive out of here and go back to Boston? Or do you want to make a run for it and hope we make it inside the hotel without a microphone being shoved into our faces, and our faces somehow finding their way on the front page of tomorrow's newspaper? Your call Genna?"

"Are you nuts? That's all I would need. My face plastered all over the goddamn newspapers! Guy would divorce me for sure! If one of the kazillion male strippers that I've sneaked around and kicked it with sees my face on the goddamn television or in the goddamn newspapers, and they find out who I really am and who I'm married too...Shit for the right price they will offer to sell my husband any information about his over-sexed wife that he is willing to pay for. Or worse! They might try to blackmail me! No thank you. I pass. I will ride home with you and hook up with Guy later. How about you?"

"Let's go home, Genna. I'll deal with Ethan later."

"Sounds good to me!" Genna smiled nervously.

Nouri softly pecked on the middle glass window to get Frederick's attention. After he rolled the window down, she said, "Frederick, I'm sorry. I know how tired you must be, but I'd like to go home, please. If you're too tired to drive just drop us off at the airport and spend the night here, and drive home tomorrow."

"I'm fine, madam. Are you ready to leave now?" He smiled.

"Yes, thank you, Frederick, if you please."

THE LAMBERT SERIES

THE *COLORFUL* CAST OF CHARACTERS

NOURI ST. CHARLES SOMMERS: The main character in the Lambert Series. Nouri is the heart-stoppingly beautiful, but bored wife, to one of the wealthiest men in the world, Ethan Sommers. Nouri's secret passion is romance. And her favorite pastime is writing in her fantasy journals.

ETHAN SOMMERS: A dashingly handsome and powerful, but mysterious and ruthless billionaire businessman – that seems to have less and less time for romancing his beautiful, hot-natured wife of only two years. Ethan is a man surrounded by mystery, and skeletons from his past. His secret passion is revenge. And his favorite pastime is beautiful super-young women.

CLINT CHAMBERLAIN: Ever so sexy, but hot-tempered and sometimes hard to control best friend and high-powered attorney to Ethan Sommers. Also quite the ladies man. And secret lover from Nouri's past – that her husband was never told about. Clint holds the key to Nouri's heart. A man with a few skeletons of his own. His secret passion is Nouri. And his favorite pastime is catering to his one true weakness: beautiful women.

CHARLES MASON: Incredibly manly, but obstinate, private eye extraordinair! The best private dick in the country. Quite the ladies man himself. Charles is also a man from Nouri's past (her first real man) that she will always have deep feelings for. His secret passion is also Nouri. And his favorite pastime is trying to win her back.

GABE BALDWIN: Not only the sexiest, but also the best homicide detective on the Boston Police Force – that is, after Charles Mason left the force. His secret passion soon becomes Nouri. And his favorite pastime is nailing the bad guys.

BECKA CHAMBERLAIN: The incredibly beautiful, but whacko wife to Clint Chamberlain. Becka is also Nouri's ex-partner in an Interior Design business – who happens to hate Nouri with a purple passion. Her secret passion is to become the next Mrs. Ethan Sommers. And her favorite pastime is to destroy Nouri or anyone who tries to get in her way.

RENEA CHANDLIER: A seductive temptress who is hired by Ethan Sommers to help him destroy someone close to him. With Renea's unbelievable beauty, she has zero problems getting close to her intended mark.

GENNA MATTHEWS: Beautiful, but wild and zany best friend of seven years to Nouri Sommers. They had met while attending the Fine Arts Academy in Boston. Genna has a dark side that Nouri isn't aware of. Genna's secret passion is Charles Mason. And her favorite pastime is to settle a score!

MAI LI: Originally from China where she worked for the House of Chin – China Royalty. Now, she runs the Sommers' Estate. Mai Li is a beautiful, but mature woman who is as mysterious as the well-kept secrets she manages to hide so well.

STEVEN LI: A character with a lot of mystery surrounding him. One of which is his association with the Chinese mob – a.k.a. THE RED DEVIL.

TONYA DAUGHTERY: The District Attorney of Boston. She's also Charles Mason's "EX." And even though engaged to someone else now, Charles Mason is still her one true passion in life.

OLIVIA & OTTO LAMBERT: Own and operate the exclusive Lambert paradise. A truly one-of-a-kind couple, that takes tremendous pleasure in *serving* themselves, as well as their guest elite.

KIRSTEN KAMEL: Ethan Sommers' super-young new mistress.

KIKI: Super-young, super-sexy special service employee in Lambert.

THOMAS: Super-sexy, special service employee in Lambert. Thomas' special skills make him and his unique service very much in demand on the island elite.

KIRT JARRET: An employee in Lambert with special connections to Otto Lambert, Kirsten Kamel, and Ethan Sommers. His secret passion is Kirsten Kamel.

STACY & STUART GUILLAUME: Close friends to the Sommers, the Chamberlains, Matthews, and Lamberts. Also a couple on the rocks.

GUY MATTHEWS: Billionaire oil tycoon who is married to Nouri's zany best friend, Genna - even though he's thirty years Genna's senior.

CHRISTOPHER GRAHAM: An over-priced attorney that is engaged to the DA of Boston, Tonya Daughtery.

AL BALLARD: Young, inexperienced police detective the Gabe Baldwin takes under his wing.

LACEY ALEXANDRIA BONNER: Charles Mason's old flame. Also, ex-lover to Gabe Baldwin. Not just another pretty face. Lacey Bonner is also a famous star of stage, screen, and television. A lady with a few skeleton's and secrets of her own.

KIMBERLY MICHELLE: International Super Model. And Charles Mason's current love interest.

LISA CLAYBORNE: A front page socialite – The Baron's Daughter and police detective, Gabe Baldwin's on again – off again fiancé.

CELINA SAWYER: Gabe Baldwin's sexy new neighbor in Connecticut – where he owns an A-frame cabin in the woods – the detective's new little hideaway for a little down time between cases.

ISABELLA BEDAUX: Connecticut Police Department's new bombshell detective from France who just happens to have the hots for sexy detective, Gabe Baldwin.

JIN TANG: Ethan Sommers' Asian connection to THE RED DEVIL.

ANNA McCALL: Ethan Sommers' private secretary.

VIOLET SMITH: High-priced attorney, Clint Chamberlain's beautiful Malaysian private secretary.

TESS: Charles Mason's private secretary.

FREDRICK: The two-generation chauffer for the Sommers.

ROBERT BARNET: Stationed in Boston, Robert works undercover for the FBI.

RICK HOBNER: The young police officer in Boston.

PIERRE DuVALL: Famous French clothing designer.

HEIDI: The Sommers' downtown maid.

JAMES: The Sommers' downtown chauffer.

TALULA: Charles Mason's pet feline.

Printed in the United States
18950LVS00001B/439